If Frogs Could Fly

A psychedelic romp with a 60s undercurrent
strangely relevant to our times

E.B. Mendel

Sunbridge Books

Deerfield Beach, Florida

Reality is more complex than we would like. If we insist upon it making sense, we will find ourselves despairing. Reality cannot be neatly packaged. Reality is all there is. And it's often at odds with what it should be.

Rabbi Yannai

Early Jewish sage who lived in Israel during the 3rd Century

1

October 5, 2016

In Miami Beach at seven o'clock in the morning, fifty-year-old Ron Levine stood barefoot on the platinum-gold sand and silently watched a full orange sun rise above the cloudless horizon. A glimmering bridge of light stretched across the placid ocean while he flexed and extended his athletic 5' 8" frame. A mild breeze tousled his brown curls. Ron took three deep breaths, then waded through the surf, swimming several feet beneath the surface where a school of tiny yellow fish, a graceful stingray, and a wary sea turtle swiftly migrated through the undercurrent. The swimmer propelled himself upward, feeling something slick and rubbery rake the back of his thigh. He turned his head and saw a hammerhead shark lumbering in the water nearby; close enough for Ron to see its healthy white teeth. He rapidly distanced himself from the predator and reached dry land. His heart pounded out of his chest while he dried off and noticed blood drip behind his left leg. He washed it off a few moments before walking to a high-rise condo a quarter mile up the beach.

In front of her bedroom mirror, Ron's forty-eight-year-old wife, Rachael, threw on a pair of blue bikini underwear, cutoff jeans, a purple tank top, and yellow flip-flops. After brushing her straight blonde hair and sniffing a recently shaved underarm, she rolled on some Tom's lavender-scented deodorant, made the bed, folded her husband's paisley pajamas, and then read her emails on a desktop before going downstairs to juice some carrots, beets, celery and baby kale.

After Ron emptied his shorts of seashells and unusual stones with holes he found at the beach, he stepped into the shower and washed the sand and salt from his skin. He closed the water, toweled off, and disinfected and bandaged the minor injury on the back of his thigh. He donned a pair of white Bermuda shorts and a tropical shirt designed with Islamorada conch shells, pink flamingos, and coconut palms; the typical outfit he frequently wore for work. Ron was a successful freelance writer for popular magazines and currently immersed in an article for *Time* concerning the dangerous effects of global warming on South Florida. He graduated from New York University with a master's degree in journalism. On his first writing assignment with *National Geographic,* he went to Asia where he'd written a six-page spread about the Great Wall of China. That's where he met and fell in love with Rachael. She was in Beijing, studying to be a Doctor of Oriental Medicine. The year before she'd graduated from the University of Alabama with a master's degree in language. Two years later they got married. Ron spent the next ten years travelling all over the world and writing for National Geographic. His wife frequently accompanied him on his travels. They never had children.

Ron attached the Velcro straps on a pair of Teva sandals, and he leisurely strolled to the kitchen with a laptop and a Time magazine in hand. He sat at the table where a fresh cup of coffee and the Miami Herald awaited him. His wife turned off an electric juicer and poured fresh vegetable juice into two glasses.

"How was the ocean, sweetie?" Rachael asked.

"It was nice. I saw a shark."

"Oh yeah?"

"A good size hammerhead. It almost had me for breakfast," Ron mentioned as if it was an everyday occurrence.

His wife raised her eyebrows and gave her husband a displeased look.

"You better be more careful, Ron. I heard yesterday a surfer lost his arm in a shark attack."

"Where was that?"

"Vero Beach," Rachael replied while she dismantled the juicer and placed the parts in the sink. She rinsed it off with a spray of hot water.

"I'm going to the mall after work," Ron announced.

"What for?"

"Have to get a birthday present for Earl. You want anything while I'm there?"

"Maybe a good flashlight and batteries. Candles too. Just in case the power goes off tomorrow."

"No problem."

Rachael poured more coffee into their mugs.

"I still think we should've evacuated," she said. "It's supposed to be a bad hurricane. I just hope it doesn't make landfall like the last one."

"We'll be fine. The Weather Channel said it's blowing toward Texas."

"Hope you're right, Ron. Get two bottles of red wine. I invited the Applebaums for dinner."

"What are you making?"

"Spaghetti and meatballs. We're eating at seven. Don't be late. And please don't stop at the casino."

He rolled his eyes. "I won't. Have any appointments today?"

"I have a consultation at 10:00, and an acupuncture treatment afterwards. I'll be at the office 'til 2:30. Call me later."

"Have a great day, sweetie."

"You too."

Ron grabbed his shades, a cold bottle of water, a coffee thermos, and then rode the elevator several floors down to the parking garage. He sat behind the wheel of his black and white Cadillac convertible and pressed a button on the console for the top to open. He left the garage and cruised down Collins Avenue, heading over to the public library where he spent the next four hours doing research for his upcoming magazine article.

Ron packed up his laptop, checked out some library materials and left. He hopped in his car and stopped at a drive-thru and ordered a large black coffee. He carefully poured it into his thermos, put on his prescription Ray-Bans, and then drove to the Lincoln Road Mall.

At the intersection of Lincoln and Washington, a traffic light took forever to change. Dressed in a light brown military uniform, a man hobbled off the median and started collecting money from the driver ahead of Ron's antique Cadillac. He finished with that car and approached the Caddy. Ron noticed the man's hand was badly mangled from an old war injury perhaps. He took out his wallet and found a wrinkled $2.00 bill. He ironed it with his thumb and forefinger before giving it to him.

"Thank you, sir!" the military veteran shouted.

Ron dropped the money into a small white bucket with a decal of an American flag stuck to it. The man stood at attention and admired Ron's car.

"Haven't seen one a those in ages."

"A two-dollar bill?" Ron asked while he put away his wallet.

"No, your Caddy. What year is it?"

"1956."

"The year I was born," the man stated. "It's a sweet looking machine."

"Thanks. You fight in Iraq?"

"No, sir! Afghanistan. Marines, sir!"

"It's really shameful how this country treats their war veterans," Ron mentioned.

"You can say that again, sir!"

The military vet slowly hobbled back to the concrete median, and he drank from his water bottle.

The traffic light finally turned green. Ron proceeded down Lincoln, hung a right into the Lincoln Road Mall and then found a parking space beneath the shade of an overhanging banyan tree. He turned on the radio and listened to an emergency broadcast on IRKME FM. The announcer said that Hurricane Bessie was approximately 265 miles southwest of Jamaica. The hurricane had been classified as a category three, and Governor Scott ordered everyone in the Keys to evacuate immediately. The Seven Mile Bridge was already bumper-to-bumper from Little Duck Key to Marathon. And many residents south of Homestead were high tailing it north. The announcer ended the broadcast by saying: "If Hurricane Bessie stays on course, there's gonna be some major problems for Key West by tomorrow morning. My name is Louis Hermosa, reporting live, for IRKME FM News."

Ron turned off the radio and pressed a button that closed the convertible top. He grabbed an umbrella, the bottle of water, and shut the car door and locked it with the key. He strode briskly along the sunburned pavement and entered the mall through Sears. The store felt terribly hot. An unpleasant odor made him feel light-headed. He approached a security guard who was sweating profusely and coughing into his plaid handkerchief.

"Excuse me, why is it so hot in here?" Ron asked.

He put away his hankie and replied, "They're fixing the AC. It's about a hundred degrees in here."

The man removed his cap and wiped his face, forehead and neck with a paper towel.

"Thanks."

On his way through the store, Ron nearly passed out. He guzzled his water and tossed the bottle in the trash before taking an escalator one floor up. He found a flashlight with a lifetime warranty, a pack of batteries, and a box of unscented candles. In the camping and fishing supply section of the sporting goods department, he grasped a fishing rod from a catchy display. He put that one back and chose another rod with a comfortable cork handle and a fancy turquoise reel. Ron mimicked a fisherman who had a bite on his line, excitedly reeling in his prize catch. *This should make a fine birthday present for Earl.* (Ron's close friend who lived up in the Adirondacks in upstate N.Y. Earl Tosh, loved the outdoors and was an avid fly fisherman.) Ron brought the merchandise to the checkout counter, where a young saleswoman stood fanning herself with a glamour magazine. She looked as if she wanted to peel off her perspiration-soaked blouse right then and there. Ron held the fishing rod upright and admired the woman's beauty.

"It's dreadfully hot in here today," he said. "Like a sauna.'

"That's for sure. All our bait and fishing supplies are twenty-five percent off the regular price. It's our big hurricane sale this week."

The woman managed to put on a thin smile despite the horrendous heat. She repositioned a desk fan.

"That includes our hooks, decoys and sinkers," she added.

"I don't need any bait. Or any of that other stuff. Can I pay for the flashlight and the batteries here too?"

"Of course."

The blue-eyed, bleached blonde wiped some sweat from her forehead and adjusted her button-popping blouse. Ron noticed her tongue had been pierced with a silver-blue ball, and one side of her nose with a tiny diamond. Her bare upper left arm had been tattooed with three blue butterflies. It was quite colorful, he thought.

"My Uncle Hymie uses bread for bait. Is that what you use?" she inquired.

"I don't fish. It's a birthday present for a friend of mine. Are Pfluegars decent quality poles?"

The saleswoman exposed her pierced tongue while receiving another text message from her ex-boyfriend. She closed the phone and looked up at Ron.

"Pfluegars makes some of the best fishing rods on the market," she replied with a professional demeanor. "This model has a stainless-steel six-ball-bearing reel, instant anti-reverse one-way clutch bearing, and a smooth cork handle with a soft-touch knob. Made with excellent craftsmanship, sir."

"I'll take it then," Ron said, holding the rod so she could easily scan it. He opened his wallet and gave her his credit card while gazing at the deep-cut ravine between her breasts. "Do you gift wrap?" he asked while she ran his card.

"I'm sorry we don't. Try customer service."

The saleswoman could tell where Ron had his eyes fixed. She finished the transaction and gave him his card and receipt.

"Thanks for shopping at Sears."

"Have a good night," he said.

"You too. Stay safe."

Ron gathered his shopping bag and fishing pole and headed for the exit. Outside, he immediately noticed a tower of dark gray clouds moving in from the west. A man in front of him was also looking at the sky. He was dressed in a long black coat, a fancy fedora, pair of casual trousers tailored above his ankles, and a vintage pair of worn-out Nike's. From behind the man could have easily been mistaken for a boy, until he turned around to face Ron. He revealed a long grayish brown beard and mustache. A pair of wire-rimmed glasses made him look intelligent, yet hipster. A flash of lightning and a loud thunderclap broke, just when Ron spoke to the man.

"They're cumulonimbus."

"What did you say?" the bearded man asked with an accent typical of Jews from Brooklyn, New York.

"I was referring to the clouds," Ron replied. "Cumulonimbus is the scientific term for a towering cloud formation that often produces a heavy rainfall."

"Oh? I wasn't aware of that. You wanna know someting?"

"What?"

"You don't need a weatherman to know which way the wind blows. Are you a meteorologist?" the Chasidic Jew asked.

"No, but it looks like we're in for some rather nasty weather soon."

"I was only joking about the weatherman," he said, giving Ron a friendly smile.

"Are you a rabbi?"

"Why? You work for the IRS?"

"No, I don't."

Ron chuckled as he glanced at the menacing black clouds once more.

"Pardon me for not properly introducing myself. I'm Rabbi Mandelson."

"Ron Levine."

"You're from the tribe of Levy. It's an honor meeting you, Mr. Levine."

"Likewise."

The two men shifted their shopping bags to their other hands and shook. A flash of lightning lit up the sky while another boisterous thunderclap vibrated the ground beneath their feet.

"Loud thunder," the rabbi said.

"I can help you with your bags, if ya want," Ron said. "Where'd you park?"

With his insightful green eyes, the rabbi studied Mr. Levine. "I didn't drive. I walked here. I live in the condominium across the street."

"Deerfield Beach Gardens?"

"Yes."

"An old friend of mine once lived there," Ron mentioned.

"Oh yeah? One too many loud motorcycles if you ask me. And the damn maintenance fee keeps going up."

"I can give you a lift home."

"I need the exercise."

"I wouldn't want you to get struck by lightning, Rabbi."

"Me neither. I'll take your offer."

"My car isn't far," Ron said as a powerful blast of wind shook the royal palms along the promenade.

Shoppers ran out of the mall, and they frantically searched for their vehicles in the windswept parking lot. A torrential downpour soon got underway.

"Let's make a run for it!" Ron exclaimed.

The men opened their umbrellas and sloshed through puddles, reaching the antique Cadillac just when a lightning bolt struck the top of the banyan tree near Ron's vehicle. He unlocked the doors and hurriedly placed everything in the back seat. They closed their umbrellas and ducked inside the car.

"I can't see anything through the windshield," Ron stated. "We should probably hang tight for a while."

"That's a wise decision," the rabbi said while drying his bifocals. "You have a nice honker, Mr. Levine."

"What's a honker?"

"It's Yiddish slang for a big comfortable car. A nice ride, shall we say? It's in great condition. You should drive it only in good health."

"Thanks."

After ten minutes or so, the thunder and lightning tapered off. The rain and wind still hammered the windshield but even with the wipers on full blast, it made no difference; the men saw nothing but a barrage of water outside the car. Ron turned the wipers off and the radio on. The broadcaster announced his name and the current location of Hurricane Bessie.

"Live, from IRKME FM, this is Louis——."

Ron turned the knob to a station that played classical music.

"I hope we don't get too much of this hurricane," the Chasidic Jew spoke.

Ron unscrewed the cap on his coffee thermos.

"I'm afraid we already are. You drink coffee? I have an extra cup. There's no milk or sugar in it though."

"Why not. It doesn't look like we're going anywhere too soon."

Outside, the forceful wind blew across the parking lot while branches of the banyan tree struck the hood of Ron's car. He filled a paper cup with coffee and handed it to the rabbi.

"Be careful, it's hot."

"Thanks. So, what do you do for a living, Ron? — I don't think you're a fisherman — are you?"

"I'm a freelance writer for magazines."

"No kidding. Which magazines?"

"I'm presently working on a project for Time. I've done articles for Life, Reader's Digest, Sports Illustrated, National Geographic, Rolling Stone and Playboy."

"That's impressive. What kind of articles do you write?"

"Human interest stories, interviews, travel, the environment, outer space, etc."

"That's terrific."

"You like Pink Floyd?" Ron asked.

"They're one of my favorite bands."

Ron inserted a *Shine on You Crazy Diamond* CD into the CD player, and he turned up the volume.

"I saw them at Madison Square Garden in 1971," Rabbi Mandelson mentioned.

"Oh, yeah? How were they?"

"Fantastic."

"I bet. I wrote an article about them in Rolling Stone ten years ago. I met their guitarist, David Gilmour. We talked for two hours in Central Park."

"That's great. Have you been writing a long time?"

"Nearly twenty-five years. How long have you been a rabbi?"

"Almost forty years."

"The whole time in Florida?" Ron asked.

"No, I had my first job at a small synagogue in Greenwich Village, New York. The shul was on Bleeker Street."

"How was that?"

"They were the best times of my life, the sixties. A trip as they say. *Peace, love and happiness.* Bob Dylan lived near the synagogue. And I used to hear Jimi Hendrix jam in Washington Square Park quite often. You know he came from nice a Jewish family?" the rabbi inquired.

"Who? Jimi Hendrix?"

"No! Bob Dylan. His real name was Robert Zimmerman."

"I know. I was only joking. That's wild. You ever drop any acid, Rabbi?"

"LSD?"

"Yeah."

"Never. But I had enough acid indigestion learning how to read the Torah. Back at the yeshiva we used to smoke a good joint now and then."

"How was that?"

"Took me sky high. What about you?"

"I had a few mind-altering experiences in my day," Ron replied. "I haven't done any drugs in years."

"Did you go to Woodstock?" the rabbi asked.

"The music festival?"

"Yeah. The one at Yasgur's farm."

"I was too young," Ron said. "What about you?"

"We were on our way there, but they closed the New York State Thruway. Hey, if you're interested, I might have some work for you in the near future."

"What kind of work?" Ron inquired, as he lowered the volume on the music.

"A friend of mine owns a fishing boat up in Lung Island. Seriously. I could have a great writing assignment for you."

"Tell me more," Ron said.

"I'm putting together a team that will go on an expedition to the rain forest in Peru. We'll need a journalist to do a cover story."

"What kind of expedition?"

"We're going to search for a lost tribe of Israel."

"That's pretty funny," Ron said.

The rabbi remained straight-faced.

"I wasn't joking."

"You're not?"

"No."

"When's this expedition happening?"

"Next year. The middle of January."

"I'm all ears. Tell me more about it," Ron said as he poured the remaining coffee into the rabbi's cup. Outside, a wall of rain fell. The wind increased.

"The expedition team will be based in the city of Iquitos," the rabbi began. "The Amazon River runs through there. Two good friends of mine, an archaeologist and an anthropologist have been working in the rain forest since 2010. They heard about the lost tribe from some local rubber farmers. We're really excited about it. I flew down there a couple of years ago. We saw them briefly," he described.

"Who — the lost tribe?"

Ron turned off the music.

"Yes," the rabbi said. "It was only for a minute or two but long enough for us to tell they were wearing yarmulkes and tallis. The rain was falling hard that day. By the time we got near them they were gone.

They're a nomadic tribe and only inhabit the deepest parts of the jungle."

"That sounds pretty incredible to me."

"Yes—"

"It could make for an interesting story," Ron stated. At the same time wondering if this guy was legitimate or not. He'd come across his share of charlatans in his day.

"If I hired you, I couldn't pay you anything. But I'd cover all your expenses. The airfare, taxis, hotels and meals. Here's my e-mail. Send me a couple of articles you've written. I have a good feeling about this, Mr. Levine."

"Interesting. A lost tribe of Israel in South America." Ron was thrilled yet hesitant. "I'd have to think it over and talk to my wife before I made any decisions."

"Of course. Take your time. Just be sure your passport is up to date. And you would have to get shots for Malaria and Dengue Fever. If we decided to use you, that is."

The parking lot continued to flood, rising halfway up the tires on Ron's Cadillac. An ugly green slime floated along the surface of the water. Police and fire-engine sirens wailed in the background. Ron's phone rang.

"Excuse me, I have to take this call. Hi, Rachael."

"I hope you're not at the casino, Ron."

"I'm still at the mall. It's raining cats and dogs here — I can't go anywhere."

"The Applebaums just arrived," Rachael said. "Don't forget to pick up the wine. Two bottles."

"I'll get it right after I take the rabbi home."

"What rabbi?"

"I'll explain it later, Rachael."

2

January 2017

At Lima International Airport, Ron and Rachael waited in the departure lounge for a two-hour connecting flight to Iquitos, Peru, a small city bordered by rain forest and the Amazon River. A few seats away from the American couple, a tall blonde photographer attached a telephoto lens onto his 35-mm camera. He looked through the lens a moment, removed it, and then placed everything back inside a leather case.

Dressed in a business suit, an olive-skinned gentleman sat across from the Levines. He was reading *The Jerusalem Post* while combing his goatee in a scholarly manner. He put away the comb and folded the newspaper. Not far from him, a Chasidic Jew stood in front of a plate-glass window with a panoramic view of the runways. He rocked back and forth while devotedly reciting the afternoon prayers, occasionally raising his eyes to watch a jet take off, or land.

"Now boarding passengers who are seated in section B," a man from Peruvian Airlines called over the intercom in English, then Spanish.

Rachael heard the announcement, and she nudged her husband to get up.

By 6:30 that evening, the Peruvian Airlines jet touched down in Iquitos and taxied to the gate. The doors opened.

Ron and Rachael disembarked and retrieved their luggage. They exchanged three hundred dollars for Peruvian currency before going outside to flag a cab. A taxi driver quickly responded to Ron's wave by opening the window of his Mercedes Benz.

"Where to, *amigo?*"

"The Palacio Hotel. Downtown Iquitos."

"Get in. I'll take care of your luggage."

Ron and Rachael climbed into the back seat while the cabby threw their bags in the trunk. He closed it, sat in the car, and then started the meter. He drove around some traffic and left the small airport behind.

Rachael felt a rumbling in her stomach while the taxi quickly traveled along a bumpy road lined with thick jungle on both sides.

"I'm really hungry, Ron."

"Me too. We'll get some dinner after we check in. Excuse me. Can you recommend a good place to eat?" he asked the cab driver.

"*Si amigo.* There's a number of good restaurants by the hotel you're staying at. Depends on what kind of food you like. Plaza De Armas has the best restaurants. A little pricey though."

"Gracias."

"De nada."

Ron turned to his wife. "Rabbi Mandelson said the food at the Palacio is halfway decent."

"How does he know?"

"He's eaten there before," Ron replied. "The food is strictly kosher."

"It is?"

"That's what the rabbi told me in an email."

"We can decide when we get there," his wife said.

The cab driver made a sharp left turn and drove along an avenue lined with trees, boutique shops and sidewalk cafes. He headed toward the river and parked in front of the Palacio Hotel; the antiquated lodging the members of the expedition team would be staying. Ron paid the fare, and the cabby removed their bags from the trunk. They stretched for a moment as the taxi drove off. The couple looked up at the hotel's old facade. It reminded Ron of a place he stayed at in France.

"Mr. Levine!" a man yelled and waved from the hotel entrance.

Holding the handle of his laptop case, Ron saw Rabbi Mandelson standing by the front door. The couple approached him.

"It's great to see you again, Rabbi," Ron said as he shook his hand.

"I'm glad you were able to make it," he said.

"This is my wife, Rachael."

"Pleased to meet you, Mrs. Levine."

"It's a pleasure to finally meet you, Rabbi. And please, call me Rachael."

She smiled, just about to offer her hand when she suddenly remembered that Chasidic Jews refrained from touching women, other than their own wives.

The slightly embarrassed rabbi asked, "How was your flight?"

"Not too bad. A bit crazy with the delays," Ron replied.

"Go get yourselves checked in," Rabbi Mandelson said. "I've arranged a little welcoming party and orientation. It's in the dining room now. There's plenty of good food and an open bar. See you soon."

The rabbi smiled, turned away, and walked across the lobby to greet a gentleman who was dressed in a blue suit and holding a briefcase.

"He seems nice," Rachael remarked as the couple tiredly approached the front desk.

They checked in, received their room key, and then took an old elevator upstairs.

In their room, Rachael felt the soft mattress and plopped her Louis Vuitton handbag on the double bed. She opened the curtains to a spectacular ocher sunset on the Amazon River below. The room was modestly furnished with a coffee table, tiffany lamp, two upholstered chairs, a potted plant, and a small fridge.

"I'm gonna freshen up before we go downstairs," she said.

Inside the bathroom, Ron unzipped his pants and released a steady stream into an old-style toilet. He noticed a big claw-footed bathtub and a sink fitted with old brass faucets. A large wood-framed mirror covered the wall over the sink. He flushed the toilet and washed his hands.

"This place looks like it's about two hundred years old, Rachael."

"You think we should change?" she asked.

"I think we're all right with what we have on. It's casual."

The couple went downstairs and walked through a hallway and entered a dining room where they found the expedition team's welcoming reception. Hot and cold food was laid out on a long rectangular table.

"Want a glass of wine?" Ron asked his wife.

"Sure."

A Chasidic Jew approached the Levines and introduced himself. "Hello, my name is Rabbi Karpadah. I'm the biblical expert on the expedition team."

"*Shalom*, Rabbi. I'm Ron Levine. I'll be doing the cover story for the expedition. This is my wife Rachael."

"It's a pleasure meeting you," Rabbi Karpadah said.

"Likewise."

Rachael smiled and noticed the young man's attractive brown side locks, handsome face, and a strong physique.

"Where you from, Mr. and Mrs. Levine?"

"We live in Miami Beach," Ron answered. "I'm originally from upstate New York. Rachael comes from Alabama."

"With a banjo on her knee? Just kidding."

"Something like that. Where you from, Rabbi?"

"Crown Heights, Brooklyn."

"No shortage of Jews there, huh?"

"That's for sure."

"Excuse us. We're gonna grab us a bite," Ron told his new friend.

"Eat—there's plenty of good food," Rabbi Karpadah said with a broad smile.

3

Four days later, a motorboat ferried the expedition team upriver about 30 kilometers from Iquitos. They disembarked at a small city called Tamshiyacu, and the group of seven men and two women boarded a van that drove them to a dark edge of town. Ron, Rachael, Rabbi Mandelson, and the other team members organized themselves for a long-wet trudge into the jungle. Nobody appeared to be in good spirits as the rain came down in buckets. The jungle felt more humid than Miami Beach, even in the hottest months of summer. To make matters worse, the mosquitoes were having a field day. Rabbi Karpadah bitched and moaned while he swatted the mucky air, slapping his bug-bitten arms and neck several times, he loudly exclaimed: "Damn these bastard mosquitoes! They're driving me nuts."

"Try some more bug repellent, Sam," Rabbi Mandelson told the biblical expert. He handed him a spray bottle. "We're taking a half-hour break. And if you don't mind, could you tone down your language, please. There are women present."

"Sorry."

Rabbi Karpadah sat on a tree stump and doused himself with the bug repellent.

"I'll take some of that when you're done," Ron said as he approached the rabbi.

Dr. Zevardia announced: "The guides said to watch out for poisonous snakes around here."

Ron pointed to a black snake that was slithering around the trunk of a rubber tree. "There goes one now. I don't know if it's poisonous or not."

Rachael held onto her husband's arm. "I hate snakes." He sprayed her arms and legs with the insect repellent before applying it to himself.

Howard Sternfinger, the photographer, held up a bunch of ripe bananas and asked, "Anyone care for one?"

"I will," Dr. Zevardia said.

"Save it for the monkeys. I've had four already," Rabbi Karpadah replied. "Maybe all this talk about a lost tribe of Israel is just a bunch of baloney."

"Or corned beef, perhaps," Ferdinand Tudela suggested. "I have a strong craving for a tall deli-sandwich on seedless rye. The kind you can get in a Brooklyn deli. With brown mustard, half-sour pickles, a side of potato salad, coleslaw, and an ice-cold root beer perhaps. I can just see it now. Delicious!"

"Stop it, Ferdinand. "You're making me hungry," his wife Sadie told him.

"Yeah, right, Mr. Tudela," Rabbi Karpadah said. "Good luck finding a Brooklyn deli in this swamp."

"What's the matter, Rabbi? You getting wet feet?" Ron asked with a chuckle.

"Very funny, Levine. Do you honestly believe there's a lost tribe of Israel here? I'm having some serious doubts myself," the biblical expert postulated.

"It's possible a lost tribe could be here," Ron said. "Jews have been known to inhabit some pretty desolate environments you know. Don't forget, our ancestors lived in the Sinai Desert for forty years."

"That's true, Levine," Rabbi Karpadah said. "But this is our fourth day here and we haven't found anything but hot humid jungle, mosquitoes, monkeys, snakes and—"

"And what?" Dr. Zevardia asked while attempting to light his cigarette with a damp wooden match.

"I think he means bananas," Ron said, as he peeled one, broke the fruit in half and then gave it to his wife. She voraciously ate it in two bites.

"You don't sound very optimistic this morning, Rabbi," Dr. Zevardia mentioned as he finally got his cigarette lit.

"I can't see how Jews would wanna come here and settle," Rabbi Karpadah stated. "There's no running water, or electricity, or indoor plumbing for heaven's sake."

"Our biblical expert has a good point there," Mr. Tudela said while slapping a few mosquitoes of his own.

"Listen up everyone," Rabbi Mandelson said with a stern look on his face. "I know this heat and rain is a pain in the neck, but it wouldn't hurt if we were all a little more optimistic today."

"I still wouldn't call this place the promised land," Rabbi Karpadah said while he tied the laces on his waterproof hiking boots.

While the men and women rested a few more minutes, the rain stopped completely. A splendorous sunlight penetrated the forest canopy and shone upon Rabbi Karpadah's white shirt; it illuminated a red-eyed creature which slowly crept along his back and shoulder. There, it stopped and planted its sticky orange feet. It stared at Dr. Zevardia who was puffing on his fag.

"Something stinks," Rabbi Karpadah said.

"It's the doctor's cigarette," Howard Sternfinger stated.

"Will you look at that!" the anthropologist declared while he focused his attention on the frog that had landed on Rabbi Karpadah's shirt.

"Don't touch it," Rabbi Mandelson warned.

"Why not?" the anthropologist inquired.

"It could be poisonous," Ron answered.

"Is it a snake?" Rabbi Karpadah asked.

Dr. Zevardia laughed and nonchalantly replied: "It's only a friendly, red-eyed tree frog."

The scientist curiously poked the amphibian's side with his index finger. It didn't move an inch.

"It's cute," Rachael said as she watched the frog turn its head her way.

"Are you sure it's not poisonous?" Rabbi Mandelson questioned with a worried look on his face.

"Will everybody mellow out. Since when are tree frogs poisonous?" asked Rabbi Karpadah.

"You can never be too careful — certain frogs are — you know," Ron lectured.

"Oh yeah, Levine? And which frogs would that be, the ones in fairy tales?" Rabbi Karpadah brashly questioned the journalist with a puff and a snicker.

"How ridiculous. Poisonous frogs," Howard Sternfinger said while he snapped a close-up of the vibrant green creature.

"I believe I saw a poisonous tree frog in Bali," Ron said. "Or was it Madagascar? I can't recall now."

The frog bravely stared at Dr. Zevardia while he touched it with his fingertip again.

Mr. Sternfinger took more pictures of the creature, then posted them onto his Facebook page.

"Everyone can relax," Dr. Zevardia said. "This particular frog species is nonpoisonous. The only poisonous frog I know of in Peru is the *tinctorius azureus*. Otherwise known as the dart frog. And it's rarely seen in the wild by humans."

"You see, Mr. Levine," Rabbi Karpadah said. "There's absolutely nothing to worry about."

The fearless amphibian traveled across the biblical expert's shoulder, upper arm, elbow, down his forearm and wrist. It stopped and squatted on his hand. To examine it better, the rabbi raised his arm and brought the frog closer to his face.

"It's a beautiful specimen, huh, Dr. Zevardia?" Rabbi Karpadah asked.

"Absolutely."

"Is it a male or a female?" Ron inquired.

"It's too hard to tell by just looking at them," the anthropologist replied. "The males usually make noise though."

"This one must be a female then — it's not talking," Rabbi Karpadah stated.

While everyone watched, Rabbi Karpadah closed his eyes, puckered his lips, and then gently kissed the amphibian on its thin yellow mouth. When he opened his eyes, the frog was still sitting on his hand, undauntedly staring back at him. The rabbi slowly lowered his arm, and the free-spirited tree frog jumped upon a rain-soaked banana leaf, before it vanished into the jungle.

4

The lobby in the Palacio Hotel had been furnished with antique furniture and other Parisian style decor befitting a fine hotel in Paris. Oil paintings adorned the walls, including an original Van Gogh, Monet, Dali, a Picasso, and a portrait of Gustave Eiffel, the renowned architect who had designed the iron-built Palacio and the Eiffel Tower in Paris. Framed and signed photographs of famous actors, actresses, authors, politicians, artists, athletes and musicians covered the plastered white walls of the lobby and hallways throughout the building. They were former guests who had once frequented the fine establishment.

Ron, Rachael and the other members of the expedition team left their wet umbrellas on the porch, and they entered the hotel lobby. Ron stopped to admire a black and white photo of Groucho Marx and his brothers, Chico, Harpo and Zeppo. The Three Stooges were next to them while a glowing Marilyn Monroe, and a ravishing Elizabeth Taylor were framed alongside.

Ron turned to Rabbi Karpadah and asked, "My wife and I are having a drink at the hotel bar before we eat. Care to join us?"

"Thanks, Levine. But I'm gonna grab myself an extra-long shower. We'll see you at dinner."

"Yeah sure."

Ron went upstairs with his wife while Rabbi Karpadah went to the front desk to retrieve his room key. He approached an attractive Peruvian woman named Rosa Florentina. She had long jet-black hair that was slicked with coconut oil, and a white-rice complexion with lips painted a primrose shade. A thin yellow blouse accentuated her pointy breasts. The man stared at them. The receptionist closed the book she was reading and admired the rabbi's muscular arms and barrel chest underneath his soggy shirt.

He caught a whiff of her jasmine scented perfume while he drummed his fingers on the front desk.

"*Hola, señorita.* I need the key for room thirteen, *por favor.*"

"*Hola*, Rabbi."

The receptionist charmingly smiled and handed the handsome rabbi a silver key. She suddenly grabbed his muscular forearm and stated in a hot Latin accent,

"You have such strong arms, Rabbi."

He looked at the women's manicured white hand. Startled by her sudden touch; it was soft, warm and inviting. She released her grip, smiled, and then winked at him.

"Maybe you would like to have a drink with me, later?" she asked. "I know of a nice place in town. They have dancing there, too."

Her brusque behavior caught the rabbi off guard.

"Possibly. What time is dinner served tonight?"

"Seven as usual, *señor.*"

"*Gracias.*"

"*De nada.*"

Rosa straightened her posture and pushed out her high shelved breasts. She smiled at the rabbi once more.

"I get off work at nine. Stop by the front desk if you would like."

The rabbi smiled behind his moist beard but said nothing.

She combed her fingers through her hair. And went back to the book she was reading.

The rabbi placed the key into his pants pocket and rode the old elevator up to his room. He unlocked the door and plotzed on an armchair, removing his hiking boots, socks and the rest of his dampened garments. He poured himself a shot of whiskey before having an ice-cold shower.

After he dried off, the rabbi put on a black-velvet kippah, trimmed his beard and mustache, and then he dressed for dinner. Before going downstairs, he rested on the bed, opened a prayer book and read a short passage from Proverbs. He shut the book, kissed it and placed it on a nightstand. He stretched out on the bed and laid his head on a pillow. He closed his eyes and reflected on his day in the rain forest.

The rabbi suddenly opened his eyes when he heard someone knocking on the door. The room seemed much brighter now.

"Who is it?" he asked.

"Ron."

"Give me a minute."

Still in his dressy clothes from last night, the rabbi crawled out of bed and caught a glimmer of light trailing through a crack in the mauve curtain. He stepped into his slippers and shuffled across the wood floor. He turned the doorknob and pulled the door open.

"Rise and shine," Ron greeted. "The team is downstairs already. Are you joining us for breakfast?"

"Breakfast? What time is it?" the rabbi asked while yawning and rubbing the sand from his eyes.

"It's 6:30. We're leaving for the rain forest soon. How come I didn't see you in the dining room last night?"

"Guess I fell asleep. Boy, I feel lousy. I don't think I'm going on the expedition today."

"You sure?"

"Positive."

"Want me to bring you up some breakfast?"

"Maybe a tea with lemon. You have any aspirin, Levine?"

"Rachael has a bottle in the room — I'll be right back."

At seven o'clock in the morning a delicate breeze descended upon the Amazon River. It was a cool 89 degrees in Iquitos and the heavy rainfall had ended. The subtropical air smelled fresh and fully oxygenated while a cloudless sky was rendered the most spectacular blue. A colorful variety of birds noisily sang and flew overhead.

On the dock in the back of the Palacio, two muscular Peruvian men whistled as the lazy river meandered by. They busily loaded a barnacle-encrusted motorboat, hauling on jugs of gasoline, a large ice chest filled with sandwiches, fruits and cold water. Afterwards, the two men rested on the pier and drank robust coffee and ate a Peruvian style flatbread called pan chuta.

Meanwhile, the expedition team and their wives had breakfast in the hotel. Ron reviewed his notes from the previous days of exploration while his wife enjoyed a glass of fresh-squeezed orange juice. He put his pen down and softly placed a hand on her shoulder.

"You coming with us, today, sweetie?" Ron asked.

"I don't think so. Sadie and I are going shopping at the Belen floating market."

"Do me a favor and pick me up a couple of shrunken heads while you're there. Just kidding."

Dr. Zevardia looked up from his paper, "Hey, where's our biblical expert this morning?"

"I saw him earlier," Ron said. He wasn't feeling well. Pass me the cream cheese please. So, where we headed today, Doctor?"

"We're gonna take the boat downriver a few miles. To a place called Mazan, Mr. Levine. From there we'll trek to an area of the jungle where the lost tribe was supposedly last seen."

"That sounds like a plan."

Ron poured himself another coffee and asked the anthropologist if he could look at his newspaper.

"Help yourself."

Howard Sternfinger approached the table where the Levines and Dr. Zevardia were sitting. He had his long blonde hair pulled back in a ponytail. The American hippy sported a white pair of shorts, a colorful tie-dyed tee shirt, and a floppy sun hat with a mosquito netting around it.

"Excuse me, Dr. Zevardia," the photographer said.

The anthropologist put down his fork and looked up.

"Yes, what is it, Mr. Sternfinger?"

"The captain said the boat is ready to shove off soon."

"Tell him we'll be out in ten minutes."

Minus the biblical expert, the lost tribe expedition team put on their life jackets and carefully boarded the barnacle-encrusted motorboat. They settled in as the Peruvian boat captain started the motor and chugged away from the dock. He deftly navigated the vessel past dinghies, houseboats, fishing boats, custom-built cruise ships, commercial freighters, and the exotic Belen floating market, bustling with early morning merchants, housewives, and tourist groups.

Banks along the murky green river grew lush with tropical flowers, palm, banana, cassava, pineapple and rubber trees. Loquacious parrots glided over the water while an inquisitive troop of red-faced and bald Uakari monkeys ate a breakfast of bananas and nuts. The monkeys shrewdly watched while the blue and yellow motorboat passed their tree-filled habitat.

After an hour and a half on the river, the ruddy skinned boat captain maneuvered toward the shore, docking at a small fishing village. The captain's first mate secured the vessel, and the expedition team slowly disembarked. Everyone stretched their arms and legs before two Peruvian guides led them into the rain forest.

Rabbi Mandelson yanked on a long hanging vine, causing an unexpected shower to fall on top of him. A clan of tree monkeys noisily chattered above, apparently amused by the incident. He looked up and wagged his finger at the rude creatures; that only caused a bigger commotion. The rabbi shook the water off his hat, then caught up with the others.

As the team of explorers trudged deeper inside the lush wet jungle, Ron detected a strong fragrance.

"What's that odor?" he questioned the anthropologist.

Dr. Zevardia stuck his nose up and intelligently raised his eyebrows.

"It smells like the Prosthechea fragrans. It's a common orchid that grows around here, Mr. Levine."

As the flowery scent pervaded the jungle air, the team gradually came upon a dense growth of white orchids clinging to trunks and tree branches. Not far ahead, a hanging garden of intensely red and yellow plants came into view. Ron admired them.

"Those are beautiful. What are they, Doctor?" he asked once more.

"Those are called Heliconia flowers, or the lobster claw."

"Pretty."

Ron snapped a series of photos with the camera on his cell phone. He drank some water before moving ahead.

Mr. Tudela yelled out, "I think I see something!"

"Where?" Rabbi Mandelson asked.

"Over that way," the archaeologist answered while pointing to a gold light that shot through the trees and bisected the dense forest canopy.

"What do you think it is, Mr. Tudela?" Ron asked, his nose still absorbed with the flowery odor.

"I'm not quite sure. We'll have to get a better look," the archaeologist replied.

While the expedition team excitedly approached the mysterious light, Rabbi Mandelson accidentally knocked his hiking boot against a hard flat object. He bent down and saw a wooden door and a doorpost.

The blue paint on it was chipped and faded. The wood was warped, and the hinges and handle were badly rusted. He read the Hebrew words, *Beit Yisrael,* plainly written on the door in flaking red paint.

"House of Israel," he translated. "Come look at this," Rabbi Mandelson called to the team.

A burnished gold mezuzah had been nailed to the doorpost. The sunlight struck the religious door ornament at just the right angle, causing the beam of light to shoot up through the trees. The rabbi stood and stared at the light. Intensely mystified him.

"I found something else," the team's archaeologist announced. He had just discovered a tarnished seven-branched candelabrum that was stuck between some ayahuasca vines. Ron helped him untangle the menorah, and they inspected it.

Dr. Zevardia walked over and closely studied the blue door with Rabbi Mandelson.

"You think it's a door from a synagogue?" the rabbi asked him.

"It's a good possibility. Looks like it's been here for a very long time."

"Mr. Sternfinger?"

"Yes, Rabbi?"

"Why don't you get some photos of all this?"

"Excellent idea," the photographer said while he prepared to focus his high-tech camera on the brilliant gold light.

"This is some find huh, Rabbi?"

"Most definitely, Mr. Levine."

"Shit!" the photographer cursed.

"What is it, Howard?" Rabbi Mandelson asked the photographer.

"I'm not sure."

"Maybe it needs new batteries," Dr. Zevardia told him.

"I replaced them this morning," the photographer stated.

"May I suggest something, Mr. Sternfinger?"

"What is it now, Mr. Levine? —I don't have time for your dry humor."

"It might help if you removed the lens cap," Ron answered, pointing his finger at the long nose of the camera.

"Christ!" the photographer lamented while his face turned a carnelian red. He removed the lens cap and quickly snapped several shots of the gold light, old door, mezuzah, and menorah.

"How about a picture of the whole team?" Rabbi Mandelson suggested.

"Yes, of course. C'mon, let's get everyone together," the photographer urged.

Mr. Tudela held the silver menorah in front of his chest while everyone beamed broad smiles. Howard

Sternfinger squinted through the camera lens, said "cheese", and then captured the team's proud moment.

5

The following day, Rabbi Karpadah stared at his ill-looking reflection in the bathroom mirror. He turned his head sideways to the left, the right, and then back to center. For some strange reason he didn't look like his normal self that morning. His throat felt like it was lined with coarse-grained sandpaper; it was painful when he swallowed two tablets of aspirin and water. He also noticed a collection of red spots on his stomach. They irritated him. The more he scratched, the more they itched. He buttoned his pajama top, shut the bathroom light, and then crawled back to bed.

Rabbi Mandelson walked down the hall with a breakfast tray. He set it down and knocked on his colleague's door.

"Come in," a tired voice announced.

Rabbi Mandelson opened the door, picked up the food tray, and then entered the room.

"Good morning, Sam. Brought you some breakfast."

"Set it on the table. I can't eat right now."

"Feeling any better?"

"Worse. I woke up with a sore throat and a rash on my stomach."

"Oh, dear. Well, at least have a hot tea. I spoke to a doctor last night. She's coming to examine you today."

"Really?"

"She's a specialist in infectious diseases."

"Why? —I don't have an infectious disease. It's only a sore throat and a little rash."

"I know but she was the only doctor available in Iquitos," Rabbi Mandelson informed. "Besides, maybe you'll need an antibiotic. I have some exciting news for you."

"Let me guess. You found an old box of matzos and a jar of gefilte fish in the jungle."

"At least your sense of humor is still intact," Rabbi Mandelson stated. "We discovered a menorah and an old door with a mezuzah on it."

"Mazel tov. You happen to see any rabbis running around in loincloths?"

"No. But the archaeologist believes there might be the remains of an old Jewish community buried underneath the jungle floor. How 'bout that?" Rabbi Mandelson asked.

"Next thing you know you'll be finding some Chinese Jews."

"If we dig far enough, I suppose we might," Rabbi Mandelson said while the men heard someone knocking on the door. "Maybe that's the doctor."

The ill rabbi rustled about, organizing his hair, beard and pajama top. "Do me a big favor before you open the door? Hand me my deodorant it's on the sink."

"Sure."

On the other side of the door: a freckle-cheeked, light skinned, big-busted, red-headed woman checked her watch, and a slight run in her pantyhose. She knocked again while the sick rabbi quickly applied the deodorant to his smelly armpits.

His colleague walked to the door and opened it.

"Can I help you?" he asked.

"Are you Rabbi Mandelson?"

"I am."

"Hi, I'm Dr. Maggie McKermy. I believe we spoke on the phone yesterday."

"Oh! It's a pleasure meeting you, Doctor. Come in, please."

"Likewise."

Rabbi Mandelson escorted her over to his colleague's bed.

"This is Rabbi Karpadah. He's your patient. Rabbi, meet Dr. McKermy."

"Hello."

"Hello, Rabbi. I understand you're not feeling well," she said.

"No, I'm not."

"Have a seat, Doctor. Would you like a tea or a coffee?" Rabbi Mandelson offered.

"No, thanks, I've had three cups already. Let's get down to business shall we."

While the two Chasidic Jews eagerly x-rayed Dr. McKermy's well-proportioned anatomy: she opened her black day pack and laid a towel on the bed, placing on it a stethoscope, thermometer, tongue depressor and a blood-pressure gauge. She put on sterile gloves and leaned over to examine her patient.

"Open your mouth and say ah."

"Ah."

She observed the rabbi's discolored tongue and throat.

"How long has your throat been swollen like that?" she asked.

"Since this morning. I have these too," the rabbi replied as he lifted his pajama top and showed her the unusual red spots on his belly.

She took out a magnifying glass and inspected the rash on his tightly muscled abdomen.

"Those are odd," she commented.

"What is it, Doctor?" Rabbi Mandelson inquired.

"Jungle rash. Do you have a fever?"

"A little," Rabbi Karpadah answered while scratching his stomach. "I have the rash on my genitals also."

"There's no need to show me," the doctor said. "Have you had all your inoculations?"

"Yes, Doctor."

"I hope it's not dengue fever," she said while shaking a glass thermometer and placing it underneath his tongue. "So, I heard you rabbis are here on an expedition."

"How did you know?" Rabbi Mandelson asked.

"Iquitos is a small city. It doesn't take long for news to travel around here." She waited a few moments before removing the thermometer. "You have a 101.5 temperature." The doctor wrapped a blood pressure cuff around the rabbi's muscular bicep and pumped. "You lift weights?" she asked.

"When I was younger."

"You have good muscle tone. Have any allergies?"

"Monkeys and bananas. I'm only joking."

"Where you from, Rabbi?"

"Brooklyn. And you?"

"Ireland."

"What part?"

"Belfast. Ever been?"

"Never, but I love corned beef and cabbage," Rabbi Karpadah replied.

"I hate it," the Irish doctor said with a grimace. "I'd much rather eat Jewish food. Your people know how to cook. Mine just know how to drink. Your blood pressure is normal, but I don't like those spots on your stomach. If it's all right with you, I'd like to get a blood sample and send it over to the lab."

"That's fine," Rabbi Karpadah said.

Dr. McKermy reached into her day pack and took out a sterile syringe with a clear plastic tube attached. She tied a rubber tourniquet around the rabbi's arm and wiped his skin with alcohol. She stuck a needle into his vein and drew a vial of blood.

"I'll write you out a prescription for your fever and have someone bring the medicine to the hotel. I should have the results of your test by tomorrow afternoon."

The doctor zipped her bag, stood, and then gave the ill rabbi a comforting smile.

"What about the bill, Doctor?" Rabbi Mandelson asked.

"I'll have to calculate it later. I need to see some patients at the hospital right now. Have a great day, gentlemen."

6

Dr. McKermy showered, had a late breakfast, dressed for work, and then went outside and straddled her Rocket Goldstar motorcycle. She used the mirror on the bike to apply her makeup, eyeliner, and a cherry red lip gloss. She waved and smiled at a neighbor who was watering his flower garden next door.

At five feet and five inches, 140 pounds, and the measurements of 37-22-35, Maggie McKermy wasn't what I'd call your typical medical doctor, but a woman more likely to be found in the centerfold of a girly magazine.

The good doctor put away her makeup kit and secured her helmet and goggles. When she kick-started and revved the powerful engine on her bike, a bevy of parakeets madly shrieked and flew out of a carambola tree across the street. She torched some rubber and opened the throttle on her polished chrome monster, gunning the motorcycle down Putumayo Road, past La Casade Fierro, Plaza de Armas, hung a sharp right onto Prospero, and then parked in front of the Espinoza Medical Laboratory.

The doctor entered the foyer and took the elevator to the third floor. She walked into an office and greeted a smartly dressed receptionist with a close-cropped hairstyle.

"How's it going, Rana?"

The receptionist looked up from her work.

"Fine, thanks. How 'bout you, Doctor?"

"Fabulous. My lab results ready?"

"They just came in five minutes ago," the receptionist replied, handing the doctor a manila envelope with Rabbi Karpadah's name printed on it.

"How's the family?" the doctor asked while she took out the lab report and reviewed it for a minute.

"*Muy bien gracias.*"

"We should have lunch next week," Dr. McKermy suggested, "A new Thai restaurant just opened up on La Casade Fierro. Some nurses I know said the food was outstanding."

"Is Thursday good for you?" Rana asked.

"I'll have to check my calendar and give you a buzz on Monday. Have to run. Ciao, Rana," the doctor said while placing the report back into her day pack.

"*Hasta la vista*, Doctor. And drive safe."

After the expedition team spent a morning and afternoon exploring the archeological site they had discovered the previous day, they returned to Iquitos, where Ron, Rabbi Mandelson, and Dr. Zevardia relaxed on the hotel's back porch that overlooked the Amazon River. The men sat at a table under the shade of a large red and white umbrella. The sun scorched above while they nibbled on fresh-fried plantain chips and quenched their thirsts with frozen pisco sours, a traditional Peruvian cocktail made with brandy and citrus juices.

While a silver-scaled fish jumped in the air then back into the river below, Ron raised his glass for a toast, "To your health, gentlemen."

"And to yours also, Mr. Levine," Rabbi Mandelson said.

"Yes, and let's not forget about a successful expedition," Dr. Zevardia threw in, tapping his glass against the other two. He tasted the pisco and reached for his pipe tobacco.

"When can we start excavating the site?" the Rabbi asked the anthropologist.

"Soon as the Ministry of Foreign Affairs in Lima grants us the permission. We can't do any archaeological digging 'til then."

"That could take several days," Ron stated discouragingly.

"I hope not," Dr. Zevardia said, lighting his pipe and blowing the smoke downwind.

"Perhaps we should inform the Department of Antiquities about the menorah," the rabbi suggested.

Dr. Zevardia put down his pipe, stroked his goatee and thought seriously for a moment. "I will contact them in the morning."

"Good," the rabbi said as he wiped the sweat from his forehead. He sat down again.

Ron opened the voice recorder app on his phone and tested it.

"One, two, three." He played it back and heard his voice. "Doctor, I'd like to ask you a few questions for my article. Mind if I recorded the conversation?"

"Go right ahead."

Ron pressed the red button on his cell phone to start the recording.

"So, how do you figure this lost tribe of Israel ended up in Peru?" the journalist inquired.

"That remains a mystery, Mr. Levine. It's my speculation that sometime before, or after the destruction of the second temple, the twelve tribes of Israel dispersed and made their departure from the land of milk and honey. A couple of staunch tribes stayed in ancient Israel. My guess, they lived near a body of water with an ample supply of fish. Most likely at the Sea of Galilee, or the Red Sea. I presume a few tribes migrated to other areas of the Middle East and North Africa. Particularly Yemen, Syria, Egypt, Algeria, and Morocco."

Ron nodded. "That's pretty interesting, Doctor. But where do you suppose the remaining tribes went?"

A waiter interrupted their conversation by placing a fresh bowl of plantain chips and a replenished pitcher of frozen pisco on the table.

"On the house," the waiter said.

"*Muchos gracias*, Jorge," Dr. Zevardia told the waiter.

"*De nada.*"

The anthropologist continued.

"There are various schools of thought on this subject. But according to my lost tribe of Israel theory, these wandering Jewish tribes had traveled in all directions. Some left the country on foot, others left on horseback, or with camel caravans. Two or three tribes had to be highly skilled shipbuilders and sea navigators. They must have gathered enough courage to sail across the waters for Europe, then eventually South America. Probably settling and forming Jewish communities along the coasts of Peru, Argentina and elsewhere. More adventurous tribes connected with inland areas of Peru, discovering the Amazon River and following it north. It's possible they encountered the dwindling Inca and Mayan civilizations. A colleague of mine believes that a Native American Indian tribe might have descended from one of the lost tribes of Israel. Who knows? Apart for some scattered hieroglyphics and broken pottery, no written records were left behind to tell us what really happened."

"That's truly fascinating, Doctor. But how can you be sure this actually took place?" Ron asked.

"I don't know, Mr. Levine. It's only a theory of mine."

"Your lost tribe of Israel theory?"

"That's correct. Some ancient artifacts, and whatever else we may find in the jungle could tell us another story perhaps. The door, the mezuzah, the menorah and the Torah ark we discovered are a good start, but if there's truly a lost tribe of Israel surviving in the rainforest somewhere, they won't be too easily found. It's my belief this Jewish tribe moved on to a more secluded area of the Amazon. Like other primitive tribes living in South America and Africa, I'm certain they would prefer not to come in contact with modern civilization. To be honest with you, I can't blame them," Dr. Zevardia explained behind an intellectual cloud of tobacco smoke.

"I see. I think that's a good place to stop for today," Ron said, pausing the voice recorder and saving the file.

Siesta in Iquitos was half-way through when Dr. McKermy drove her loud motorcycle up to the Palacio. She cut the engine and dangled her crimson helmet on the shiny chrome handlebar. Before running up the steps to the hotel, she shook out her wild red hair, tied it in a ponytail, and then straightened her pink V-neck scrub top. The shirt highlighted her freckled cleavage a bit more than she would've preferred that day. Still, it was boiling hot out, and she enjoyed the airflow riding the bike. The good doctor smoothed some wrinkles on her white skirt and walked into the hotel.

"Good afternoon, Rosa," Dr. McKermy greeted the half dozing receptionist.

Inside the Palacio's lobby, ceiling fans spun around a few times before the receptionist half-opened her eyes and responded.

"I love your outfit, Doctor," Rosa said.

"*Gracias.*"

"The rabbi and two other men are waiting for you out on the porch."

"*Gracias*, Rosa."

Rosa leaned back in her chair and shut her eyelids again. The ceiling fans whirled above her head. The receptionist took a cloth out of a bowl of ice water; without opening her eyes she rung it out and covered her face with it.

Dr. McKermy walked outside to the porch and passed a table where four American women chatted and drank mint juleps. She approached the table where the three men sat.

"Hello, Rabbi. I see you're enjoying our gorgeous weather in Iquitos," she said while the afternoon light glowed upon the woman's freckled countenance.

The anthropologist looked up and admired the doctor's fair-skinned complexion and strong-boned figure.

"It's a pleasure seeing you again, Dr. McKermy," Rabbi Mandelson said. "Please, have a seat. This is Dr. Zevardia, our anthropologist. And Mr. Levine, the journalist doing the cover story on the expedition."

"Nice meeting you both," she said and smiled.

"Care for a nice cold drink?" the rabbi offered.

"Pisco?" she asked.

"Yes."

"I'd love one, thanks."

She retreated under the protection of the umbrella and seated herself on a wicker chair next to Mr. Levine. The rabbi filled a glass with the cold liquid, and he handed it to the doctor.

She smiled and toasted, "*L'chaim.*"

"*L'chaim,*" the three men responded in unison.

"So, how's the expedition coming, Rabbi?" the woman asked.

"We're making good progress, thanks."

"That's wonderful news."

The Irish doctor threw back her drink and poured herself another. Her sensually smelling perfume caught the anthropologist's attention.

"I love the way the Palacio makes their pisco," she stated. "They know how to use just the right amount of brandy."

"So, I heard you're a specialist in infectious diseases," Dr. Zevardia mentioned.

"That seems to be the rumor going around."

"How'd you end up in Peru?" Ron asked her.

She put down her drink and replied, "After medical school, I did my internship at a hospital in Lima. I worked with Doctors Without Borders for three years, then I decided to open up my own practice in Iquitos. I've been here ever since."

"That's interesting," Ron said. "How do you like Iquitos?"

"I love it here. It took some time for me to get used to the rainforest environment though."

"I bet."

"Have you brought the results of the blood test, Doctor?" the Rabbi Mandelson inquired.

"I have it in my pack."

"Is everything okay?"

"I sure hope so."

"What do you mean by that?" the rabbi asked.

"It's rather complicated to explain in a few words," the doctor replied.

"Does the rabbi have dengue fever?" Dr. Zevardia asked.

"I doubt it," she replied. "The symptoms are different."

Dr. McKermy noticed that one of the women at a table nearby had turned her head to listen in on their conversation.

"Perhaps it's best we finish these drinks and discuss it upstairs in private. And if it's okay with Rabbi Karpadah, I think Dr. Laguardia might be interested in joining us. I trust you'll find his prognosis especially thought provoking."

"I'd like a that, Doctor. But my name is pronounced Zevardia."

"Oh, I'm sorry."

"Fuget a about it," Dr. Zevardia said.

. . .

After Dr. McKermy and the three men drank another pitcher of pisco, she, Dr. Zevardia and Rabbi Mandelson visited Rabbi Karpadah. The medical doctor and the two men entered his room.

"I see you brought an entourage with you today," the sick rabbi said.

"My apologies, Rabbi. Would you mind if Dr. Zevardia joined us?" Dr. McKermy asked.

"Not at all. Pull up a chair."

"Feeling any better?" the doctor asked as she set down her black pack and sat on a chair next to the rabbi's bed.

"I think my fever went down. My throat still feels a little sore, though."

The doctor put on sterile gloves, a mask, and then took out a tongue depressor.

"How 'bout we start by examining your throat. Stick out your tongue and say ah."

When Rabbi Karpadah opened his mouth, his tongue limply hung out of it. There was a noticeable silence in the room.

"Ah . . ."

Dr. Zevardia's brows lifted while Dr. McKermy's brown eyes bubbled wide. At a table by the window, Rabbi Mandelson knocked over a glass of ice water he had just poured.

"Holy Mary, Joseph and Jesus!" the doctor declared while she placed her palm onto her upper chest. She looked above and made the sign of the cross.

"What is it, Doctor?" the healthy rabbi asked as he wiped up the spilled water.

"Come see for yourself."

Rabbi Mandelson rushed over and saw that his colleague's tongue had practically doubled in length. It hung well below his chin.

"Oh, mine God!" the healthy rabbi exclaimed. "May we all see the messiah in our lifetime."

"Truly fascinating, Doctor," the anthropologist scientifically stated. "How do you suppose this happened?"

"I believe it's from the condition he's acquired," she answered while moving closer to examine the elongated lingua. "You can put it back in your mouth now."

"I've something else to show you," Rabbi Karpadah told the doctor of infectious diseases.

"What is it?"

He pulled the blanket off his legs and revealed a thin algae-colored webbing between the toes of both feet.

"Now that's very unusual," she said in a professional monotone.

"Oy vey," Rabbi Mandelson said.

"That doesn't look like a good sign either," Dr. Zevardia mentioned.

"It's not. Rabbi Mandelson?"

"Yes, Doctor?"

"Do you have something strong to drink?"

"I have a bottle of whiskey in my room."

"Go get it, please."

While Rabbi Mandelson left for his stash of booze, the doctor photographed her patient's feet with the camera on her cell phone. She examined the rash on his stomach before checking his vital signs.

Rabbi Mandelson returned with a bottle of Seagram's 7 whiskey. He unscrewed the cap, and asked before pouring the liquid into three glasses: "Would anyone like ice?"

"Straight for me," the doctor replied.

"Two cubes, *por favor*," the anthropologist said.

Rabbi Mandelson handed a glass to Dr. McKermy and one for Dr. Zevardia.

She downed the whiskey, and prepared to speak:

"Judging by the lab report, the rabbi's hemoglobin count tested normal. There's a slight decline in his iron level. However, I'm more concerned about his white blood cell configuration. Evidently, he's acquired a rare type of virus. And I've only seen two or three cases of it."

Rabbi Mandelson chugged his whiskey. "A rare virus?" he coughed out his words.

"That's correct."

"What's the virus called, Doctor?" Rabbi Karpadah inquired.

"In Spanish it's known as *El Virus Anfibio Humano*. In English that translates to—"

"The Human Amphibian Virus," Dr. Zevardia spurted.

"That's correct, Mr. Zevardia. I see that you know some Spanish."

"I'm fluent in it. Along with Hebrew, Latin and Swahili."

"You're multi-lingual. That's very impressive," she said.

"Thanks."

Rabbi Karpadah frowned while pulling on his long side lock. He adjusted the black-velvet yarmulke on his head while reaching for his tea.

"Where the hell would I get such a terrible thing from? I've had all my shots," Rabbi Karpadah stated.

"Most likely it came from the rainforest," she replied.

"*Oy vey*. Is the virus contagious?" Rabbi Mandelson asked.

"Not to my knowledge. The Human Amphibian Virus can only be contracted by coming in contact with the host."

"Which is?" Dr. Zevardia asked.

"Certain types of amphibians. A frog or a toad. Perhaps a salamander or a gecko may carry the contagion as well."

The doctor flipped a page on the prognosis.

"Like I was saying. I've had little experience treating this virus, but medical experts believe that the FEDS may play an important role in its development."

Dr. Zevardia cocked his head and scratched his goatee in a scholarly manner. "The Feds?" he asked.

"The Frog Enzyme Deficiency Syndrome," Dr. McKermy replied.

Rabbi Karpadah turned his head away from the window and asked, "The what?"

"The Frog Enzyme Deficiency Syndrome," she pronounced louder and slower.

"Shit!" the biblical expert loudly groaned.

"Try to contain yourself, Rabbi," the doctor said. "In the few cases I've come across, the virus seems to affect the skin on the face, the neck, chest, belly, tongue, hands, feet, and sometimes the male and female genitalia. Toady bumps, warts and other growths may also arise. In the advanced stages of the disease, the ears, lips and nose may shrivel. And eventually the patient's facial appearance may become unrecognizable. The voice can change pitch and tone also. To put it bluntly, the patient will gradually acquire the distinct features of a frog. Rabbi, would you mind refilling my glass please?"

"And you've treated patients who've had this virus?" Rabbi Karpadah asked.

"Only two or three cases."

"Is the virus fata, Doctor?" Dr. Zevardia inquired.

She took the glass from Rabbi Mandelson and thanked him. The Irish doctor laughed before she downed half the glass.

"Um. I always appreciate a good whiskey," she said.

"Did I say something funny?" Dr. Zevardia asked.

Dr. McKermy crossed her legs and covered the meaty part of her thighs with the hem of her cotton skirt. She replied with a straight face: "I've never heard of anyone croaking from the disease, gentlemen. Sorry, I couldn't resist that. No, it's not fatal."

"I like a your sense of humor, Doctor," the anthropologist said.

The scientist finished his drink and flippantly threw a glance toward the doctor's cream-cheesy leg. His intellectual mind simmering up some lustful fantasies no doubt.

"The virus is normally treated with an anti-viral medication, similar to what's used for the common cold," the doctor stated. "I just happen to have a few samples in my bag. We should have it cleared up in no time."

"Well, that's a relief," Dr. Zevardia said as he nonchalantly swirled the ice in his glass, becoming more intrigued with the doctor's acute curvatures. "Do you have any children, Dr. McKermit?"

"It's pronounced McKermy," she said and gave the anthropologist a long hard stare. "I'm not married if that's what you're asking me. Rabbi Karpadah has fallen asleep. I think we should let him rest now. I'll drop by Monday afternoon. Be sure he takes the medicine with some food, drinks plenty of liquids, and stays in bed."

"If you have a couple minutes, Doctor. I need to speak with you in private," Rabbi Mandelson spoke.

"Why don't we go downstairs," she suggested.

In the lobby, Dr. McKermy and Rabbi Mandelson sat on cushioned chairs in a quiet corner. Next to them was a small square wood table with a Tiffany lamp on it. Colorful gladiolas decorated the glass shade of the antique light.

"What's on your mind, Rabbi?" Dr. McKermy asked.

"I'm extremely concerned about my colleague's condition."

"That's understandable. It's not life threatening though."

"Something happened that may be important for you to know," the rabbi stated.

"What is it?"

"A couple of days ago while we were in the rain forest. The expedition team stopped to rest."

"And?"

Rabbi Mandelson leaned across the table and whispered through his hand: "A frog jumped onto Rabbi Karpadah's shirt."

"I couldn't hear you—what jumped onto his shirt?"

"A frog!" the rabbi shouted.

Everyone in the lobby turned their heads toward the noise.

"Not so loud, Rabbi. What kind of frog was it?"

"A red-eyed tree frog."

"So?"

"The expedition team stared at it. Then Dr. Zevardia started poking it with his finger."

She leaned in closer. "Then what happened?"

"He kissed it."

"The frog?" the doctor asked.

"That's correct."

Dr. McKermy incredulously pondered a Salvador Dali painting on the wall beside her. (The painting the artist did of the clocks hanging limply in a surreal desert landscape.)

"I can't believe I'm hearing this. He struck me as being kind of queer. You mean to tell me that, Dr. Zevardia kissed the frog?"

"No. Rabbi Karpadah kissed it."

"Is this some kind of sick joke, Rabbi?"

"I wish it was," he replied.

The rabbi removed his glasses and squinted.

"Did anyone else kiss the frog?" the doctor inquired.

"No."

Dr. McKermy slapped her forehead and declared, "Oy gevalt! Why didn't you tell me this earlier?"

"I didn't know it was so important until now," the rabbi replied.

"Excuse me, Rabbi. Dinner will be served in five minutes," Howard Sternfinger announced.

7

That Friday Evening

In the Palacio Hotel's kitchen, Chef Ranita dropped two matzo balls into a deep white soup bowl; and she poured a ladle of piping-hot chicken broth into it. She placed the bowl on a dinner tray while Rabbi Mandelson watched the steam rise from the soup.

"That smells like my mother used to make," he said.

"*Gracias.* Rabbi."

The chef placed a portion of beef brisket, carrots and a square of hot potato kugel onto a dinner plate. She covered it, put it on a tray, and then gave the rabbi an envelope containing a get-well card for his colleague.

"Make sure he eats. And don't forget to give him the card," she told him. "A waiter will bring the tray upstairs. Have a restful Sabbath, Rabbi."

"You as well, Ranita."

The next morning at the Palacio, in a small makeshift synagogue: a few members on the expedition team, their wives, some guest rabbis, men, women and children of the local Jewish community gathered for a Sabbath morning prayer service.

Mr. Tudela pulled a curtain and opened the ark, where a small velvet covered Torah was shelved. He removed the scroll and gave it to Rabbi Mandelson, who stood with it, faced the congregation, and then lifted up his voice and chanted a Hebrew prayer. The Shema.

"Sh'ma Yis'ra'eil Adonai Eloheinu Adonai Echad."

(In English, that prayer translates to 'Hear O' Israel, the Lord is our God, the Lord is One.)

The congregation repeated the prayer and said amen. Rabbi Mandelson recited another prayer, then carried the Torah and walked among the congregation. He returned the scroll to a table on the bimah (podium), where it was opened, unrolled, and then read from.

Jorge Kohani, Ron Levine and Dr. Zevardia were individually called up to the bimah to receive an aliya, an honorary blessing said during the Torah reading. After the blessings were recited, the Torah was raised aloft, set down, and then rolled up again. Mr. Tudela slipped a red-velvet skirt over the scroll and hung a decorative silver breastplate on the front. A special reading from a passage followed. Afterwards, Rabbi Mandelson stood at the podium and delivered a ten-minute sermon.

After the prayer service ended, the congregants greeted one another with a "Good Sabbath".

Everyone went into the hotel dining room to enjoy an after-service meal.

Dr. Zevardia and Rabbi Mandelson met each other by the entrance to the dining hall.

"Good Shabbos," the rabbi greeted his colleague.

"A good Sabbath to you, Rabbi. I really enjoyed your sermon."

"Thank you very much."

"And how is our biblical expert feeling today?" Dr. Zevardia asked.

"I haven't seen him this morning, but he was in good spirits last night. At least he managed to eat some of his dinner."

"That Chef Ranita sure knows how to cook good Jewish food," Dr. Zevardia mentioned.

"She sure does."

"Are you joining me for lunch, Rabbi?"

"That's an offer I can't refuse."

After Rabbi Mandelson ate, he prepared a plate of creamed herring, challah, and gefilte fish with beet horseradish. He brought it upstairs to Rabbi Karpadah's room. When he entered the half open door, he noticed that his colleague wasn't in his bed.

"I brought you some food, Sam. You hungry?"

He only heard water dripping from the bathroom sink. The get-well card was open on a pillow. He picked it up and read it:

Dear Rabbi Karpadah,

I spoke to my husband about you. He's a healer, or what we call a shaman. He may be able to alleviate your condition. Enjoy your dinner and have a blessed Sabbath.

Sincerely,

Chef Ranita

The rabbi dropped the card, went into the bathroom and closed the brass faucet on the sink. He quickly left the room and hurried downstairs to the lobby, where he approached Rosa at the front desk.

"Have you seen Rabbi Karpadah anywhere?" he nervously asked.

She lazily raised her eyes while filing her fingernails.

"And which rabbi would that be, señor? There appears to be several of them here today."

"Rabbi Karpadah. He's supposed to be in room thirteen."

"Is he the handsome one with the muscular arms?"

"Yes—"

"I saw him earlier this morning," Rosa said. "I believe he went to the market. He left the hotel in a hurry."

"Did he walk there?"

"*No, señor.* I called him a taxi."

"On the Sabbath? I need to use your phone *por favor.*"

"Of course—"

Rabbi Mandelson took out Dr. McKermy's business card and dialed the number from the telephone on the desk. It rang five times before she answered.

"Hello. Dr. McKermy speaking. Can I help you?"

"Doctor, this is Rabbi Mandelson," he said with a voice that revealed panic.

"Is there something wrong?"

"Rabbi Karpadah is not at the hotel."

"I'll be there in twenty minutes."

8

Baba Ganoosh, an Indian gentleman from Calcutta, was the proprietor of a health food store in Iquitos, called Baba's Holy Foods. He was also close friends with Carlos Calaveros, a short, lightweight, black-haired and kind-faced Peruvian gentleman, who was the local shaman and married to Ranita, the head chef of the Palacio Hotel. Carlos owned a holistic retreat center in town that offered ayahuasca ceremonies and various other healing modalities. Baba and Carlos occasionally drank coffee together and shared in-depth conversation. Wearing his familiar multi-colored skullcap, the shaman happily strolled through the market and stopped when he arrived at his friend's health food store.

"*Buenos dios*, Baba," Carlos greeted.

"*Buenos dios* to you, *amigo*. I haven't seen you in ages—where have you been hiding?" Baba asked.

"Ranita and I were enjoying a quiet little retreat up in Machu Pichu."

"How was that?"

"Excellent. It's always a very spiritual experience when we go up there," Carlos told his friend.

"That's nice. I just brewed a fresh pot of coffee. Will you be joining me?"

"Sure, why not."

Carlos sat at the counter and put his hand in his pocket to see if he remembered to bring the grocery list he'd scribbled on a piece of brown paper bag.

"So, what's new in the shaman's world these days?" the Indian man asked while he poured a Colombian roast into two cups. He handed one to Carlos and pushed the sugar bowl his way.

"Business is rather slow right now," he sighed and inhaled the robust coffee aroma. "I held my last ayahuasca ceremony about two months ago."

"Who attended? More hippies from Haight Ashbury?" Baba asked. "They were a trip."

"No. Four Japanese businessmen from Osaka."

"I suppose the Japanese men danced naked in the jungle, climbed trees, ate bananas and acted like a bunch of baboons?"

Carlos laughed while stirring a teaspoon of brown sugar into his coffee.

"They weren't any trouble really. More behaved than the hippies, I'll tell you that much."

Baba turned to a gas stove behind him, where cheese blintzes cooked in a large frying pan. He rolled them over, revealing a lightly browned surface, and then lowered the flame.

"Try a cheese blintz?" Baba asked while placing one on a plate and handing his friend a fork. "I made them with goat cheese this time."

"Sure, why not."

While Carlos taste-tested the blintz, Baba couldn't help noticing a customer checking out the homeopathic medicines on a shelf. The man wore a lengthy beard, a black fedora, a long coat, and a black and white prayer shawl was wrapped around his neck and shoulders. Because he hadn't worn any trousers, his hairy lower legs were exposed underneath his knee-length coat. It was Rabbi Karpadah.

"Are you in need of any groceries today?" Baba asked his friend.

"*Si.*"

Carlos reached into his pocket and took out the shopping list and placed it on the countertop.

"I hope you can read my chicken scratch. I'll need some pretty flowers too. It's Ranita's birthday today."

"Oh, how nice. Tell her I said happy birthday."

"I will."

"These roses came in this morning," Baba stated.

Carlos leaned over and caught a whiff of the pleasant fragrance.

"Give me a dozen of those. And wrap them in that fancy yellow paper por favor."

"Gladly. And I'm not charging you," Baba said.

Carlos put up a fuss, but his friend eventually won the argument. The white roses were wrapped in yellow paper and placed in water for Carlos to take with him later. Baba gently removed the cooked cheese blintzes to an oblong platter.

"Hey, I heard that lost tribe of Israel was seen running around naked in the rainforest," Baba said.

Carlos wiped his mouth with a napkin. He looked skeptical. "Eh, that lost tribe stuff is probably just a bunch of crazy rumors," he said.

"You're probably right, amigo. How are the blintzes?"

"Delicious. They have a different taste with the goat cheese."

"Good."

Baba scanned the shopping list.

"I'm out of mung beans by the way," he stated. "Should have some in next week. How's your supply of ayahuasca holding up?"

"I have enough to last me for the time being," Carlos replied.

"You sure? I just got a fresh batch yesterday. It's a new product. Primo quality. And extra-extra potent. The guy who I order it from said that all the shamans from Peru to Ecuador were raving about it."

"How much is a half-gallon, Baba?"

"Twenty nuevos. I'm giving you a ten nuevo discount."

"I'll take a gallon then."

"Excuse me, Carlos. I need to help this customer."

Baba walked over to the gentleman in the hat, beard, and long black coat.

"Are you looking for something special, *señor?*" Baba asked him.

"Does this stuff really work?" Rabbi Karpadah questioned the proprietor about a bottle of Dr. Shapiro's cure-all skin cream.

"That's an excellent product," Baba touted. "All my remedies are homeopathic, certified organic, kosher, and all-natural. What are you using it for may I ask?"

The rabbi unraveled the prayer shawl from his neck and revealed a puffy green throat sack that startled the dark-skinned Indian man.

"What the!"

The rabbi looked at Baba and asked him: "Is there something wrong?"

"That's an awfully strange looking throat you have there," Baba said. "Have you seen a doctor about your condition?"

"Yes. But the medication I'm taking doesn't seem to be working too well."

"I have faith Dr. Shapiro's remedy will do the trick. Here's a test bottle. Try a little on it."

The rabbi pumped a glob of white ointment on his palm and rubbed it onto the front part of his neck.

"It feels nice and cool," he stated.

"See . . . it's working already," Baba said with the confidence of a snake-oil salesman. "Cover up your neck, though. I wouldn't want you to scare off any of my customers."

The rabbi re-wrapped the prayer shawl around his neck.

"I'll take two bottles then. And a cup of that strong black coffee, please."

"Certainly, *señor.*"

The rabbi followed Baba to the counter where he sniffed a delightful aroma. "Are those cheese blintzes?"

"They are," Baba replied. "And they happen to be kosher. Would you like an order?"

"Yes, please. May I use your sink to wash my hands?"

"Be my guest."

Carlos asked from the front counter, "You're not a rabbi by any chance?"

Dr. McKermy abruptly stopped her motorcycle by the entrance to the Palacio Hotel. Rabbi Mandelson had been patiently waiting for her in the parking lot.

"You find him?" she asked.

"Not yet. The woman at the front desk said he might have gone to the marketplace earlier this morning."

"Hurry—we'll take my bike. I have an extra helmet—put it on."

"But I'm not allowed to drive on the Sabbath, Doctor."

"That's okay. I'm driving. And it's an emergency. God will understand. Ever ride on a motorcycle before?" she asked while mounting the bike.

"Never."

"Hop on the back and wrap your arms around my waist. And don't let go—whatever you do."

He settled in behind the doctor, feeling the warmth of her soft body pressed against his. He smelled a hint of her perfume.

"Where should I put my feet?"

"On the pedals. Hold on tight!" the doctor shouted above the thunderous motor. She peeled out of the parking lot, leaving a long trail of dust and smoke behind.

At the outdoor market in Iquitos, a young rat sat on the top of a wooden pallet and relished the sweet and pungent odors of chicken, beef, and fish barbecued on charcoal grills.

Meanwhile, Rabbi Karpadah drank his second cup of coffee and polished off another plate of cheese blintzes at Baba's Holy Foods. Afterwards, he, Baba, and Carlos delved into the ancient Jewish mysticism of Kabbalah.

Dr. McKermy screeched to a stop and she and Rabbi Mandelson got off the motorcycle and searched the marketplace for nearly ten minutes until they found Rabbi Karpadah sitting at the counter of Baba's Holy Foods.

"There he is," the Irish doctor announced, startling a young rat that was in the midst of a savory shish kebob odor.

"Greetings, Dr. McKermy. As always, it's so nice to see you," Baba said.

"Hi, Baba, Carlos," she greeted. "You're supposed to be in bed, Rabbi."

"I wanted to get some fresh air. All cooped up in that stupid hotel room all day and night. Besides, it's not often I get to eat cheese blintzes that taste this good."

"C'mon, Rabbi, let's find you a taxi and get you back to the hotel," the doctor said.

9

Two days later

On a late afternoon in the tranquil habitat of the shaman's courtyard, Dr. McKermy, Rabbi Karpadah and Dr. Zevardia sat around a circular wooden table. The twelve astrological symbols of the zodiac were ornately carved into the walnut furnishing. Coconut palms and fruit-bearing cacao trees provided ample shade for the three guests while they refreshed themselves with iced mint tea the shaman's assistant had brought them earlier.

Nearby, three morpho butterflies displayed their iridescent blue wings while flying above a garden planted with plump red tomatoes, eggplant, bell peppers, a variety of herbs, chili peppers and yellow summer squash. In a cloistered corner of the wooded retreat, beside a small fishpond, twelve bamboo trees swayed in the late afternoon breeze. The tall reeds made a haunting rhythm as they pinged against one another, sounding as if someone was playing a primitive musical instrument.

Although Rabbi Karpadah had recovered from his high fever, he still showed signs and symptoms of the bizarre virus he'd contracted from kissing the red-eyed tree frog. To make matters worse, Dr. McKermy and Dr. Zevardia now had the infectious disease, while Ron and Rachael were presently laid up in bed with high fevers, sore throats, achy muscles, crimson spots on their bellies and slightly webbed feet.

"Will you leave your hands alone already. You'll only make them worse," Dr. Zevardia told Rabbi. Karpadah.

The rabbi kept rubbing his hands and wrists. "I can't help it — they itch like crazy."

"Want me to put some more cream on them?" Dr. McKermy asked.

"Yes, please. I knew I shouldn't have come to this Godforsaken place," the rabbi lamented. "None of this would've happened if it wasn't for me."

Dr. Zevardia puffed on his pipe and held up his hand. "Oh, stop talking like that, Sam," he said. "It's not going to help us one bit. Besides. It was just as much my fault. I first touched the frog. And I should've known better and stopped you from kissing the damn creature."

"Well, it's a little late for that now," Dr. McKermy said while she applied the homeopathic remedy to the rabbi's hands and wrists. She smiled reassuringly. "Does that feel better?"

The rabbi set his hands in his lap. "Yes, thanks."

"Good."

She rubbed the medicine on her hands before passing the ointment to Dr. Zevardia.

Dr. McKermy took a cigarette and a lighter out of her bag, and she walked over to the fishpond by the tall bamboo. A nectarine light between the trees refracted from the setting sun, enabling the doctor to see her reflection in the pond's lucid water. She lit her cigarette and took a lungful drag. Exhaling, she disgustedly turned her face away from the repugnant image of herself. A large bronze carp glanced up; fearful but inquisitive, the fish caught the last glint of sunlight before it swam away. The sun set and the sky quickly turned an eggplant black. A crescent moon appeared in front of a half-a trillion stars. The doctor dropped her burning cigarette and smashed it under her shoe. She rejoined the two men who were sitting at the round table.

Jorge Kohani, the shaman's assistant, carried a brightly lit lantern and hastily walked through the shadowy courtyard. He approached the woman and the two men at the table.

"The ceremony will begin in a few minutes. Follow me, *por favor*," Jorge announced.

10

In the shaman's retreat center behind his house, his three guests sat on low cushions while he burned some white sage, causing a thick herbal smoke to linger in the air a few moments.

The shaman explained, "The sage is burned to clear the air of any negative energy before the ceremony begins. The bundle of leaves Jorge is holding is called the chacapas. He'll be shaking it throughout the ceremony, in order to restore the balance of energy."

Jorge demonstrated then put down the chacapas. He reached for an opaque bottle and pulled out the cork. He poured a brown liquid known as ayahuasca into five porcelain cups, and he gave everyone a cup, keeping one for himself.

Carlos chanted something in Spanish as he placed the smoldering sage into a brass bowl. The room fell silent, and the Peruvian medicine man drank some water and cleared his throat.

"I know that Dr. McKermy has experienced a couple of these ceremonies in the past, but I will explain some important information before I proceed. The liquid in these cups contains a sacred, sense-heightening, and hallucinogenic medicine known as ayahuasca. It's made from two plants that grow in the rainforest, the ayahuasca and the chacruna.

The three guests looked at one another, then back at Carlos. He continued.

"The word ayahuasca means 'spirit vine,' or 'vine of the soul.' It's been used in these ceremonies for thousands of years. The medicine can help heal us from disease and opens our minds to the unseen. The drug can cause you to experience intense dreams, hallucinations and visions. These may frighten you but cannot harm you. You may get sick to your stomach, have to vomit, or go to the bathroom. Please answer these calls when necessary. Everyone has a pail nearby in case you must unexpectedly throw up. If this happens, flush the contents in the toilet I showed you earlier. Before rejoining the ceremony thoroughly wash out your pail in the bathtub with the liquid soap and hot water."

Carlos opened the top of an ice-chest.

"If you get thirsty there's plenty of cold juices and bottled water to drink. No one should get dehydrated. The effects of the medicine will last approximately six to eight hours. If either of you experience any physical problems during the ceremony, please inform me or Jorge. Is that understood, gentlemen?"

"Yes, of course," Rabbi Karpadah answered.

"Absolutely," Dr. Zevardia replied.

"If you get tired and need to lie down there are cots over there," Carlos said, pointing. "Are there any more questions or concerns before I begin?"

"Do we have to stay inside throughout the entire ceremony?" Dr. Zevardia asked.

"It's okay if you go out for some fresh air, Doctor. But don't stray too far. We've had some problems with that in the past. People have wandered off and managed to get themselves lost all night. Let's begin."

Jorge dimmed the lights and shook the chacapas. He sat on his cushion again. The shaman tapped on a hand drum and chanted some incantations in Spanish. Everyone watched him slowly drink his cup of ayahuasca. By the look on his face, he wasn't relishing the taste. The others reluctantly drank the unsavory liquid from their cups. Jorge shook the chacapas once more. The shaman tapped on the drum.

11

The Ayahuasca Ceremony

In Rabbi Karpadah's first vision, a sugar maple sapling sprouted from a bright yellow seed, then turned into an adult-size tree which blossomed an abundance of electrified flora. This was a highly unusual occurrence, because the sugar maple, or any other maple tree for that matter doesn't normally grow in the rainforest of Peru. Yet, here was a big upside-down tree, its roots embedded in the shaman's ceiling. Although the tree appeared to be real, the rabbi was only hallucinating of course.

He watched the glowing leaves gradually turn an ecstatic yellow followed by a vivid red, moonlight pink, orange, magenta, various brown tones, and a whiter shade of pale.

A wind blew the leaves off the tree and formed a colorful carpet above. The room smelled of autumn, reminding the rabbi of the wonderful times he had spent during the High Holy Days in the Borscht Belt, in a quaint little bungalow at Kiamesha Lake, in upstate New York. While the effects of the ayahuasca grew more intense, a puffy gray cloud appeared directly above the rabbi's head. Water droplets fell and bounced off his hat and onto the table beside him. He contemplated the sparkling blue and red molecules of hydrogen and oxygen. They beamed an astounding brilliance while a clear aqueous bubble encapsulated each molecule. The bubbles formed a mirror-like surface on the tabletop.

"The shaman must have left a window open somewhere," the rabbi said to Dr. McKermy.

She glanced over at him and smiled. "What makes you say that?"

"I just felt some raindrops on my hand."

"How does it feel, so far?" she asked.

"Warm and wet."

The doctor laughed. "I meant the ayahuasca, silly."

"It's definitely a strong medicine," he stated, still sensing a bitter aftertaste in his mouth.

The doctor reached for the rabbi's hand and stroked it in a soothing manner.

"Just go with the flow, you'll be fine," she reassured him.

As the shaman curiously watched candle flames dance across the floor, he also felt the powerful influence of the ayahuasca kick in. He paused from tapping the hand drum. "Excuse me a few minutes," Carlos told the group. He got up and left the room.

The shaman walked down a hall and turned a light on in the bathroom. He was immediately surrounded by a multitude of long-legged spiders that crept everywhere. Despite the hallucination, the spiders looked very much alive. Carlos had led many of these shamanic healing ceremonies in the past, but this one felt uniquely different. He wondered if it was because of the new ayahuasca he was using. Baba told him it was primo quality and extra-extra potent. Perhaps it was much stronger than the ayahuasca he was normally used to. When the shaman turned the sink faucet on to wash his hands, the water ran only after a torrent of blackbirds escaped from the tap. They crazily flew in circles around the room. He ducked his head and opened a window, watching the birds fly out one by one. He went to the sink and scrubbed his hands with soap and water, noticing a collection of green and yellow spots on his palms, wrists, and fingers. No matter how hard he scrubbed, they wouldn't wash off. Instead, more of the rash appeared and spread to his forearms and elbows at an alarming rate. The shaman soon felt a strange sensation between his toes. He turned off the bathroom light and rejoined the ceremony.

When Rabbi Karpadah gazed at his reflection in the watery surface of the table, his face resembled an amphibian. He dipped his hand into the water and felt something clamp onto his wrist and pull him through the table. The claw of a gigantic lobster pulled him down through an underwater cavern filled with octopus, starfish, grandiose seahorses, ink-spilling squids and an odd variety of sea creatures he'd never seen; that included some large rotund oysters dressed in dapper gray suits, white shirts and black bow ties. They sat with their shells wide open, on chairs made of scintillating pearls. A woodwind section of scallops and shrimp blew on flutes, clarinets, oboes, piccolos and bassoon, while a string section of bottom feeders played violin, viola, double bass, cello, harp and timpani. They feverishly performed interludes, intermezzos, arpeggios, and then a climactic arrangement from Beethoven's Violin Concerto, in D Major. The deep-sea orchestra finished their selection with a boisterous crescendo. The giant lobster released its grip on the frogman, then it and the other sea creatures applauded the outstanding performance.

A strong current propelled the rabbi through the subterranean cave and swiftly pushed him up and out of the waterfilled grotto. His webbed feet landed on the sandy bottom of an immense black lake in Peru. Lake Titicaca. A gypsy moon precariously hung above the dark waters. High snow-capped mountains loomed in the distance. The hallucinating rabbi could still hear the chanting, the drumming, and the shaking of the chacapas, but it all sounded much fainter now. As if it came from a farther end of the lake.

Brilliantly colored lights darted across the sky, etching kaleidoscopic patterns throughout the heavens. A sanguineous rain of molten brimstone fell upon the mountains, moon and lake. The rabbi gazed upward and trembled tumultuously. He put on his fedora and quickly moved to avoid the white-hot chunks of hurtling brimstone.

12

Farther along the shores of Lake Titicaca, Rabbi Karpadah met a man who held a gold cup filled with a bubbling elixir. A bright white aura surrounded him, and a double-edged sword was in his other hand, raised toward the moon. He handed the gold cup to the rabbi.

"Drink," he ordered.

The rabbi drank the elixir and threw the cup on the ground. He watched as black, white and yellow spotted lizards crawled from the cup and scurried along the beach.

"Who are you?" the rabbi asked the man encircled by the glowing white aura.

"Jorge Kohani. The shaman's assistant."

"Are you a high priest? A Kohein?"

"*Sí, señor,*" Jorge replied. "Come with me, Rabbi."

"Shouldn't we stop to pray?"

"There's no time for that, *señor*, the others are waiting for us."

The rabbi followed Jorge to a large wooden fishing boat, where Carlos, Dr. McKermy, and Dr. Zevardia were laughing hysterically from inside.

The rabbi noticed their skin was translucent, enabling him to see everything inside their bodies. He watched their hearts pump, and their other organs function. Blood flowed through their veins, arteries, and capillaries; he saw that too. Their livers, gallbladders, churning stomachs, and snaking intestines radiated a psychedelic blue, green, red and yellow. Their brains moved like purplish blobs inside a lava lamp.

"Don't just stand there, Rabbi, climb aboard," the shaman said as he secured the multi-colored skullcap on top of his head.

"Where are we going?" the rabbi asked.

"On a little fishing trip," the shaman replied. Put on your life jacket."

Carlos laughed hard while he handed the rabbi an orange life jacket lined with more holes than Swiss cheese.

"We're ready to go, Carlos," Jorge announced.

The shaman's assistant stood at the stern and cut the line with his sword. He planted the sword in the sand, and it turned into a blossoming white lilac bush. Jorge pushed the boat into the water, and he jumped aboard.

The boat sailed through a narrow strait with high jagged cliffs on either side. From the heights, fire-breathing dragons glared down at the five passengers inside the flimsy wooden vessel. The weather turned nastier than a Halifax winter storm; the boat shuddered from bow to stern while a monstrous black wave washed over the side and threatened to capsize it at any moment. A brackish liquid filled the hold while everyone laughed hysterically.

Dr. Zevardia closed his eyes and wallowed in a mindless slumber as incandescent night crawlers burrowed deep within his wavy-gravy brain. The glutinous worms squiggled past the protective membrane of his florescent blue meninges, his brain's inner sanctum, the pons, amygdala, the ridges and ruffled cerebral cortex before they voraciously devoured the tender gray matter of the scientist's medulla, cerebrum and cerebellum. Meanwhile, a disciplined regiment of army ants rampaged the scientist's dendrites, biting off brisket-like chunks from his pituitary, pineal, thalamus and hypothalamus glands. After the invaders depleted his hormones, they left his inter-brain, traveled through his spinal cord, and then wreaked more havoc there.

Jorge adjusted the mainsail while another tall wave crashed over the boat. Dr. McKermy and the shaman were immediately knocked overboard and sucked into a corkscrewing quagmire. The rabbi held on for dear life and the shaman's assistant lost his balance and teetered to the starboard side; he was thrown into the lake.

Dr. Zevardia awoke from his worm-filled delirium, reaching out his hand for Jorge to grab, but he yanked the anthropologist into the turbulent water as well. Rabbi Karpadah watched helplessly while Dr. McKermy and the three men battled a tumultuous sea that eventually engulfed them. A ravenous school of piranha attacked the foursome. And the water turned a blood-red salmagundi.

13

On the dark and silent waters of Lake Titicaca, Rabbi Karpadah sat alone in the fishing boat and contemplated an amethyst light that radiated from the middle of his forehead. This illumination originated from his Ajna chakra, or third eye. The chakra grew brighter and larger until it levitated outside his body, eye-level. The heliotrope orb rapidly spun clockwise, becoming the size of a deep-sea diving bell, large enough for a man or a woman to fit inside of. The purple bathysphere slowly dropped to the water's surface and gradually stopped spinning. It knocked against the boat's starboard side every now and then. The rabbi watched this strange nautical capsule, curious to know if anyone was inside. A mucky layer of seaweed partially covered a large round window. A soft amber light burned within. He pressed his ear against the window and distinctly heard the constant hum of the ocean. Next, he stuck his nose inside a narrow crack and smelled a strong odor of vetiver, anchovy, grouper, Italian clam tacos, nori seaweed and ambergris. A most erotic essence. The light dimmed inside the bathysphere while something pinched the end of the rabbi's stunted green nose.

"Ouch!" he exclaimed.

He heard a woman's laughter inside the diving bell.

"I can't open the window because it's jammed with seaweed. Could you try from your end, please?" a female voice implored.

The rabbi untangled the oleaginous green gunk and yanked the handle on the round glass portal. It popped open, and out came the manicured fingers, slender arms and face of a ravishing young woman who wore nothing but lipstick, rouge, makeup and eyeliner.

"Take my hand and help me out of here," she said. "Be careful, I'm very slippery."

The rabbi cradled the woman's lithe body in his arms and gently placed her in the boat. Her large fishtail flopped excitedly and splashed water everywhere. His clothes got soaking wet.

"I thought you were a woman at first," he said, noticing her fish scales and throbbing tail.

"My better half is."

She giggled and revealed a set of straight white teeth, full red lips, and big bouncy breasts that were slicked with algae slime.

"Are you a mermaid?" the rabbi inquired.

"I am. And I'm terribly sorry I got your clothes wet. If you take them off and hang them on the mast they should dry quickly in the wind."

"Good idea."

The man stripped off his garments and hung them up. Except for the hat on his head, he sat naked next to the beautiful sea-nymph. She stared at him. And he swiftly covered his manhood with the black fedora. He smiled bashfully and blushed. When the mermaid moved, her blue-green scales scintillated. The rabbi found that oddly exciting.

"It's big," she said.

"Huh?"

"Your hat. May I try it on?" she asked.

"Sure."

He handed it to her, and she placed it on her head. Her long red hair still dripped with sea water.

"It's lovely. How does it look on me?"

"To be honest it looks kind of funny on you."

She moved closer to him. "Would you kiss me, Rabbi? —I've never been kissed by a real live man before."

"And I've never kissed a mermaid."

He chuckled.

While the boat rocked gently, he and the mermaid kissed awhile.

"That was nice. Could we try it again?" the mermaid asked.

"If you so desire."

The rabbi wrapped his arms around the misty-eyed sea nymph, and he kissed her briny lips. When he opened his eyes this time, however, a most startling surprise confronted him. The mermaid's face had been transformed into the face of his mother. She looked at him, and immediately gave him a guilt complex.

"I can't believe what I'm seeing!" the mermaid who was now-his-mother declared.

The rabbi sat back in shock. He couldn't believe it either.

"Mother! What on earth are you doing here?"

"Why aren't you wearing any clothes, Samuel?" she questioned her surprised son.

"They got wet when I put you in the boat—don't you remember?"

"And why isn't your head covered?" she asked.

The rabbi snatched the hat from her head and covered his own. His penis turned into a snake, and it sprang up and bit his nose.

"Ouch!"

The mermaid scowled.

"What happened to your face? It looks terrible."

"It's from a virus," he replied while placing his hands over his now shrunken privates.

"I told you to go see a dermatologist. Your father would have a stroke if he saw you right now."

"But Mother, I can explain—"

"Explain why you're not praying in the synagogue. You're still eating kosher, I hope?"

"Of course. I met a really nice woman. She's a doctor."

"A doctor? Mazel tov. And, is she Jewish?"

"No—"

"She's not Jewish? I'm going to cut you out of my will if this keeps up."

"But mother."

"Don't mother me! Shame on you. My son the big rabbi. Vhat a shlemiel he is. Just vait till I tell your father. He'll disown you."

The rabbi shamefully lowered his head while the mermaid laughed and flopped out of the boat. She splashed into the water and vanished under the murky undercurrents of Lake Titicaca.

14

A variety of fish and other sea creatures swam to the surface of Lake Titicaca, and they gathered for an official powwow around the rabbi's fishing boat. Everyone placed their undivided attention on an eloquent fish named Johnny Mac: a large, loud-mouth bass who was an authoritative figure within the deep-sea community. He organized his notes and prepared to speak.

"Good evening. My name is Johnny Mac. Welcome to our annual meeting on the environment."

The multifarious assembly gave the large-mouth bass a most lengthy and boisterous applause.

"Thank you. Thank you. Thank you. Thank you very much. I'm pleased to extend a warm welcome to the members of the community, and our most honored guest, biblical expert, Rabbi Samuel Karpadah. He came all the way from Brooklyn, New York. Welcome to our annual meeting on the environment, Rabbi," Mr. Mac's voice boomed clear across the lake.

When the applause died down, the rabbi spoke, "Thank you. It's an extraordinary honor to be here, Chairman Mac."

"So, tell us, Rabbi. Why is man polluting the world's streams, rivers, lakes and oceans?" Mr. Mac inquired.

"With all due respect, chairman. I didn't have anything to do with it."

"Quiet! You'll have your time to speak after my discourse."

Mr. Mac wiped the excess spittle and seaweed off his notes while a school of catfish swam to the surface. They positioned their tiny ears above the water and listened to the bass's ballyhoo.

"Our people haven't harmed your environment, but you humans have turned our watery homes into oily cesspools filled with blue-green algae, harmful red tide, garbage, plastic this and that, chemical, nuclear and pharmaceutical wastes. Not to mention tons of your shit! Our food is tainted now—and we can hardly breathe anymore—let alone swim."

The rabbi interrupted, "I'm sure there must be an explanation for all this."

"Silence! You most insignificant hierophant," the loudmouth bass shouted. "One more interruption and I'll have you removed from this meeting. Whether it's by cruise ship, freighter, barge, pleasure yacht, or a fishing boat like the one you're on, humans continue to endanger our species and the environment by dumping toxic waste into the oceans. Sea turtles, manatees, whales, tuna, shark, stingrays and numerous other sea creatures and fish get entangled in your treacherous nets. They become mangled, or die because of boat propellers, jet skis, and other dangers in the waters such as offshore drilling and poisonous oil spills. Seabirds and fish get coated with this thick black oil and die. Floating islands of garbage inhabit the oceans now. This is an extremely shocking sight to see. Pardon me."

The bass hiccupped and paused a moment to eject a small tadpole from its gullet. The tiny creature happily swam away and reunited with its family.

"Your factories pour industrial pollutants into lakes, rivers, and oceans of the world. The Great Creator's benevolent waters have provided human beings, birds, land animals, and sea creatures with valuable food and clean drinking water for eons. And this is how the human race shows its gratitude? If these harmful practices are continued at the present rate, most, or all of the clean water on Mother Earth will be too contaminated for animals and humans alike."

The rabbi sighed.

"And need I mention that my fellow fish and shellfish will eventually become unsuitable for human consumption? What do you have to say about all this, Rabbi?" the bass inquired.

All eyes focused on the man while he stroked his long white beard, loosened his necktie, and then cleared his throat.

"Good evening, members of the community, and Chairman Mac. I am most honored and privileged you have given me the opportunity to speak here tonight. But I can assure you, I've had nothing to do with these environmental travesties you're referring to. I deeply sympathize with your cause but as you can see, I am not a fisherman myself."

The large-mouth bass leaned on his floating lectern. He shook his silver-green head in disbelief.

"Would you kindly repeat that last phrase, sir?"

"I am not a fisherman myself."

"Is that the truth?" the bass interrupted.

"Yes, Mr. Mac."

Johnny Mac arched his scaly neck back and spit a stream of water high into the air. The dolphins, fish, sea urchins, and crustaceans dropped their mouths and took in water; they also spit fountains in the air. From the shore, a group of jellyfish quivered. Crabs cowered and ran for cover while seagulls and other seabirds squawked, screamed, and whistled. Mr. Mac banged his gavel on the floating lectern once more, and it became quiet again.

"Let me get this straight, Rabbi. You're holding a fishing rod, yet, you say you're not a fisherman? For some strange reason, I feel like we're not on the same page here."

The rabbi looked down and saw that he was indeed holding a fishing rod with a craftily made handle and a smooth blue reel; its thin silver line trailed above the water cast far out of sight. The rabbi's face turned beet red as he dropped the fishing rod. Discontented schools of trout, orestias, blackfish, blind fish, bluefish and bullhead consorted among themselves. Many of the schools left the gathering utterly disgusted.

"I'm terribly sorry, chairman, but that's not my fishing pole," the rabbi protested.

"Then whose is it?" the bass snorted.

"It's a long story. But it all started out with this tremendous wave."

"Enough! I, nor anyone else here is interested in hearing your long story."

"Let me explain—"

"Don't waste your precious breath, Rabbi. The human race better clean up their act before it's too late," Johnny Mac lectured.

"But, but . . ."

"And no more buts, Rabbi. There's plenty of 'em on your sunny beaches. Farewell, and safe travels. This meeting is now adjourned," the loud-mouth bass declared, as he banged his gavel.

15

The ayahuasca ceremony continues

Rabbi Karpadah envisioned a thin outline of land along a dusky horizon. High above Lake Titicaca, an Andean condor with a ten-foot wingspan, gracefully flew toward the fishing boat and landed on the top mast. Its neck was wrapped with a collar of white feathers. It called down in a voice which sounded exactly like Dr. McKermy's.

"Mind if I caught a ride with you, Rabbi? I'm awfully tired."

He briefly opened his eyes but ignored the bird's query, thinking it was only the wind stirring from the bow. He lowered his hat, clasped his hands behind his neck, and then fell asleep again. With its sharp beak, the enormous bird broke off a small barnacle from the mast and dropped it on top of the rabbi's hat. It made a thump-like sound and bounced off and plunked into the water. He looked above and saw the bird smiling at him. It had the perfect likeness to Dr. McKermy.

"Is that you, Doctor?"

"Yes. In a slightly different form obviously. Are you having a nice trip, Rabbi?" the bird-doctor inquired.

"I am. But where's the shaman?"

"I believe he's on the island," she replied while preening a feather.

"What island would that be?"

"The one right in front of you," the bird answered. She spread her long black wings and flew off the mast toward the tropical pink paradise.

The rabbi adjusted the sails, and the winds gradually blew him in the direction of the island. The sky turned yellow while a blazing blue sun appeared. Tantalizing smoke from cooking fires mingled with sweet and zesty fragrances of mango, pineapple, lemon, nutmeg, cinnamon, orange and coconut. Children's laughter filled the air while mothers shouted, babies cried, dogs barked, and parrots chattered in a cacophony.

Scantily dressed natives ran from their wooden huts and rushed down to the beach to curiously watch the fishing boat approach the shore. The jubilant natives gathered along the beachfront and prepared to welcome the visitor to their lush pink paradise. The men, women and children danced, sang, and happily waved their arms in the air while other natives blew conchs, hollowed-out ram's horns (shofars), and loud brass trumpets that heralded the visitor.

The rabbi put on his dry clothes and ran an abalone comb through his hair, beard and mustache. He dropped anchor, waded through the sparkling surf, and then stepped onto land. From the large group of skimpily attired men, women and children: the Chasidic rabbi immediately recognized the shaman by his rainbow-colored skullcap and wiry physique. The bare-chested man wore a plaid loincloth, his left arm was tattooed with a blue and gold Star of David. He held a long-pointed spear by his side.

Extremely overjoyed to see a familiar face, the rabbi approached the shaman and gave him a warm hug. After releasing his embrace, he declared: "Boy, am I glad to see you again!"

"Who are you?" said the man who looked like the shaman.

"Rabbi Karpadah. Don't you recognize me?"

The man grinned and shook his head.

"No, but welcome to our island paradise, Rabbi."

The clergyman looked confused. He twisted his side-lock a moment. Then four black-nippled beauties cheerfully placed flower garlands around his neck. The women's grass skirts blew from the ocean breeze while the man who looked like the shaman kissed the rabbi firmly on his lips.

"Hmm. You're a good kisser, Rabbi."

The natives cheered and joyously gathered in a large circle around the two men. The crowd grew quiet.

"Where are the others?" the rabbi asked.

"Others? What are you talking about?"

"Dr. McKermy, Jorge, and Dr. Zevardia."

The native shrugged.

"I don't know these people."

A few of the men in the circle looked at one another and also shrugged their shoulders. They mumbled something under their breaths. Some of them looked rather hungry.

"But aren't you, Carlos, the shaman?" Rabbi Karpadah asked.

"Who is he? My name is Chief Bug O' Levy."

The man shifted the spear to his other hand, grinned and showed a full set of teeth. He scratched his balls underneath his plaid loin cloth.

"Chief Bug O' Levy?"

"Yes, Rabbi. We're the Fuck-are-wee."

"You're asking me? —I'm lost myself."

"You don't understand, Rabbi. That's the name of our tribe. We are the Fuck-are-wee. The lost tribe of Israel," he proudly announced.

"The lost tribe of Israel?"

"That's correct. Shalom aleichem," the chief spoke in Hebrew.

"Peace on you, also," the rabbi said. "Are you really one of the lost tribes of Israel?" he asked in a somewhat skeptical tone.

"Of course, we are. What's the matter? —you don't look too convinced."

The rabbi confusingly combed a hand through his beard.

"I just expected the lost tribe of Israel to look more," the rabbi's voice trailed off.

"What? Jewish?"

"Yes."

"Looks aren't that important, Rabbi. I understand you've traveled a long way. You must be tired and hungry."

"I am," the hallucinating rabbi admitted. Although he wasn't sure of how far he'd traveled, or where he was now.

"Come, Rabbi. We've prepared a wonderful lunch for you," the tribe's chief said. "Afterwards, three of our most beautiful young concubines will bathe you. Then they'll make passionate love to you. How does that sound?" Chief Bug O' Levy asked with a salacious grin.

"Too good to be true," the rabbi replied.

"You'll see."

The chief grabbed hold of the rabbi's arm, and they walked toward the village. A group of natives followed behind.

"And tomorrow, we'll have a big feast and celebration in your honor," the chief spoke.

The tribesmen mumbled their approval.

"That's very kind of you," said the rabbi.

The lost tribe's friendliness impressed him, and he felt much more at ease.

"You will eat now," the chief said as he handed the rabbi over to his trusted envoys.

They escorted him to a dining hall lavishly furnished with oak tables and chairs, crystal chandeliers, fancy velvet wallpaper, stained-glass windows and a polished marble floor. The vaulted ceiling had been painted with incredible murals comparable to the ones the rabbi had once seen in the Sistine Chapel. He gazed up and admired the exquisite works of art.

"Those are extraordinary," he told one of the tribe's emissaries.

Grinning from ear to ear, the native said, "Paint-by-numbers."

The tribe's musicians played a celebratory canticle on the trombone, theremin, bongo drums, ukulele, hurdy-gurdy, Jew's harp and kazoo, while the honored guest was taken to a long rectangular table covered by an immaculate white tablecloth set with gold-plated cutlery, proper plates, and narrow-stemmed wine chalices. Bouquets of roses and sweet magnolias embellished the setting. The flowery scents pervaded the room, along with a distinct odor of animals and animal dung.

Three long-armed red-faced monkeys sat at the rabbi's right side. One monkey wore a brown fur coat; another sported a red fur coat; the third monkey flaunted a black fur coat. A male and a female pig sat on their haunches beside the monkeys. They stank. The porkers squirmed, oinked and ogled as they impatiently waited for food. Sitting across from the pigs, a dark-eyed ewe and a ram, who occasionally whacked his hard head against the table. A straggly pair of horny goats sat next to them, chewing on fine linen napkins and long strips of tablecloth. At the far end of the table, a lion and a lioness roared while grooming each other's rust-colored manes.

Attired in a crisp white tuxedo shirt, a black bow tie, a top hat and loincloth: a waiter happily strutted across the room and attentively stood beside the table where Rabbi Karpadah and the smelly animals were seated.

"Do you care for something to drink, Rabbi?" the waiter inquired.

"A glass of dry red wine would be nice. Why are these animals sitting at the table?"

The waiter smiled and bowed slightly.

"It's our custom, sir. It would be extremely rude for our guests to sit alone."

The waiter poured the rabbi a chalice of red wine and stood there, politely waiting to help.

Meanwhile, three fair maidens entered the dining room carrying platters of hot and cold delicacies. The women wore long grass skirts, star flowers in their hair, and nothing else. The servers placed the platters of food on the long table, and the stinky animals unabashedly helped themselves. The rabbi held his nose shut while he inquisitively watched. He pointed to a pile of sliced meats and another unfamiliar food steaming in front of him.

"What's on that plate?" he asked the happy-go-lucky waiter.

"That's slow-cooked squirrel and possum on the half shell."

"Are you serious?" the rabbi asked.

"Two of my favorite dishes."

"And what's on that platter over there?"

"Smoked salamander, peacock breast, corned-feet, pig's ears in a blanket, curried dog's tongue and brisket of yak."

The waiter adjusted his bow tie and smiled again. The rabbi swallowed a bit of bile that had crawled up his esophagus. Afraid to ask, but he pointed to another tray which the monkeys and the pigs had no interest in whatsoever.

"What's all that?" the rabbi inquired.

"Those are deep-fried fisheyes, Swedish goat-balls, marinated snake tripe, chopped alpaca liver, seagull knishes and pickled monkey brains. Why do you ask? Are you a vegetarian, Rabbi?"

"No, but none of this food looks, smells, or sounds very kosher to me."

"Oh, not to worry, sir. It's all been blessed and certified kosher by our chief rabbi. Rabbi Korowai."

Just then, one of the monkeys put its hands over the rabbi's eyes, another monkey covered his ears, and the third monkey placed its hand over the rabbi's mouth. The goats belched and politely nibbled on their appetizers. The pigs wore their food and vociferously snorted. The lion and lioness roared for more meat while the ewe and the ram shamelessly fornicated underneath the table.

Rabbi Karpadah lifted his wine glass and said the blessing. He tasted the wine and almost gagged when he swallowed it.

"Are you okay, Rabbi?" the waiter asked.

"This wine has the most peculiar taste. What type of grape is it made from?"

"We don't produce our wine from grapes," the waiter answered. "Grapes don't grow on the island. We make our red wine from fermented ram's blood."

The waiter proudly crossed his arms over his crisp white tuxedo shirt. The rabbi coughed and spat out a mouthful of wine and sprayed the goats that sat across from him.

"Ram's blood?" he shouted.

The animals briefly looked up from the table, then went back to what they were doing.

"That's correct, Rabbi. Would you prefer a glass of white wine instead?"

"What's that made from?"

"Fermented yak semen. And it's chilled to just the right temperature."

"What the?"

After the rabbi's bizarre dining experience, three voluptuous maidens accompanied him to the tribe's luxurious bathhouse. They undressed the rabbi, helped him into a hot bubble bath and scrubbed him from head to toe. After that they dried him with plush cotton towels and swaddled him in a purple silk robe reserved for extra special guests.

Those three beauties left the bathhouse and were replaced by three of the fattest, ugliest, and most ill-tempered ladies of the tribe. They escorted the rabbi to a candlelit chamber burning with frankincense and myrrh. A large brass bed had been decorated with silk sheets, pillows, and a red velvet spread. On a table, bananas, oranges and papaya filled wooden bowls while exotic aphrodisiacs and scented lubricants were made available. An abundance of primitively fashioned sex toys hung from the walls and ceiling. The highly perfumed concubines undressed themselves and disrobed the rabbi. They laid him on the soft mattress and tantalized him with the fruits, pleasured him with the aphrodisiacs, massaged him with the oils, and then teased him with the sex toys.

16

In the tribe's communal kitchen, women and older girls cheerfully sang traditional Fuck-are-wee melodies while they prepped for the rabbi's feast and celebration. Outside in back of the kitchen, under pleasant shade of plum-colored hemp blossoms and broad-leafed umbrella trees: The alter-kakers of the tribe amused themselves with card games, checkers, and a primitive version of shuffleboard played with shrunken human heads. The men talked about what they had for lunch, their aches and pains, bowel movements, or lack of, and other important matters.

At a ceremonial fire pit nearby, three strong young tribesmen filled a huge black pot with buckets of water. One of them rubbed two sticks together. And soon, a small fire was ignited underneath the cauldron.

Back at the lost tribe's guest lodge, Rabbi Karpadah hallucinated on flying frogs, ice-skating turtles, laughing armadillos, dancing blue giraffes and two snowy owls playing chess at a small table in the corner of the room.

Smoke from the fire-pit entered an open window of the rabbi's guest room, tickling his nose and causing him to sneeze repeatedly. Three tribesmen entered the room and sat next to his bed. One of them took a sharp pair of scissors and cut off his hair, sidelocks, beard and mustache. Another tribesman gave him a clean shave while the other swept all the hair off the floor with a broom and a dustpan. Amazingly the rabbi slept undisturbed throughout the procedure. They poked his belly, pulled his ears, nose, fingers and toes. One of them threw a bucket of ice-cold water onto his face. He opened his eyes and saw the gloating tribesmen standing over him. The rabbi felt his hairless face and head.

"What happened to my hair, my beard, and my side locks?" he asked the savages.

The tribesmen flashed him primeval grins. One of them replied, "We cut it off."

"Why on earth for?"

"To prepare you for the big feast and celebration. In your honor."

"How long have I been asleep?"

"Twelve years."

The rabbi rubbed his face where his beard had been.

"I still feel a little intoxicated. Perhaps I should sleep it off some more."

The savages slapped their thighs and laughed uproariously.

"Who are you kidding? You're drunk as a skunk. We heard you finished off two bottles of vodka, one of whiskey, three bottles of wine, and a full liter of schnapps," a tribesman said.

The rabbi didn't recall drinking all that much. "I did?"

"Don't worry. This way you won't feel too much pain," a tribesman explained.

"What do you mean?"

"At your feast and celebration soon."

"I won't have to eat for a couple days. I'm stuffed to the gills."

"That's okay, Rabbi. You won't be eating. We'll be eating you. Ha ha."

"You're cannibals?"

"Bingo."

The rabbi jumped from the bed and tried to escape, but he was too wasted to get anywhere. The lost tribesmen tied his ankles and wrists and covered his naked body with the purple robe. They led him outside and escorted him to a luxurious living quarters. The tribesmen pushed him onto the floor at the feet of Chief Bug O' Levy and head Rabbi Korowai. Both men had already dressed for the joyous occasion to take place outside. Rabbi Korowai got angry with the two tribesmen.

"Untie him! That's no way to treat our guest," he declared.

Rabbi Karpadah recognized the face and the voice of the man who had just spoken to the two savages.

"Rabbi Mandelson! Thank God, you're here," he said to his bearded old friend and colleague. A feeling of hope rose from his chest.

"What did you call me?" Rabbi Korowai asked.

"Rabbi Mandelson. You look exactly like him."

"I don't know this man you speak of. I am Rabbi Korowai. Are you satisfied with our tribe's hospitality?"

Rabbi Karpadah had to admit he'd been treated quite well. Up until recently that is.

"I am satisfied with your hospitality. Although I didn't care much for the pickled monkey brains. And I'm a little confused to why you'd want to kill and eat me. Especially after treating me with such kindness."

"Simply because we are cannibals," Rabbi Korowai explained, as he crossed his arms over his chest. And licked his lips.

"And it's considered a great honor for our guests to be sacrificed," Chief Bug O' Levy added.

"Says who?" the biblical expert vehemently asked.

"Tradition!" Rabbi Korowai sang in a robust manner. His voice cracked on the higher note.

"Tradition?"

"Yes. Tradition!" the chief burst out singing too. He and Rabbi Korowai got up and started dancing around the room.

"Bup, bup-a-bah-dah, bup, bup-ah-ba-dah, bah bah bah. Tradition!" they loudly chanted.

"You're both out of your freakin minds," Rabbi Karpadah said. "You're going to sacrifice me by cutting my throat?"

The two men stopped singing and dancing and they blankly looked at Rabbi Karpadah.

"Oh, no. That would be too bloody," the chief said.

"And unkosher," Rabbi Korowai added, "You'll be cooked in a pot of boiling water."

"Like a Maine lobster?" Rabbi Karpadah inquired.

Rabbi Korowai and the chief sat down again. They looked at each other puzzled.

"What is Maine lobster?" the chief inquired. "We've never heard of such a thing."

"What kind of lost tribe of Israel are you anyway?" Rabbi Karpadah asked. "Jews don't have such barbaric customs."

"Human sacrifice is still practiced by our tribe," Rabbi Korowai stated. "Should I tell our gods anything before we start the ceremony?"

"You have more than one God?" Rabbi Karpadah asked.

"Of course, we do. The Fuck-are wee worship many gods. We make them out of stone, wood, bronze, brass, silver and gold. Like those two over there."

119

The head rabbi pointed to a silver statue of an orangutan. And a bronze replica of a common house cat.

"Well? Do you vant I should tell them something or not?" he asked, rolling his eyes and growing more impatient.

Rabbi Karpadah sat up straight and stuck out his beardless chin.

"You can tell your gods you'll be committing a great sin by sacrificing me. Haven't you heard of 'Thou shalt not commit murder'?"

"We can't say such blasphemy," Rabbi Korowai replied.

"He speaks the truth. Our gods would be furious," Chief Bug O' Levy stated.

"Then screw you and to hell with your idols!" Rabbi Karpadah shouted.

"We don't understand this language, Rabbi," the chief said. "What does this screw you mean?"

"And what is hell?" Rabbi Korowai inquired.

"Never mind," the rabbi said as he stared in disgust at their silver baboon god.

One of Rabbi Korowai's ten concubines called from a back bedroom: "Korowai, my darling?"

The rabbi answered over his shoulder, "Yes, my love?"

The concubine asked in a seductive voice, "Will you be joining us soon?"

"When the ceremony is over. Have patience my lovely one."

"Rabbi Korowai. Aren't you forgetting something?" the chief asked.

"How stupid of me." The head rabbi called over one of the tribesmen. "Bring in the mohel now."

"Yes, your excellency."

The tribesman went out. After a couple of minutes, he returned, guiding an elder of the tribe who was carrying a short stool and a brown box that looked exactly like a shoe box. The man set the stool by Rabbi Karpadah's feet. He sat on it, and then placed the box on his lap.

Rabbi Karpadah joked with the elder tribesman.

"You're going to fit me with a new pair of shoes before you sacrifice me?"

The man opened the shoe box, but he didn't reply.

Chief Bug O' Levy laughed. "Very funny, Rabbi, but the man you joke with is deaf. And blind. He's the tribe's mohel. He will be circumcising you now."

"I've already been circumcised."

"The men of our tribe are required to be circumcised twice," the chief stated. "Once at birth, and again after their thirteenth birthday. We've been informed you were only circumcised once."

"My lucky day," Rabbi Karpadah stated.

The mohel reached into the shoe box and removed a small bottle of alcohol, a sharp scalpel, and a thick roll of white bandage. Shortly afterwards, a loud shriek was heard by the group that had gathered outside by the fire.

When the water started boiling in the massive black pot, the tribe's chef tossed in a basket full of chopped herbs and vegetables. He seasoned the broth and stirred it with a long wooden spoon. After a taste, the chef showed his approval with a wide toothless grin.

The lost tribesmen howled with laughter while they jubilantly sang and danced around the towering orange flames. The Fuck-are-wee wore terrifying masks and headdresses their women had fashioned from furs, coconut shell, animal bones, fins, and bird feathers. The frightful disguises resembled the heads and faces of birds of prey, fish, ferocious caiman, other animals, and angry looking demons with white horns and three red eyes.

A fierce looking tribesman appeared wearing a walrus mask with ivory tusks and wily whiskers. He escorted the purple robed rabbi up a ladder and onto a platform above the boiling soup. The masked tribesman flexed his muscular chest and biceps as he tightly grasped the rabbi's arm.

In a solemn procession, the tribe's twelve elders rode their donkeys to the ceremony. The old men dressed in white ankle-length caftans, dark sunglasses, and tall black hats. They dismounted their animals and sat in twelve reserved seats that encircled the sacrificial fire.

The chief climbed the ladder and took his respective place on the platform above the simmering pot. The chief's naked back and chest was painted with green snake bile and fresh red yak's blood. He wore an ugly brown horse mask with a long black mane, crooked front teeth, and hollowed-out eyes.

Rabbi Korowai came dressed as a scruffy blue bird with tousled plumes and a narrow yellow beak. His olive-pitted eyes focused on the congregation reveling about the fiery circle. Through the steam rising from the cauldron, the head rabbi raised his droopy wings and the dancing, singing, and shrieks of laughter stopped.

The muscular tribesman ripped the purple robe off Rabbi Karpadah, and he stood there trembling in his nakedness and fear. Sweat poured from his pale face—about to pass out.

Rabbi Korowai loudly chanted in the Fuck-are-wee tongue; his blue wings flapped wildly as the circle of elders and tribesmen chanted a response.

Just when Rabbi Karpadah was ready to be immersed into the scalding liquid: a cloud appeared above the gathering. The sky turned a dark violet, and a series of thunderclaps exploded. A heavy rain poured from the cloud, onto the ceremony. Everyone raised their arms to the sky except for Rabbi Karpadah and the muscular tribesman. The Fuck-are-wee shouted with joy, because they hadn't seen rain on the island for months.

While the lost tribe fixed their eyes above, the muscular tribesman whispered into the captive's ear:

"Now's your time to escape, Rabbi."

"Who are you?"

"I am the Walrus. Quickly, follow me."

The gruesome masks rapidly flashed before the rabbi's eyes while he and the Walrus climbed down the ladder and hit the ground running. They bounded through the jungle and headed for the beachfront to where the fishing boat was docked.

When the ecstasy of the rain had worn off, the tribe's elders confusingly mumbled to one another. They peered through their masks and felt that something was terribly amiss. Rabbi Korowai and Chief Bug O' Levy stood on the platform and stared at one another.

"What are you looking at?" Rabbi Korowai asked.

"Where is our guest? And the tribesman who was guarding him?" the chief inquired.

"I don't know. They were standing here a minute ago."

"You idiot! He must have escaped. After them!" the chief shouted to the costumed tribesmen.

The freaked-out natives grabbed their poison-tipped spears, slingshots, blowguns and wooden clubs. The angry mob bolted through the jungle and sprinted like madmen.

But it was too late. For the rabbi and the Walrus had climbed into the boat and prepared to set sail. A strong wind gradually blew the fishing schooner away from the island and out to sea. The walrus kindly put a hand onto the rabbi's shoulder.

"Whatever happens, Rabbi, don't look back at the island until I say it's okay."

"Why not?"

"Because you'll turn to stone if you do."

The men who proclaimed to be the lost tribe of Israel reached the shore and watched the fishing boat swiftly sail from their pink paradise. They dashed into the shallow water, flung their spears, and aimed their blowguns and slingshots. The target had gone too far out of range. Their ammunition arched high through the air and limply dropped into the lake. The rain stopped. And the sky turned blue again. The frustrated tribesmen removed their masks and crazily pulled at their hair, and wept like small children.

Rabbi Karpadah said to the tribesman who was wearing the walrus mask, "Thank you for saving my life."

"You're most welcome."

"But why did you save me? I thought you were one of them."

"Oh, no. I was never one of them. And never will be. I saved you because you're a God-fearing man. And no one deserves to die in such a horribly cruel manner."

"Blessed be His name," the rabbi said. "Is it safe for me to turn around now?"

"I believe it is."

The rabbi looked back and saw what was left of the pink paradise. Now a parking lot. The Fuck-are-wee tribesmen stood still as soapstone statues.

"Why aren't they moving?" the rabbi asked.

He wasn't given a reply.

A powerful current drove the fishing boat rapidly through the water. It circled the island once, and then vanished. When the rabbi turned around again, he found that the walrus had disappeared. And the boat had turned back into a table.

"Where is he?"

"Who?" Dr. McKermy asked.

"The man who was in the boat."

"What boat are you talking about, Rabbi?"

"On the lake. Inside the table."

The doctor laughed.

"You must've been dreaming it," she said while adding cream to a mug filled with steaming hot coffee.

"Is the ceremony over?" the rabbi asked her.

"Yes, how do you feel?"

"Exhausted."

"That's normal," Dr. McKermy stated.

The rabbi felt his face, joyful his beard and side locks were still there. "Where's the shaman?"

"I'm right here," Carlos replied, arriving with two cups of hot coffee.

"Where's Dr. Zevardia and your assistant?" the rabbi asked.

Carlos gave the rabbi a cup.

"Dr. Zevardia is sitting in the courtyard, and Jorge is preparing us a delicious breakfast."

"Have we been cured of the disease?" the rabbi asked.

"It's too early to tell," Carlos replied. "Why don't we take our coffees and sit outside? Jorge will bring out the breakfast when it's ready."

"Great idea," the rabbi said, picking up a stone with a perfectly round hole in the center. He gazed through the opening and viewed the morning light. "It looks like a gorgeous day out."

He sipped the hot coffee, and slowly came to his feet.

After breakfast, Jorge harvested vegetables from the garden inside the courtyard. Three blue morpho butterflies hovered nearby before they disappeared over a stone wall. A crescent moon faded in the morning sky while Jorge placed the vegetables into three paper bags; he gave one each to Dr. McKermy, Rabbi Karpadah and Dr. Zevardia. While everyone conversed and drank more coffee at the round table outside, the medical doctor's cell phone rang.

"Hello, Dr. McKermy?"

"Speaking."

"*Buenos dias*, Doctor. This is Dr. Gutierrez at the old medicine hospital in Iquitos. You better get over here asap."

"What's the matter?" she nervously asked.

"We need your assistance in the emergency room. Around fifty men, women, and children just walked in with a very unusual skin condition."

17

Once the majority of Iquitos's population had contracted the Human Amphibian Virus, it wasn't long afterwards, the disease spread pell-mell to other parts of Peru, bordering countries, the rest of South America, Central America, Mexico, the United States, and then north to Canada. Next, the global pandemic blazed through Europe, the Middle East, Africa, Thailand, Vietnam, India, China, Japan, Malaysia, Australia and New Zealand. Before the disease was brought under control, it had afflicted nearly eight-five percent of the world's population. Despite the dramatic changes the H.A.V. made to each individual's anatomy and physiology, it never proved fatal to anyone. And the people of the world continued living relatively happy, normal, and productive lives.

A cure has yet to be discovered but methods of treating the virus are currently available. Unfortunately, none of them are covered by health insurance. Affordable or otherwise. Skin grafting is one such treatment, although it's a lengthy and costly procedure. Another treatment involves the use of stem cells which are extracted from a male pot belly pig. Once the patient undergoes a long series of injections, their affected skin is eventually replaced by a healthy layer of pig dermis. This method has had varying degrees of success, although it has its side effects. Because of the cruel and extensive experiments, the poor pigs must endure, animal rights groups are firmly against the therapy. (The potbellied pigs usually die in the laboratory.) Muslim sects who are prohibited from eating pork, and Jewish people who follow kosher dietary laws, are both vigorously against the stem cell treatment.

Dutch seniors who sit around and get stoned off their rockers all day in the confines of nursing homes and retirement communities in Amsterdam and other parts of Holland, seem to believe that frequent smoking of medical marijuana stops, or at least slows the growth of the Human Amphibian Virus to other parts of the body.

After the onset of the global pandemic, the expedition team went their separate ways. Everyone who was on the team, along with anyone associated with it, had acquired the virus. Ron and Rachael flew back to the States. Rabbi Mandelson did too. Dr. Zevardia moved to Israel and opened a falafel stand. Mr. and Mrs. Tudela returned to their quiet little cottage in Upstate New York. While Howard Sternfinger purchased an overpriced condominium in Boca Raton, Florida. He quit working as a photographer and began a lucrative career in stand-up comedy. Rabbi Karpadah, however, remained in Iquitos. He and Dr. McKermy fell madly in love. They got engaged, married, and then eventually raised a large family. And yes! They lived happily ever after.

18

Two years after the expedition in Peru, Ron and his wife never expected to see four inches of snow in Miami Beach on a Thanksgiving morning, but the mercury had dipped below freezing the night before, and weather conditions were ideal for winter precipitation. Then again, the couple never dreamed that they and almost ninety-five percent of the residents of Florida would look like amphibians one day either.

On the 27th floor of their beachfront penthouse overlooking the Atlantic Ocean, Ron and Rachael enjoyed a little intimate foreplay while the morning news aired on the clock radio by their bed.

The newscaster announced, "Good morning. My name is Geraldo Geraldo, reporting live, from IRKME FM radio. Yesterday, over 200,000 people from the massive environmental movement, Green Lives Matter, gathered at the National Mall in Washington, D.C. to voice their concerns over the disastrous blue-green algae and red tide effecting the nation's rivers, lakes, and oceans. Beaches from

Maine, Cape Cod, theJersey shore, down to South Florida including the Keys, as well as up and down the Pacific coasts of California, Oregon and Washington continue to be closed because of high levels of toxicity in the waters. The environmental group also protested the lack of progress made by scientists and medical experts in finding a cure for the Human Amphibian Virus. G.L.M. accused doctors and pharmaceutical companies of quackery and profiting from the disease. Riots broke out between the police, the National Guard, and sporadic groups belonging to Green Lives Matter. There were several reports of demonstrators being arrested, injured and hospitalized. In other news around the nation: the gargantuan meteor that was heading straight for Mar-a-Lago—just kidding. I would like to wish everyone a happy Thanksgiving. My name is Geraldo Geraldo, reporting live, for IRKME FM News."

Rachael got on top and eased into a slow-moving rhythm.

"Is it still snowing, Ronald?"

"Just flurries the last time I looked. The radio said there was close to four inches on the ground."

Rachael closed her eyes and felt a pleasant sensation come on.

"I'm sure it'll be melted by the time we go to the airport this afternoon," she said.

"Most likely."

After making love, Rachael went back to sleep while Ron stood in front of their bedroom window and watched intricately patterned snowflakes flutter through the early morning light and melt into the ocean below. He closed the curtain, left the room, and then had himself a long and steamy shower.

With a striped towel wrapped around his waist, Ron stared in the bathroom mirror. The light green webbing between the fingers of his left hand, and the unsightly pink throat-sack were what bothered him the most about having the Human Amphibian Virus. The tropical shirts he loved wearing for work no longer fit him around the collar, so he donated them to the Salvation Army, replacing the shirts with a much larger neck size. Ron glanced at the orange-red spots on his torso. Both he and his wife had them all over their stomach, ribcage, and inner thighs. Ron even had some spots on his penis and the soles of his feet. Rachael had acquired the translucent webbing between her toes, but fortunately, Ron had not. Ideal for swimmers maybe, the webbing was such an encumbrance that some people had it surgically removed, or else they were specially fitted with orthopedic footwear like Rachael had elected to do. Ron ran the hot water and applied a lather of shaving cream to his mottled black and green complexion. He carefully ran a new razor along his face.

Ron ground some coffee beans and made a pot. He poured a cup, sat at the kitchen table, and opened the Miami Herald. Ruby, one of their three English terriers, lapped milk from a bowl in a corner. Rachael walked in with her bathrobe on, helped herself to a cup, and then sat opposite her husband.

"You finish packing, Ronald?"

"I just have a few things left."

Ron kept reading the funny papers. Their fat terrier trotted to the living room where she spun in circles for a while. The other two dogs, Rufus and Bridget, patiently waited by the front door for their morning walk.

"Don't forget to pack your wool socks and long johns," his wife reminded. "It'll be freezing in New York. What time are the Applebaums coming over?"

"Nine-thirty," Ron answered while looking up from the newspaper. He turned back to the front page. "I hope it's not too late for him."

"Who are you talking about?"

"The Pope. Take a look," Ron said while showing his wife the morning news.

Frog Virus Runs Rampant in Rome

Vatican Quarantines the Pope

"The Catholics are screwed now," Rachael quipped.

"Yeah, right."

The buzzer rang from the front entrance downstairs.

"That's probably Vivian. Let her in sweetie, I'm gonna hop in the bath," Rachael said.

Ron sluggishly stood and walked to the intercom on the wall. He heard the voice of their house sitter, Vivian Greenbaum; he buzzed her in, and she took the elevator up to the 27th floor and strolled down the hallway with a paper bag and a couple of white boxes from Arnie's Bakery. She rang the doorbell.

"Morning, Mr. Levine."

"Good morning, Vivian. Got the bagels, I see."

"Brownies and cream napoleons too. God, it's freezing out!"

"I know. C'mon in," Ron said. "Here, let me help you with that stuff."

"Crazy weather, huh?" she mentioned.

"That's for sure. Don't think it's ever been this cold in Miami Beach."

"Happy Thanksgiving by the way," Vivian said.

"Same to you. Your sister coming over?"

"Probably later. Where's Rachael?" Vivian asked.

"Having a bath. Can you make a pitcher of Bloody Mary when you get the chance?"

"Love to."

"There's a bottle of Grey Goose in the freezer," Ron said to his house-sitter. "I put everything else on the counter for you. Go easy with the Tabasco."

Ron finished preparing a Thanksgiving breakfast, while his wife opened the front door for their friends and neighbors who lived in the apartment two floors below. Rosco and Rita Applebaum.

"Good morning," Rachael greeted.

"Morning. And Happy Thanksgiving."

"Same to you," Rachael said. "You guys are a bit early. C'mon in. Ron's in the kitchen."

"Figured we'd come over and drink some of that delicious Peruvian coffee your husband likes to make," Rosco said while unzipping his down jacket.

"I made a key lime pie," Rita said, placing a brown box into her best friend's hands. She pulled her arms out of her fur-lined overcoat and draped it on a chair.

"Ron's favorite. Thanks."

"You're welcome. It's really from Publix," Rita said with a grin. "You guys excited about going to New York?"

"We're thrilled," Rachael replied. "Haven't had a vacation since we were in Peru. Well . . . if you wanna call that a vacation. Something to drink? Vivian made Bloody Marys."

"Black coffee for me please," Rosco replied.

"I'll take a Bloody Mary," Rita said as she plopped on a couch near the warm fireplace. The Levine's three terriers came over to greet her. "How are the darlings, today?" she asked the dogs.

Ruby showed off by spinning in circles while Rufus hobbled over on his three legs. He cordially licked Rita's wart-covered hand. Bridget couldn't be bothered. She went off by herself after her back was stroked once.

Rachael went to the kitchen and announced to her husband the Applebaums had arrived. He smiled while stirring a pan of home-fried potatoes, seasoning it with fresh-ground pepper, parsley and sea salt. His wife fixed a cup of coffee and a bloody Mary before returning to her guests in the living room. Ron put a pan of vegetarian bacon and sausage into the oven before scrambling a dozen eggs.

After the Applebaums and Levines ate breakfast, they schmoozed with their coffees and deserts in the dining room.

19

The owner of Regis Airport Limo, a copper faced gentleman, drove over a mound of slushy snow and stopped by the entrance to the luxury high-rise on Collins Avenue. He loaded the Levine's and Applebaum's luggage while they got inside the limo. He closed the doors, sat behind the wheel, straightened his posture, and then headed east towards the J. Tuttle Causeway. He turned up the volume on a station that played Beatle songs.

"What's the name of that airline you folks flying out of?" Mr. Regis inquired.

"FLA!" Mr. Applebaum hollered from the back seat.

"Never heard of Florida Air. Is that in terminal three?"

"It's Flying Leap Air. And no, it's in terminal two," Rosco replied with a freeze-dried look on his face.

Mr. Regis nodded. "Must be a new airline." He put on his turn signal, tapped his fingers, and then once again attempted to sing. "Strawberry . . ."

"You mind lowering the volume?" Rosco asked.

"No problem," the driver said as he merged onto the lane for departures.

Rosco whispered into his wife's abridged ear: "He should invest in some singing lessons."

"We're almost there," Rita said as she gazed out the window at a Bright Line train.

"Thank God for that," her husband said.

"Forever," the driver crooned. "Here we are. Flying Leap Air."

He pulled up to the curb, got out, and unloaded the luggage.

"That should do it then," the limo driver said. "You folks have a safe trip."

Mr. Levine thanked him and slapped a twenty-dollar bill into his amphibilous palm.

The Levines and Applebaums rolled their luggage into the terminal and approached a curiosity of Japanese tourists who were wielding maps, carry-on bags, and sophisticated cameras. The astronaut-like travelers wore silver-blue space suits; their heads were protected inside clear plastic bubble helmets. They breathed through a tube connected to an apparatus equipped with a portable oxygen tank strapped to their backs. The AVPS (Anti-Virus Protection Suit), guarded them against any Human Amphibian Virus germs floating around public places, the airport terminal, and the aircraft itself.

Rita stopped and stared at the Japanese tourists who were focusing their camera lenses on her. She smiled and stuck out her long red Rolling Stone tongue. The flashes on their Nikon cameras went off like crazy. Rosco placed a hand on his hip and shook his head in a scolding manner.

"Stop it, Rita, you'll scare them half to death."

"They seem to like it," she stated.

"Let's get our boarding passes," he urged his wife while pulling on her coat sleeve.

"Shame they have to travel in such cumbersome suits," Rachael mentioned to her husband. "They must be awfully warm inside."

"It's either that, or risk catching the virus," Ron stated. "I'm quite sure the suits are cooled by a battery-powered thingamajig. But I do agree. They look extremely uncomfortable."

After the global pandemic had occurred, major airports around the world, including Miami's, had been modernized to accommodate travelers' special needs. People who hadn't acquired the Human Amphibian Virus traveled in the UC, or the Unaffected Class. Those with the disease traveled in the AC or Affected Class. Specially protected areas had been built inside terminals for the sole protection of the UC customers and employees. These areas were 99.9 percent guaranteed virus-proof, bacteria and germ-free. A six-inch-thick plate-glass barrier divided the two classes. The UC passengers weren't required to wear their Anti-Virus Protection Suits or breathe using their oxygen tanks while in this section of the airport. The security checkpoints had been modified as well. Travelers still showed their passports or photo identification, but were no longer required to take off their shoes, belts, jewelry etc., and place it into those awkward plastic bins. Instead, travelers lined up to get onto a conveyor belt. They'd lie on it, on their backs; the conveyor belt would start moving and take them through an MRI type of chamber which enabled a Homeland Security robot to see every hair, pimple and hemorrhoid on a person's behind.

A young mother and her five-year-old son passed through the security checkpoint for the Unaffected Class. They got up off the conveyor belt and removed their protection suits. They stowed them inside secure lockers. The young boy cradled his computerized toy while his mom hung a handbag over her shoulder, and they walked down the hall past the departure lounges, stopping for lunch at a Burger High fast-food eatery. The mother checked out the selections on the menu board while her son habitually tapped the keys on his digital toy. He was blissfully oblivious to the decontaminated world around him.

"What do you want to eat, Bobby?" his mother asked.

He ignored her question while he stopped to adjust the screen resolution on his gadget.

"Bobby! What are you eating?"

Without looking up or stopping his amusement: he said he wanted a fish sandwich and fries.

The young mother told a purple-haired gentleman wearing a dress: "I'll order a double-High bacon cheeseburger with everything, a fish sandwich, onion rings, a large order of fries, a medium black coffee and a large coke, please.

The fast food employee smiled behind his brass nose-ring. "Is that for here or to go?"

"To go, please."

"Your order comes to $49.99."

The mother placed the inside of her wrist over a bar-code reader. The device read the chip implanted under the surface of her skin while the adding machine clicked, zinged, and then spit out her receipt.

"Mommy, am I a boy or a girl? —my teachers said I could be whatever I wanted."

"Bobby, like I told you before. You're a boy. Boys have penises and girls have vaginas. Why can't you remember that?"

"Johnny in my class who sits in front of me said his name was changed to Jenny. And that's what I should call him, or he would punch me in the nose."

"Don't worry, I'll have something to say to Jenny's mother. And if your teachers ever talk to you about this again. You tell me. I will come to your school and have a word with them. Here, Bobby, hold onto your soda. Let's go."

"Boys have penises and girls have vaginas. Boys have penises and girls have vaginas," Bobby quietly repeated to himself.

They walked over to a waiting lounge near the protective glass barrier. The young mother set the food on a sterile plastic table; they sat and unwrapped their meals.

On a wide-screen TV, his skin colored a lime green, and his throat bloated out, Dr. Phil touted his latest and greatest cure for the Human Amphibian Virus. The studio audience applauded, and the program rapidly switched to a commercial break.

After Bobby eagerly devoured half his fries but reluctantly swallowed a bite or two of his fish sandwich, he slurped some sugary pop from a straw. Because his mother had taken away his digital toy, the boy grew antsy-pantsy; his eyes darted about the terminal.

While his mother became heavily distracted by her onion rings and the talk-show host, her son put on his red and gold baseball cap, picked his nose, and then silently escaped from the table. He walked over to the plate-glass barrier that divided the UC from the AC. He removed his cap, pressed his face against the cold plate-glass and looked through it a few moments. He fogged up the glass with his breath and drew a squiggly little portrait with his index finger. Bobby wiped the glass clean and watched some children playing on the other side. He breathed on the glass a second time, and then drew another squiggly portrait.

His mother drank her coffee and looked up. "What are you doing over there, Bobby?"

"Nothing."

"I told you to stop picking your nose. Why aren't you eating your fish sandwich?"

"I'm full."

"You haven't touched it. You'll be hungry later."

"It tastes fishy."

"It's supposed to, it's a fish sandwich. Stop making a mess on that glass."

"Mommy?"

"What?"

"Is today Halloween?" the little boy inquired.

"No, it's Thanksgiving. Why?"

"All the kids are wearing Halloween masks," the boy said.

"What kids?"

"In there through the glass. The grown-ups have 'em on too. They're really scary looking."

The boy's mother got up and looked through the glass partition.

"What did I tell you about picking your nose? And put on your hat. Those aren't masks."

"Then why do they look like that?"

"Because they have a disease."

"Are they gonna get better?"

"I don't know—now get away from there!" his mother exclaimed while she grabbed the boy's hand and pulled him back to the table.

"Is that what happened to Daddy?" the little boy inquired while staring at his mother's angry face.

"Yes—now sit down."

"Can we get some ice cream now, Mom?"

"Only if you eat some of your fish sandwich. We'll need to put our suits back on soon. It's almost time to board the plane."

Boys have penises and girls have vaginas. Boys have penises and girls have vaginas.

"Mommy, how do you spell vagina?"

"Never mind, Bobby. What kind of ice cream do you want?"

"Good afternoon. This is Captain Carl Zuck speaking. Welcome aboard Flying Leap Air's non-stop Flight 1040 to Albany, New York. On behalf of FLA, I'd like to wish everyone a happy Thanksgiving. Flying conditions are perfect today. The temperature in Miami is a balmy 49 degrees, with the wind speed at 12 miles per hour. Be sure all your carry-on bags are properly stowed in the overhead bins, or under the seat in front of you. Those passengers seated in the Unaffected Class, please double-check that your oxygen is turned to the *on* position. Secure your seat belts. We'll be in the air shortly."

Close to where Ron and Rachael sat, a blonde and busty flight attendant stood in the aisle and demonstrated the flight safety procedures. She momentarily glanced at Ron. He smiled back at her, then opened a recent issue of National Geographic.

Inside was the feature eight-page article he'd written about the expedition in Peru. It included numerous color photos of the Amazon River; creatures, plants, and flowers of the rainforest; Iquitos; the archaeological site; the expedition team; and a man who claimed to be the last surviving member of a lost tribe of Israel: ninety-nine-year-old Yitzhak Arnon Ben Mendel. He wore a blue velvet loincloth, a skullcap, a prayer shawl, and a white beard that hung down past his bellybutton. He held an upright spear in one of his hands, a black prayer book in the other.

Ron closed the magazine and placed his undivided attention on the flight attendant with the prolific chest and pear-shaped hips. He saw that she forgot to fasten two top buttons on her white uniform blouse, revealing a canyonlike cleavage speckled with creamy white and cabbage green blemishes. Rachael looked up from her in-flight magazine.

"Do you know where Rosco and Rita are sitting?" she asked.

Mesmerized by the shapely flight attendant, Ron answered, "I think they're a few rows behind us."

Rachael frowned and looked at her husband.

"What's so interesting, Ron?"

"Nothing. I'm just listening to the flight safety instructions."

"It's not like you haven't heard them a hundred times before," she said.

"That's true."

Ron put on his headphones. Just then the cargo doors banged shut. Along the tarmac an airport worker waved a yellow flag, and the airbus coughed into reverse. It lethargically taxied to the runway and stopped. A baby shrieked while Captain Zuck hoarsely announced:

"We're next in line for takeoff. Just waiting for air traffic control. Be sure your seat belts are securely fastened. Flight crew please prepare the cabin for departure."

The behemoth aircraft nudged forward. Increased speed. And rock and rolled down the runway. It finally became airborne.

As the jet flew at an altitude of 40,000 feet, an airspeed of 650 mph, the curvaceous blonde flight attendant finished serving the UC passengers and pushed the beverage cart through the aisle, stopping by the section where the Applebaums were seated. She served them and moved on to the next set of passengers.

"Good afternoon. My name is Ms. Butters. Do you care for a beverage, ma'am?" the flight attendant asked Mrs. Levine.

"Cranberry juice—no ice, please."

She served her juice and asked if she wanted a snack. Rachael declined.

"What would you like to drink, sir?"

Ron remained engrossed in the magazine.

The flight attendant's hands impatiently rested on the superior iliac crest of her undulant hips. She cleared her exaggerated throat sack, croaked, and then repeated the question. "A beverage, sir?"

His wife elbowed him. "Ron?"

He removed his ear plugs.

"Oh, I'm sorry." He closed the magazine and gazed up at the flight attendant. "I'll have a Scotch on the rocks."

"What brand of Scotch?"

"What do you have?"

"Dewar's, Johnny Walker, Black Label, and Ribbet," she googled.

"What was that last selection?"

"Ribbet—"

"Ribbet?" Ron asked.

"Yes, sir."

"I've never heard of that brand."

"It's a new Scotch made in France," she said.

"I didn't know the French made Scotch," Ron said.

"Yeah, go figure."

The flight attendant chuckled.

Ron asked: "How do you spell the name of that Scotch?"

"R-i-b-b-e-t," the flight attendant mouthed.

In the row behind, a couple of teenage girls had a loud guffaw.

"Pardon me, Mademoiselle, Monsieur," said a woman across the aisle who was wearing a dark red burka and a matching face veil. "I'm quite certain the proper way of pronouncing that Scotch, is Ribay. The 't on the end is silent. Like the name of the great French impressionist painter. Claude Monet."

The flight attendant thanked the French woman and looked at Ron again.

"Sorry, I was wrong about the pronunciation."

"I'll take the Johnny Walker, please. And not too much ice," he said while handing her his American Express.

While Ms. Butters made Ron's drink and performed the transaction, Rachael informed the well-endowed flight attendant of her undone uniform top.

"Excuse me miss, you forgot a couple of buttons on your blouse."

She blushed. "Darn, I was in such a hurry this morning. Thanks for telling me."

"No problem."

The flight attendant cordially handed Ron his drink and credit card.

"Enjoy your Scotch, sir."

"Appreciate it."

"Can I have a taste?" his wife asked.

"Sure."

He handed her the plastic cup, then flipped another page on the magazine.

"You find her attractive?" Rachael inquired.

"Who's that?"

"Your girlfriend. The flight attendant. That's a smooth Scotch. Ribbay," she mimicked.

After the plane flew through an air pocket, Ron took the plastic cup from his wife.

"What makes you say that?"

"I saw how you were looking at her tits," Rachael crossly replied.

"Are you serious?"

"Why wouldn't I be? I'll admit—she does have a nice figure. Wish you paid that much attention to me sometimes."

He quickly changed the subject.

"I found an interesting article."

"On what?"

"Medicinal herbs and plants of the medieval era. I'm reading about a plant called the mandragora. It's Latin for mandrake. The plant grows around the Mediterranean Sea. Here's an illustration of one."

"They're pretty weird looking," his wife remarked.

Ron returned his focus to the text.

"It says that the mandrake is a narcotic that was once used by doctors for its medicinal properties," Ron stated. "They'd mix an extract of the plant with wine and use it as an anesthetic before operating."

"That's interesting."

"Shakespeare wrote about the plant in Romeo and Juliet," he said.

"What did he have to say?"

"And shrieks like mandrakes torn out of the earth, that living mortals hearing them, run mad," he quoted.

"I need to pee like a racehorse. Excuse me, dear," his wife announced while unbuckling her seat belt. She squeezed by, then rushed down the aisle.

Ron finished reading the article and viewed a page with the parting shot: twelve large pelicans flying low above a sparkling blue ocean. The humongous jet penetrated a flurry of pencil-thin clouds then slipped out the other side. He drained the Scotch and reclined his seat.

The gregarious flight attendant juggled her hips through the aisle; she stopped and collected Ron's empty cup and asked him if he wanted another drink. He smiled, said no, closed his eyes, and then fell asleep. He woke up to the pilot's goatish voice over the intercom.

"Attention all passengers. Please discontinue the use of all electronic devices at this time. We're in for some pretty nasty weather in the next half-hour or so. If you're up, please return to your seat and fasten your seat belt."

Ron reached for his wife's hand. Through the window she observed some twinkling lights from a fleet of minuscule boats far below. At an altitude of 35,000 feet, the jumbo jet cruised over the turbid Atlantic, the Jersey coastline, Flushing Meadows, Brooklyn Heights, the former site of the World Trade Center, Wall Street, Soho, Greenwich Village, Chinatown, Midtown, 5th Avenue, uptown, crosstown, Central Park, and the George Washington Bridge. The plane made a sharp right above Hoboken, N.J., cruising north toward the outer banks of the Milky Way. Up around West Point: the jet smacked into a wall of snow — ten miles thick.

"Pardon the rough ride, folks," Captain Zuck announced. "We'll be making our final descent into the Albany metropolitan area in just a few minutes. Please remember to use caution when disembarking the aircraft. Safe holiday. And thanks again for flying FLA. Flight crew please prepare the cabin for landing."

While a baby's piercing cry shattered the sound barrier again, the cabin lights darkened, and the airbus vaulted all of a sudden. It dipped sharply and vibrated so hard, Ron felt as if the windows and doors were going to be sucked out of the jet. A few of the overhead bins popped open. He took a deep breath. And prayed.

The large flying machine made a lengthy and choppy holding pattern around Albany. The cabin

remained dark, while the airbus abruptly descended at
a high rate of speed.

20

An Arctic wind slashed across Albany International Airport while work crews cleaned 28 inches of snow from runways, roads, ramps and sidewalks. At 7:45 pm, the temperature outside was a smidgen above zero. Inside the warm terminal that housed Delta, Jet Blue and Flying Leap Air: people waited for connecting flights, departures, and arrivals delayed by the fierce Thanksgiving blizzard.

At Forblunjet Rent-A-Car a bothersome fruit fly buzzed about the bald green pate of Mr. Bufo Schlavin, a Russian-American sales agent employed at the company. The fly examined the man's messy desk as he read the newspaper under a flickering fluorescent light. The frumpily attired man looked up from his paper and checked the computer screen for the umpteenth time. He rolled up a Wall Street Journal and smacked the counter with it. The fly hovered over to Avis, then Hertz next door. The rental agent placed a sign on the counter, notifying patrons he would return in ten minutes. He waddled over to Dunkin' Donuts and procured his fourth coffee of the day.

"Evening, Bufo," a man greeted behind the counter.

"Hey, Joey. Give me a large coffee and a chocolate-chip cookie please."

"Sure, Bufo. How come you're not home eating turkey dinner with your family?"

"Hopefully soon.

The coffee shop employee asked while he grabbed a large cup: "Hear anything about Flight 1040 yet?"

Bufo rubbed his eyes and yawned.

"It should've landed an hour ago. Air traffic control said they lost sight of the jet on radar. There's been no radio communication from the pilots either."

"That doesn't sound too good."

"No," the rental agent added.

Joey fixed the coffee and rang up the purchase.

"Maybe it landed in Newburgh?" he asked.

"Stewart Airport would've told us by now," Bufo replied. He paid for his stuff and dropped the change in the tip jar.

Back at his desk, the rental agent secretively added a shot of cheap Russian vodka to his coffee. He drank a little, gobbled down the cookie, and then brushed the crumbs off the jacket of his threadbare leisure suit. The rental agent adjusted a purple clip-on necktie, and he straightened his name badge prior to checking the computer screen once more. He was relieved to finally see the blinking red arrows next to Flight 1040 from Miami. The plane had just landed in Albany. The stooge-faced man hopped off his stool and spit-polished a pair of black triple-wide Oxfords.

Flight 1040 hobbled to the gate. The pilot cut the engine, and the doors eventually opened. The first few passengers wearily emerged and slowly wheeled their carry-on bags through a cold narrow corridor, and into the terminal.

The Applebaums and Levines retrieved their luggage and walked over to the rental car kiosk. Ron walked up to the counter and greeted the man in the threadbare leisure suit.

"Hey, how's it going."

"Good evening. And velcome to Forblunjet Rent-a-Car," Bufo greeted.

"We have a reservation for a mid-size car. It's under Levine."

The bald-headed man tapped his keyboard while the fruit fly whizzed by his shrunken ear.

"How vas your flight, Mr. Levy?"

"Nerve-racking. That's the last time I ever fly FLA. And my name is pronounced Levine."

"I'm sorry you had such an unpleasant experience, Mr. Levine." He flicked a stray cookie crumb off his leisure suit, and he kept typing. "Storm vas pretty bad, huh?"

"Yeah," Ron tiredly grunted.

"I'll need your driver's license and a credit caad, please. How many passengers traveling in your potty?"

Ron cocked his eyebrow. "Four."

"I gotta nice comfortable full-size vehichical for you."

"I believe I requested a mid-sized car," Ron stated.

"I'm terribly sorry, sir, but all the mid-size cars were taken due to the holiday."

"What's the make and model?"

"A vond-a-full four-door Olds Delta 88. It's got plenty of legroom, V-8 engine, AC, power shteering, power brakes, power vindows, and an AM-FM radio vit a cassette player," he answered with a heavy Russian accent thicker than a cranberry bog on Cape Cod.

Ron thought the toady little man appeared slightly pickled. "The car sounds like a honker to me."

"It is," the rental agent said grinning.

"There's no cruise control on it?"

"Unfortunately, not."

"You said it has a cassette player?" Ron asked.

"That's right. Vhy?"

"I haven't played music on one of those since I last listened to Englebert Humperdink. What year is the car?"

"1972. But it's in great condition. Only has twenty thousand miles on it."

"Really?

"Yes, sir."

Ron thought for a moment. *This was the only car they had left? A 1972.* He noticed that Avis, Budget, Hertz and Enterprise had already turned off their lights and closed up shop.

"Guess I don't have much choice. Sure you don't have any more modern cars available?"

Mr. Schlavin replied with a sneer, "A brand new VW Bug. It's great on gas but space is limited obviously."

"We'll take the Delta 88," Ron said.

"How long do you need the caah for?"

"Until Monday afternoon. Our flight is at three."

"You vant any roadside soivice? Hoptional liability insurance maybe?"

"No, thanks."

"Sign here. Initial here, here and here. And make sure you return the vehichical vit a full tank of grass, or else vee charge a premium rate of six dollas a gallon. If you have any problems vit the caah call this toll-free number."

"Can I have my license back."

The pickled rental agent handed Ron his license and the keys.

"It's in the parking garage across the street. The dark green Oldsmobile, next to the VW. Safe travels, happy holiday, and have a good night, Mr. Levinson," the obsequious little man said.

"Levine. Thanks, you too."

The rental agent shut down the computer, hopped off his stool and then turned off the flickering fluorescent light above his desk. The wide-awake drunk put on his coat and hat and went outside and wisely took an Uber home.

As they pulled onto the highway, Ron thought the Delta 88 rode pretty comfortable for an old honker. It definitely had plenty of leg room and horsepower like the rental agent had promised. By coincidence or not, when he turned on the radio, a song by Englebert Humperdink played.

In the front passenger seat Rosco looked out the window and viewed the wintry landscape alongside the interstate. He unwrapped a stick of spearmint gum and popped it into his mouth.

"Want one?" he offered Ron.

"No, thanks."

He handed the pack of gum to his wife.

"It's sure peaceful country up here," Rosco said.

The car's high-beams illuminated two deer that were licking rock-salt on the side of the road.

"It's quite a difference from Miami Beach," Ron stated.

"It's nice to see more than just palm trees for a change," Rosco said. "So, what's this Clinton Hotel and Spa like?"

"Rachael and I stayed there about five years ago in early October. We loved it. The leaves were just starting to turn."

"As long as the rooms are clean, the beds are comfortable, and the TV works. That's all that matters to me."

"They have a gourmet restaurant," Ron mentioned. "Michelin gave it two stars."

"That's a plus."

Ron slowed down and took the exit for Saratoga Springs, a bucolic little town famous for its healing waters and health spas. Grandfatherly oaks and majestic evergreens reverently watched over the old honker while it traversed the recently plowed road. Regal mansions with sprawling front yards had already been decked with Christmas lights, carrot nosed snowmen and colorful statues of angels, three wise men, and Nativity scenes with orange halo glows. Rosco cracked his window and smelled the smokey fragrances that came from wood burning stoves and chimneys on the old estates.

They hit Broadway and drove under some giant-size candy-canes, reindeer, Santa Clauses, and silver stars that all hung from electrical wire above the street.

Rachael opened her eyes to the glittery Christmas ornaments; she declared: "I'm starving! —I hope their restaurant is still open."

"Me too," Rita chimed. Her eyes half shut.

Ron passed a flashing neon sign in the window of Ching Wa's take-out.

"We're almost at the hotel, girls," he said.

Rosco saw the sign for the restaurant, and he mentioned with a chuckle. "There's always Chinese food."

Rita's eyes popped open. "I'm not eating pork-fried-rice on Thanksgiving, Rosco!"

"We won't have to, Rita," Ron promised.

He drove into a parking lot and stopped at the front entrance to the Clinton Hotel and Spa. Thick English ivy grew on the front of the old brick building while two bronze lions adorned either side of the entrance. No doorman was in sight.

"Rosco and I'll get the luggage out. We'll meet you girls inside," Ron said.

"Great. Let's go, Rita."

Ron kept the car idling while the women grabbed their handbags, opened the car doors, and then hurriedly entered the hotel. Rachael held Rita's hand, and they walked across the lobby to a stone fireplace. A man named Mr. C, tapped the ivory keys on a baby grand piano. He sipped on a whiskey before breaking into a rousing assortment of George Gershwin melodies. Rachael snapped her fingers to the beat.

Rita pointed to an oil painting of a bright sun; under it children danced around an Indian tipi.

"That's sweet," she said to her friend.

"C'mon, let's go stretch our legs before we check-in," Rachael suggested.

The two women meandered to the other side of the lobby, where a group of hotel guests in the holiday spirit, drank wine, cognac, and hot cider. The guests had assembled in front of a wide-screen TV, waiting for the President of the United States to give his holiday address to the nation.

Rachael and Rita watched and listened while a man announced in a loud voice, "Ladies and gentlemen, I am honored to welcome the President of the United States of America."

Stiff-like, the president sat at his desk in the oval office while TV cameras zoomed in on his hard-boiled expression. He gave one of his signature 'thumbs-up' signs before speaking.

"My fellow Americans. Let me start off tonight by wishing everyone a happy and healthy holiday. When I woke up in the White House this morning. I'd come to a startling realization. I turned to my wife and said: Without checking their name badges, I'm having a tough time identifying my cabinet and staff members. It's somewhat of an inconvenience. And rather awkward for me. My wife mentioned she was experiencing a similar problem. As you can plainly see, I am not the same person I was when I took oath for office almost two years ago. In fact, I don't even look like a man anymore. And I'm quite certain that many of you have also been altered by this terrible Human Amphibian Virus. Why it gets so darn confusing around the White House sometimes, just a couple of nights ago, after having a few stiff drinks, I almost mistakenly took my vice-president's wife to bed. Because of the global pandemic the population of the planet has endured tremendous change. My main priority now is finding a cure for the virus."

The President paused to loosen his red necktie over his embroiled throat sack. He crinkled his forehead, flexed the webbing between his toes, and gave another thumbs-up sign. The cameramen focused. A cold green smile congealed onto the politician's face. He coughed into his hand, leveled his comb-over, deflated his throat-sack and then quietly croaked into a handkerchief. The president drank from a glass of water, inflated his sack with more warm air before resuming his speech.

Rita and Rachael just looked at each other and shrugged.

"It's utterly shameful what's happening to this country," Rita said. "Whatever happened to 'Make America Great Again'?"

"I don't know. C'mon, I hear the guys," Rachael said, pointing to the front desk where their husbands stood-by with the luggage. They walked over to meet them.

"Good evening and welcome to the Clinton Hotel and Spa," said a woman working at the reception desk.

"Hello, Ms. Cooper, it's so nice to see you again," Ron greeted.

"Oh, my God! Mr. and Mrs. Levine? I saw that you made online reservations. But I never imagined you would look so different now. Funny, I should talk. Sorry for not recognizing you," the woman at the front desk stated.

"No worries," Ron said. "These are our good friends, Rita and Rosco Applebaum."

"Alice Cooper. It's a pleasure meeting you both."

"Likewise," Rita said. Rosco smiled.

"Is the Escoffier Room still open for dinner?" Ron inquired.

"We closed early because of the holiday and the snowstorm," Ms. Cooper replied. "But our bar is open 'til 2:00 AM. They should have some killer turkey sandwiches tonight."

"That definitely sounds better than Chinese food," Rita said.

Ms. Cooper clicked a mouse and scanned the computer screen. The couples were given their room keys.

"Happy Thanksgiving. Our bellhop will help you with your luggage. Mr. Fowler would you please take these guests and their bags to rooms 31 and 33."

"Yes, ma'am," the bellhop mumbled while folding a Saratoga Daily newspaper. He adjusted his ten-gallon cowboy hat before loading a luggage cart and rolling it onto the elevator. The two couples followed.

Rosco looked at the short bellhop and said in a corny John Wayne impersonation: "That's a nice hat partner."

The bellhop warbled a thank you. His donkey brown cowboy hat had effectively disguised his lickspittle face, shrunken yellow ears and pressed weepy nose. Not once did he look in the mirrored walls of the elevator, nor in anyone's eyes for that matter. The door rolled open and the group proceeded down the hallway. The bellhop showed the guests to their respective suites; they tipped him, and he waddled back through the hall with the empty luggage cart.

The Applebaums and Levines quickly washed up. And afterwards they met at the hotel bar for a late-night dinner.

"We have a great pale ale on tap," the Clinton's bartender told Mr. Levine. "It's made right here in Saratoga. I think you'll enjoy it."

"I'll take a pint of that, please."

"Same for me," Rosco said.

After the bartender took their orders and walked away, Rachael spoke: "Anyone notice the bellhop tonight?"

"I couldn't see his face too well," Rosco replied. "That silly cowboy hat covered it. Why?"

"He must look awful," Rachael answered.

"Well, that stupid hat doesn't help much," Rosco said.

"I kind of felt sorry for him," Rita mentioned.

"I don't think he should be so ashamed of his appearance," Ron stated. "Whatever he looks like."

"What makes you say that dear?" his wife asked.

"Billions of people look different now. Look at us. I mean, what are we supposed to do? Hide ourselves behind masks for the rest of our lives? We'll just have to make the best of it—that's all."

Rita covered her lap with a napkin and drank a few sips of wine. "I have to agree with you, Ron," she said.

"I know," Rachael said. "He's absolutely right. But it still breaks my heart when I see people act that way."

"Great, here's our food," Rita excitedly announced. And the subject of the conversation abruptly changed.

Back in their room, Ron kicked off his shoes and undressed while Rachael stood and stared at herself in the bathroom mirror; she took a hot washcloth and wiped the flesh-tone makeup from her face. She never went out in public unless her blotchy green and black complexion was concealed under an extra thick layer of Estee Lauder cosmetics. She rinsed and wrung-out the washcloth in hot soapy water, then applied it to her cheeks and forehead again.

"Delicious food tonight," Rachael said from the bathroom sink.

"The turkey was cooked just right," her husband stated.

"— was."

Ron turned on the boob tube and rifled through the channels with a remote, finding a program and settling his head on two pillows.

Rachael shut off the bathroom light and climbed into bed beside her husband. Eerie music played on the TV while credits shown on a black and white screen.

"What's on, Ronald?"

"The Birds. An old Alfred Hitchcock movie."

21

After Rachael took an early morning yoga class, she went up to the room, showered, and then dressed for breakfast. Ron slept in.

In the hotel's dining room Rachael admired the centerpiece. The sun's rays glistened through an ice-sculpture of a mermaid. Its long-frozen arms outstretched, balancing an ice-bowl brimming with jumbo shrimp. At the base of the mermaid, inside a border of Romaine lettuce, on a bed of ice, sat lemon wedges, raw oysters on the half-shell, more cooked shrimp, cocktail sauce, California rolls, sashimi tuna, wasabi, smoked whitefish, smoked trout and smoked Alaskan salmon. The iced mermaid's eyes sparkled when the light touched them.

"How was your yoga class?" Rita asked while she approached her friend by the center piece.

"It was fun. You should come tomorrow. It'd be good for your back."

"Speaking of backs, Rosco and I have massages scheduled for this afternoon. I'm getting a mini facial too," Rita said.

"That'll be fun. Let's grab ourselves some coffee 'til the guys come down."

"Sounds good."

Ms. Cooper walked into the dining room and inspected the breakfast buffet. She bent over, picked up a stray fork, and then adjusted a bouquet of flowers before greeting some familiar guests. After that she stood in the middle of the dining room and announced:

"Good morning, everyone. I'm sorry to interrupt your breakfast, but I'd like to inform you we have a phenomenal dance company staying with us at the hotel. They're a group of whirling dervishes from Istanbul, Turkey, who've graciously offered to put on a free performance later this morning. You're all encouraged to attend. It'll be held in the main ballroom at 11 o'clock sharp. Enjoy your breakfast."

Rachael swirled some half-n-half into her coffee, and she looked up at her friend. "Feel like going?"

"The dance performance?"

"Yeah."

"I'll see what Rosco wants to do. The food smells delicious."

"It does."

22

Pierre Crepaud (pronounced Crah-po) was a noticeably overweight frog, who loved to eat. I mean a Frenchman that is. No insult intended. Pierre was the head chef of the Escoffier Room: The Clinton's swanky two-star restaurant. He graduated at the top of his class from the world-renowned Culinary Institute of America, located in Hyde Park, New York. He was sitting in his office, going over some recipes, when Ms. Cooper walked in.

"*Bonjour*, Chef."

"*Bonjour*, Alice."

"I wanna tell you, you did a fantastic job on the ice-sculpture," she said.

"*Merci beaucoup*. It's a real challenge getting the mermaid's scales just right. The fish delivery came in this morning. I put the invoice on your desk."

"Thanks. They bring the lobsters?" Ms. Cooper asked.

"*Oui*. Nice two and three pounders. Fresh from Kennebunkport."

"Excellent."

Ms. Cooper smiled and turned to leave.

"Don't you wanna hear what I have for specials tonight?" he asked.

She remained in the doorway, and suspiciously sniffed the air twice.

"Okay."

"Have a seat. Would you like a coffee. Espresso?" the chef asked.

"No, thanks."

Ms. Cooper sat on a chair by the chef's heavy iron desk. She wrinkled her leafy nose and sniffed the air again while the chef read from a note paper stained with egg yolk, tomato sauce and Burgundy wine.

"For appetizers, I have a steamed mussels in a spicy curry sauce, coquille Saint Jacques, jumbo shrimp cocktail, potato gnocchi with pumpkin, spinach and shiitake mushrooms, fried Maryland oysters, and one of my absolute favorite appetizers: Grenouilles sauté Provençale."

Alice lifted her thin gray eyebrows and asked, "What's that?"

"What's what?"

"Your last special."

"The gnocchi?" he asked.

Again, a perturbed Ms. Cooper wrinkled her preshrunk nose and replied, "No, you knucklehead. The sautéed dish. Have you been smoking again, Pierre?"

"A little. Why?"

"I can smell it, it reeks. How do you function this early in the morning smoking that dreadful weed?"

"Old habit from cooking school, I guess."

"So, what's this Provençale dish you're raving about?" Ms. Cooper inquired.

"Oh, it's unbelievably delicious! —and extremely popular back in France. I'm really surprised you haven't heard of it before. It's frogs legs sautéed in butter, minced garlic, shallots and finished with a dry white wine. I prefer to use a Sauvignon Blanc, but a Chardonnay works just as well. And I must admit the dish sounds more appealing when you say it in French," he said with his usual patriotic fervor. He bit into a chocolate croissant.

Ms. Cooper curled her top lip and asked, "You're joking, right?"

"No."

The short, but powerful woman slammed her fist on the desk and the chef's croissant somersaulted through the air while his coffee cup keeled over and further stained his recipes.

"Are you insane. Pierre?"

"What's the matter with you?" he asked while sponging off the tepid liquid with a kitchen towel.

"Isn't it bad enough we look like frogs? Now you wanna put them on the menu?"

"But they're delicious, Alice—"

"Then you can eat them yourself! And when you're done, I'll have your paycheck ready, and you can buy yourself a ticket back to France. Have I made myself perfectly clear?"

"*Oui*, but why do you have such a distaste for frogs' legs?"

"It's not their taste, I'm concerned about. It's the cruelty those poor creatures suffer, just to get on someone's plate. Did you not know their legs are cut off while they're still alive? Then the maimed amphibians are thrown back in the water to suffer a slow and torturous death," she explained.

"I didn't know. I'm sorry," he outright lied. "That's horrible. I had no idea it was done that way. I'll substitute the shrimp tempura instead."

"Fine," Ms. Cooper said while she folded her arms against her chest. "Put the rest of the specials on my desk. I'll look at them after breakfast. And have the dishwasher remove the frog legs from the walk-in and properly dispose of them."

23

We come spinning out of nothingness, scattering stars.
The stars form a circle, and in the center we dance.

Rumi, 13th century Sufi mystic and poet

Ms. Cooper entered the grand ballroom at the hotel, and she dimmed the chandeliers. She found a seat in the back near the exit doors. The Applebaums and Levines sat in the row directly in front of her.

Four musicians, a woman and three men, walked onto the stage and sat beside their instruments. The woman cradled a violin. One of the men picked up and blew air into a reed-flute called a ney. Another man lightly tapped his brass kettledrum and a tambourin, a long and narrow drum. The third man adjusted the tuning pegs on his ruddy red oud, a multi-stringed instrument related to the lute. The four musicians tuned while the guests in the ballroom waited for the performance to begin.

Twelve barefoot dervishes ceremoniously marched single file onto the dance floor; each wore a black cloak and a sweeping bone-white skirt. Tall white hats referred to as tombs crowned their heads. The dancers formed a circle, faced each other, and then stood still a few moments. They bowed to one another and lowered themselves to the floor in a kneeling position.

The drummer beat his kettle drum, and a deep-toned reverberation revived the sleepy audience inside the cathedral-like banquet hall. The flutist blew a sustained high-pitched note on his bamboo ney while the kneeling dervishes slapped the polished wood floor with their palms; a gesture which symbolizes the Day of Judgment, and the long and lonely ladder that must be climbed to get from this earth to heaven.

The violinist stroked her bow across the strings of her instrument while the oudist strummed his, creating a meditative arrangement of Middle Eastern influence.

The dancers circled three times around, removed their cloaks, kissed them, and then laid them on the wood floor; a ritual performed to signify the dervishes have left behind their earthly attachments before turning.

The dancers crossed their arms over their chests, placing the left hand on the right shoulder, the right hand on the left shoulder, and then slowly revolved counterclockwise to the music. They unraveled their arms, elevating the right arm with palm turned up to the sky to receive God's goodness. Each dancer lowered their left arm and pointed a hand toward the ground, a movement which symbolizes the dervish giving back the goodness to humanity.

The four musicians quickened the tempo. And the twelve whirling dervishes spun faster and faster. Their bone-white skirts swirled through the air, mystifying the audience with colorful spheres of light.

24

After enjoying the dance performance put on by the whirling dervishes, the Applebaums strolled over to the Clinton's spa, where Mrs. Froskenmirth, the assistant spa director, cordially greeted them at the desk.

"Good afternoon, and welcome to the spa. How may I help you?"

"My husband and I have appointments scheduled," Rita replied. "Applebaum."

The receptionist glanced at her computer screen.

"Is this your first time at the spa?"

"Yes, it is," Rita answered while noticing a distinct growth of leathery white skin protruding from the woman's chin.

Mrs. Froskenmirth self-consciously placed a hand under her mouth to hide the discoloration. She handed them clipboards and pens.

"Have a seat and fill these out. Afterwards, our spa attendants will show you to our facilities."

While Rosco baked in the sauna on the men's side of the spa, Rita tested the turbo-jetted water in the Jacuzzi on the women's side. She gradually lowered herself into the percolating hot water.

Moments later, a hefty young woman entered the spa and hung up her bath towel. She approached the Jacuzzi, stepping in and displacing a small tsunami of water when she sat opposite Rita. Her pale white legs contrasted with a blue, one-piece bathing suit with silver sequins down the sides. A white regulation NHL goalie mask blocked the view of her face.

Rita smiled and asked: "Are you a Rangers, or an Islanders fan?"

She didn't answer at first. Just coldly stared through the eye slits of her mask. "That's not funny," she murmured to Rita.

"Sorry, I was only kidding."

"And I don't like hockey. It's much too violent of a sport in my opinion."

"I agree."

But why the mask? Rita wondered.

The broad bodied woman only stayed a brief time in the water. She unhurriedly climbed out, splashing Rita in the process. She took a towel and dried her turnip-colored body. Compared to Rita's shapely but splotchy legs covered with orangey spots, the weighty woman hadn't a single blemish on her ankles, meaty calves, or thighs. Yet, Rita couldn't help noticing something extremely peculiar about the woman's feet when she stepped out of the Jacuzzi. They were deformed and shaped like a pig's hoof. The blonde woman made a high-heeled sound when she walked along the tiled floor.

"I don't mean to be rude but how did you get your legs to look like that?" Rita asked her.

The woman removed the hockey mask and revealed a flaccid face with a primrose hog-snout. She grinned and answered with an arrogance:

"I've been using the stem cell treatment for a year and a half now. Works pretty well, huh?"

"Apparently. The stem cells come from a pig?"

"That's right. Iowa pigs. Perhaps you should consider having the treatment done. Not to mention your face—but your legs and arms would improve a whole lot. And you could get rid of all those yucky spots. It only takes five injections a month—over a two-year period. I'm almost finished with my treatment plan," the woman described.

She smiled and covered her piggish face again with the mask.

"I'd do it, but I can't stand the sight of needles," Rita said while she felt the pulsating water soothe her tired muscles.

"Oh, well. It's your body."

"Yes, it is. Have a nice afternoon," Rita said.

"You too."

Rita relaxed in the water for a few more minutes before she carefully stepped out of the hot tub and got into her bathrobe. She explored the spa's relaxation area where she made herself a hot mint tea with lemon. While the tea bag steeped, she sat by a low table spread with reading material. Rita picked up a glamour magazine and noticed a photo of a fashionably dressed woman on the front cover. Undoubtedly, it was someone famous, sophisticated and charming, yet barely recognizable to Rita. The woman's facial skin and neck the color of half-ripe mango, partly red, mostly green, and streaks of yellow and black. Rita read the name below the photo, "Oh my God, I can't believe that's Oprah," she declared under her breath.

Someone approached Rita. On the floor, in front of her stood two large bare feet with a chartreuse webbing between the toes. She looked up and saw a strapping young man dressed in khaki pants and a white polo shirt emblazoned with a red capital 'C on the front pocket. His face, broad hands, and muscular arms: the color of overcooked asparagus.

"Are you Mrs. Applebaum?" he asked.

"In the flesh."

"Hello, ma'am, I'm Smiley Webster. I'll be giving you your massage this afternoon," he spoke with a strong Midwestern drawl.

Rita put down the teacup and got up to shake the man's hand.

"I see ya have good strong hands," Rita stated. "I like that in a massage therapist. I take it you specialize in deep tissue massage?"

"Yes, ma'am, I do."

"Good. I need someone who can go deep. Get my knots out. Would you mind if I called you Smiley?"

"Not at all."

"I'll be honest with you. You're the first person I've met named Smiley. Where you from?"

"Idaho, ma'am."

"Well, there's another first," Rita said. "I never had the pleasure of meeting anyone from Idaho. Let alone a massage therapist."

"Really?"

"I can't imagine an over-population of massage therapists in the great state of Idaho," Rita said.

"Last time I checked there were only about thirty-five, or forty therapists in the whole darn state."

Rita stopped to adjust her bathrobe that was about to slide off her shoulders.

"Ha, that's a laugh," she said. "I probably have more massage therapists living in my apartment complex in Florida."

"Do you need to use the restroom before we begin your treatment?"

"I'm good."

"We'll have to be quiet down here. This is where the spa treatments are done."

Smiley escorted Rita through a red-carpeted hallway and inside a semi-dark treatment room. An orange salt-lamp and battery powered candles burned within. Relaxing piano music played through a speaker on the ceiling.

"I saw on your intake form you have the Long Tongue Syndrome. Besides that, do you have any allergies, high blood pressure, or any other physical problems I should be aware of?"

"My left hip was replaced a couple years ago," Rita replied. Other than that, I'm as fit as a fiddle."

"I'll be careful not to do any range of motion for that hip."

Just then, Rita's ill-fitting bathrobe accidentally slipped off her shoulders and dropped onto the carpeted floor. A silhouette of her bare behind and breasts projected upon the wall. Smiley caught a glimpse of her naked body, and he rapidly jerked his eyes away while she bent down and placed the robe back on.

"Woops! Guess I wasn't supposed to do that. Nothing you haven't seen, right, Smiley?"

"Yes, ma'am. I mean, no ma'am," he nervously replied as he stared at the massage table and pretended to smooth out an imaginary wrinkle in the sheet. "I'm sorry, I never meant to look Mrs. Applebuns."

"Applebaum. Nonsense. That was entirely my fault. I look terrible—don't I?"

"I don't think so," the massage therapist from Idaho replied.

"Sorry if I embarrassed you, Smiley."

"Don't worry about it. Do you have any particular areas you would like me to focus on?"

"My lower back and shoulders are bothering me today."

"I'll leave the room so you can disrobe. You'll be starting face down under the top sheet and blanket. I'll knock when I'm ready to come back in the room."

"Smiley?"

"Yes, ma'am?"

"You don't look so bad yourself."

"Why that's awfully kind of you to say, Mrs. Applebaum."

25

In their cozy little suite at the Clinton Hotel and Spa, Ron bathed while his wife sat on the bed in her purple silk panties, sheer stockings, and a black and white checkered Bear Bryant hat; a souvenir she got the last time they were at her alma mater. The University of Alabama. Rachael filed her fingernails and pensively watched as the Tide kicked the living daylights out of the Florida Gators, in the last football game of the regular season. It was the fourth quarter with only eight minutes left on the clock. The Gator's coach flung his cap ten feet in the air, stomped his foot, shook his head, and then watched with one eye closed as his star quarterback, Joe Groda, fumbled the pigskin on the opposing team's five-yard line.

"Butter fingers!" the Gator's coach screamed from the sideline.

From Kerhonkson, New York, Bama's 6'8", 350 pound senior center, big Al Jolson, miraculously recovered the ball, and both teams watched dumbfounded, while he ran ninety-five yards for an easy touchdown. Big Al had a wide grin on his pasty frog-face the remaining length of the field. From inside his anti-virus protection suit, Alabama's coach,

Nick Saben, hadn't seen Mr. Jolson run that fast in the three years he played on varsity. The fans went nuts while big Al slammed the ball down in the end-zone and performed a little song and dance routine. Rachael cheered while she put on her white-lace Victoria Secret bra.

"Bama just scored another touchdown, Ron."

"What's the damage now?" he asked while coming out of the bathroom with a towel wrapped around his waist.

"Eighty-four to seven."

"Yikes. Rosco ain't gonna be a happy camper tonight," Ron stated.

"He bet on Florida?" Rachael asked.

"Yeah. Always does."

"Help me with my bra, please."

Rachael turned around so her husband could fasten it.

"When's he ever gonna learn?" she asked.

"Don't know. He graduated from Florida State, remember?" Ron replied while fumbling with his wife's bra clasp.

"What's taking you so long, Ronald?"

"Damn webbing on my hand gets in the way. There you go."

Rachael sighed and pointed to her clothes on the bed. "Which outfit do you think I should wear?"

Her husband scratched his nuts and thought for a few moments.

"I'm swayed towards the purple skirt with the herringbone jacket and white blouse. It'll look smart on you," Ron stated. "What shoes are you gonna wear?"

"The fucking red, triple-wide heels. What else do I have to wear?"

Ron shook his head. "Sorry, I asked."

"I don't care if I look smart. How 'bout this other outfit?"

"It's too loud for dinner," he replied.

"You think?"

Ron examined the colorful ensemble for a moment. He wanted to tell her, her hot-pink blouse with the ruffled collar front, black pleated skirt, and silver-lined jacket designed with screaming blue petunias on the outside, was loud enough to scare a Bengal tiger out of the jungle. He had second thoughts though.

"I believe you wore it for Mardi Gras a couple years ago," he nonchalantly stated while inserting a leg into the trouser of his pinstriped suit pants.

"That was last year," Rachael said. "And I did wear it. We ended up having a big argument. You don't think it looks good on me anymore?"

"I didn't say that, Rachael."

"But you're insinuating it's too flamboyant for the occasion."

"I didn't say that either."

She stared at him with lukewarm eyes. He tucked in his shirt and zipped up his fly.

"Wear whatever you want, Rachael. I don't know why we have to have this debate whenever you wanna wear that jacket," he said, accentuating the word {that} more than necessary.

"I rarely wear it. And I don't know why you have to refer to it as *that* jacket?" Rachael whined.

"What else do you want me to call it?" Ron asked while he bent down to tie his shoelaces.

"Asshole. I'm wearing it for lunch tomorrow then."

"Fine. We should get a move on it," Ron said. "I told Rosco we'd meet them at the bar for cocktails at five-thirty. It's twenty-after now."

Careful not to smudge her makeup-caked face, Rachael put on her pleated white blouse, dark purple skirt, herringbone jacket and custom-made heels. She sprayed on a French perfume and glanced in the mirror.

"How do I look, Ronald?"

"Like a million bucks."

"I do not. I look like a fire-belly toad, for God's sake. And these shoes look absolutely ridiculous on me."

"Do me a big favor, Rachael. Don't start that now. Please."

She pouted.

"You look handsome in that suit. Surprised it still fits you. Your socks match?"

"Yes."

"That's a miracle."

Rachael aligned her husband's jacket lapel and kissed him on the cheek.

"I'm sorry I swore at you."

"Don't worry about it."

"I love you, Ronald."

"Love you too. Almost ready?"

"Soon as I put on some more makeup."

"You already have three layers on."

26

At the Clinton's red oak bar, Rita lifted the hem on her violet dinner dress and discreetly crossed her legs. The provocative silk evening wear had a slit up the side and a haphazard neckline which easily caught the eye of Rupert Bombina, a suave Sicilian bartender who was originally from Palermo, Italy. After making the Applebaum's drinks, he went to the kitchen and scarfed down a delicious prime rib and two bites of baked potato.

Rita tasted her drink and sensually sucked on a plump green olive stuffed with feta. She gave her husband a reproving glance, just when the Casanova-like bartender returned to the bar.

"How's that martini, darling?" the bartender asked Rita.

"Perfect. Just the way I like em."

"Super, I'm Rupert."

The barman presented Rita with a manicured green hand that was clawed and webbed between his thumb and forefinger. She saw his distorted appendage but shied away from shaking it.

"It's nice meeting you. I'm Rita Applebaum."

"Sorry about the hand."

"No worries."

"It's a pleasure meeting you, Rita. Lovely dress. Violet happens to be my favorite color," the bartender suavely stated.

"Oh yeah?"

"Where you from?"

"Miami Beach."

"A Floridian!" The bartender grinned and flashed a set of bright white teeth. "My Uncle Joey owns a pizza place in South Beach. Maybe ya know it, it's called Ranocchio's."

"I've eaten there a couple times. Joey's your uncle?" Rita asked.

"Yeah, I usually fly down in February and stay with him a few days. We charter a boat and go deep-sea fishing off Key Largo."

"Small world," Rita said while she dreamily glanced across the bar, noticing the heavy-set woman who was in the spa earlier that afternoon. She wore a green velvet pants suit and still had on the hockey mask.

"You fish?" Rupert asked, gazing into Rita's blue-green eyes.

"No, but it sounds like a lot of fun."

"It's a blast."

Rosco gave the debonair bartender a sniffling glance as he drummed on his cocktail glass with a pen from the hotel.

The bartender ignored him as he wiped the highly polished surface of the bar with a dampened kitchen towel. His eyes firmly planted on Rita's leek green and red-spotted cleavage.

"Maybe we can be friends on Facebook. I'll take you out on the boat the next time I'm in Florida," he told her.

She smiled in a coquettish-like manner. "I would but I'm married. This is my husband, Rosco."

He snarled a hello and kept drumming on his glass.

"Sorry, I didn't see a ring," the bartender said.

Rita showed him her webbed hand, she would normally wear a wedding band. She smiled.

"Sorry. Give me a shout when you're ready for another martini and bloody Mary," the bartender said. "The next rounds on me."

"I will, thanks."

Rosco stewed while he rattled the ice in his almost empty cocktail glass. He watched the Italian bartender go mix a Long Island iced tea for the heavy-set blonde wearing the green pants suit. She sat next to an elderly gentleman who was drinking a whiskey sour, munching on pretzels, and laughing at his own jokes while nervously poking at the thin black membrane between his fingers. Every so often he'd glance at his reflection in a mirror on the back wall of the bar.

Rosco licked two fingers and rubbed the rim on his glass. It made a high-pitched sound.

"Stop that—it's annoying me, Rosco," his wife said with an angry sidelong glance.

He slumped on his stool and apologized.

"I told you not to bet on the game. We could've used that $500 to paint the bedrooms. You're such a jerk."

Rosco sheepishly sucked on an ice cube and put down the pen.

"That's the last time I bet on Florida," he vowed.

"Famous last words."

"Hell, I mean it this time. Order me another drink, I'm going to the restroom. Extra Tabasco please."

Rosco put away his business, zipped, flushed and then walked over to a marble sink where he washed his hands and read some wise-ass graffiti scrawled on a white-tiled wall in black magic marker.

frogs rule, toads suck

When Rosco returned to the bar, Ron and Rachael were chatting with his wife. He picked up his replenished drink and had himself a sip.

"It's about time you guys showed up," Mr. Applebaum said. "Just kidding."

"How's it going, Rosco?" Ron greeted.

"Fine. That's a sharp looking suit."

"Thanks. It's so old I wore it for my bar mitzvah," Ron chided.

"Yeah, right."

"What'll it be, folks?" the bartender asked the Levines.

"What are you drinking, Rita?" Rachael inquired.

She uncrossed her legs and replied: "A dirty martini. They're pretty good."

"I'll have one of those. Extra olives, please," Rachael informed the bartender.

"And you, sir?"

"Johnny Walker Black on the rocks."

"That's a pretty outfit, Rachael," her girlfriend said.

"Thanks. Your dress is lovely too. Silk?"

"Yeah."

"Where'd you find it?"

"At the mall in Aventura," Rita replied then whispered into her friend's shriveled ear: "You think it's too revealing for dinner?"

Rachael picked up a pen from the bar and pretended it was a cigar. She raised her eyebrows and did her best impersonation of Groucho Marx:

"That all depends on who you're revealing it to my dear."

"That's funny," Rita said while the bartender placed a cocktail napkin on the bar; he set Rachael's martini glass onto it, then served her husband's Scotch.

Rachael picked up her glass and waited 'til the bartender was out of range.

"No, I don't think your dress is too revealing. Inviting perhaps. But like that old saying goes, if ya got it — flaunt it. And you certainly have the bust to wear that low-cut style, Rita."

"That's nice of you to say." Rita raised her glass and toasted, "Here's to a fun vacation everyone."

"Cheers."

"*Li Chaim.*"

All of them tapped their glasses together. Rachael tasted her martini and turned to Rita again.

"You and Rosco enjoy the spa today?"

"Definitely. I had one of the best massages ever. A deep tissue from a handsome guy from Montana."

"How was your facial?"

"It was okay," Rita replied in a discouraging monotone.

"Just, okay? I think the esthetician did an amazing job."

"You think?"

"What's wrong, Rita? Your face looks great."

"No, it doesn't. Honestly, Rachael. I don't know what I'd do without you. You're such a great friend sticking by me through this crazy pandemic."

"What are friends for?"

"Sometimes I just hate myself looking like this," Rita moaned.

"Oh, c'mon, Rita—it's not that bad."

"Easy for you to say. At least you don't have a throat sack. I hate this puffy thing. You think they'll ever find a cure?"

"Sure, hope so. I don't wanna look like this forever," Rachael replied.

"Me neither."

The bartender leaned on the bar and crooned: Another round ladies?"

"No, thanks. We're going in for dinner soon," Rita replied while giving Mr. Bombina an eyeful of her cleavage.

With his non-prehensile hand, the barkeeper unhurriedly removed the women's empty glasses from the bar top and placed them in a rack. Rosco jealously watched the flirtation unfold from the corner of his eye. He balled up a cocktail napkin and flicked it off the bar. He turned to his friend and despondently asked, "ya catch any of the game?"

"Army Navy?"

"No, Alabama and Florida."

"Roll Tide," Ron said. "Just a few minutes of the last quarter. What a blow-out, huh?"

"It almost felt like I was watching Nightmare on Oak Street."

"I think you mean Elm Street. How much did you lose this time?" Ron asked.

"Enough."

Rosco put his credit card on the bar and told the bartender he'd cover the tab for everyone. After he signed the bill, he slid off the stool and followed his wife to the restaurant.

Wearing a pencil-thin mustache and a sharkskin suit, a maître d' greeted the foursome from Miami Beach.

"Good evening, folks, and welcome to the Escoffier Room."

"Evening. We have a reservation for four," Ron said. "It's under Levine."

The maître d' checked the list of names on his clipboard. "Right this way, folks."

They passed through a grand vestibule painted with murals portraying life in the French countryside during the early 1800's. The maître d' escorted them into an elaborately decorated dining room and seated the party at a square table beside a big window partially covered with frost.

"I hope this table is adequate for you, Mr. Levine," the maître d' said while handing them menus. He presented Ron with a wine list artistically bound in soft Corinthian leather.

"It's fine, thanks," he replied.

Ron browsed the pages of the wine list while a Mexican busboy poured everyone some chilled Saratoga water from an opaque blue bottle.

"What are you having for an appetizer?" Rosco asked his wife.

"The steamed mussels with the spicy red curry. What about you?"

Rosco unrolled his napkin and placed it on his lap.

"Think I'm gonna get the potato gnocchi."

"It's probably full of gluten," Rita said.

"Eh, who cares? A little gluten won't kill me."

A kelp-faced gentleman arrived at the Floridian's table. He sported a sebaceous black mustache, tall and quite handsome. He stood opposite Rita.

"Good evening, everyone. My name is Mr. Difda. I'll be your waiter tonight," he announced. "The dinner specials are a pan-fried halibut steak with a crisp cashew crust. Comes with a lime butter and accompanied by a garlic mashed and string beans amandine."

The waiter was briefly interrupted when he heard what sounded like a stack of plates crashing onto the kitchen floor.

"There goes his paycheck," Rosco quipped.

The waiter managed a thin smile, shrugged his shoulders and deflated his blue throat-sack. He continued:

"We also have a roasted pheasant with a cranberry peppercorn sauce. It's served with wild rice patties and a vegetable. A boiled, baked, or steamed Maine lobster with a choice of potato and vegetable, a Shaker-style stuffed flank steak with egg noodles, and a most delicious seabass baked in *papillote*. It comes with a fennel and truffle sauce, basmati rice and steamed asparagus with hollandaise. Our soups tonight are French onion, miso with shrimp and pea shoots, and a lovely cream of mushroom. Have we decided on your wines yet?" the waiter questioned.

"I believe we're ready," Ron answered. "For our appetizers we'll do a bottle of the Rothschild 2001 Sauvignon Blanc."

"That's an excellent choice, sir," Mr. Difda stated.

"Is it?"

"Most definitely. The Rothschild vintage has a delightfully lascivious, invigorating and fruity taste. The bouquet is romantic and Spring-like. It has subtle nuances of currant, honeydew, mango, peach, almond, cardamon and Bartlett pair. A white wine perfect for any appetizer," Mr. Difda eloquently described.

Rosco whispered into his wife's ear: "How can a wine taste like all that? It's kind of ridiculous. Don't you think?"

"Stop it—," his wife scolded.

"We'll take a bottle of that," Ron said.

"Certainly, sir."

The waiter lowered his voice and spoke down: "And just in case you haven't noticed. That selection is one of our steeper priced wines."

"That won't be a problem," Ron said.

"Of course not, sir. It's well worth the money. And the wine you've chosen for your entrees?"

"How's the Napa Valley Cabernet 2010?"

"It's a delightful wine, but I'm more a fan of the 2008 vintage. The earlier wine's body has had more time to mature," the waiter explained while he briefly caught Rita raising her dress a few inches above her knees, ventilating her heated inner thighs. She smiled at him. "The '08 vintage is superb with beef, poultry, and fish entrees as well. It's a robust red with a sentimental bouquet of blackberry, plum, nutmeg, coriander, and a slight hint of bilberry. There's a delicate touch of sweetness, yet not too dry. It's a full-bodied wine but won't overwhelm the palate," the blue-eyed waiter flamboyantly stated.

"Is he done?" Rosco said, placing his transfigured palm onto his ruddy-spotted throat sack; he cleared some mucous and quietly spoke to his wife again: "What the fuck is bilberry, Rita? —ribbit."

She ignored her husband's query and gave the waiter a smile as cute as a bug's ear.

"Boy, you sure know your wines, Mr. Difda," Rita said.

He smiled back and bowed slightly.

"Thank you, ma'am."

"Please, feel free to call me, Rita."

"We'll order two bottles of the Cabernet," Ron said.

The waiter quivered for a moment and tugged his eyes away from Mrs. Applebaum's provocative smile.

"Perfect. I'll put your Rothschild on ice and be back to take your dinner orders."

"Excuse me, Mr. Difda?"

"Yes, Mrs. Levine?"

"When my husband and I were here a few years ago, I don't recall seeing the murals in the vestibule. Are they new?"

"They were installed about six months ago."

"They're lovely," Rachael said.

"Absolutely. Excuse me."

"He's a good-looking man," Rita told her friend.

"Yeah, he's got that charming Clark Gable smile. I don't particularly like his mustache though."

"I do. I think he looks more like a young Marlon Brando with those baby-blue eyes."

"That's stretching it a little, Rita. What are you having for dinner?"

Rita gazed down at the menu.

"I'm torn between the lobster and the rack of lamb. What about you?"

"I'm having the sea bass," Rachael replied.

"That sounds delicious."

"It is. I had it the last time we were here."

The waiter returned with a basket of mini-French baguettes and multi-grain dinner rolls. He unveiled a white napkin from the basket and a heavenly aroma pervaded the table.

"Be careful these just came out of the oven," the waiter said while prompting a glimpse of Rita's fast plunging neckline.

Mr. Difda removed a wine bottle from a stainless-steel ice bucket; he opened it and poured Ron a couple ounces of the white wine priced at $700 a bottle. He slowly savored the vintage, then lowered the tall wine glass.

"How is it, sir?" the waiter asked.

Ron looked up at the waiter and smiled.

"Delicious."

"Excellent."

Mr. Difda demurely brushed his hand against Rita's upper arm while trickling the wine into her glass. He inhaled her Nina Ricci perfume and felt a chemistry. He served Rachael and Rosco, then took everyone's appetizer and entree orders.

With his chopsticks in hand, Ron dipped a shrimp tempura into a tangy ginger soy sauce. He ate it and chased the morsel with some grated daikon radish and a taste of wine.

"The hotel provides a shuttle bus to the casino," Ron mentioned.

"We can save on gas," Rosco said. "You girls coming with us?"

"Not me," Rachael replied. "I'm gonna curl-up by the fireplace and read after dinner. How 'bout you, Rita?"

"It's too cold out to go anywhere."

"Suit yourselves. Pass the salt please," Rosco asked.

Ron thought a moment before relishing the taste of his last shrimp tempura. He lifted his wine glass and toasted, "to life."

The two couples clinked their glasses together and drank.

Mr. Difda came back to the table and placed a lobster bib over Rita's chest. He leisurely tied the strings in a neat bow at the back of her ruddy-spotted neck.

"Eating lobster can be quite messy," the waiter informed her.

"I know," Rita said while smelling a hint of the waiter's musk cologne.

"I'll be right back with your entrees."

The Mexican bus boy removed their appetizer dishes before refilling their water glasses from an opaque blue bottle.

When a timer rang in the Escoffier Room's bustling kitchen, Chef Crepaud snatched a couple of kitchen towels and opened the door to a food steamer. He waited for the steam to escape before taking out a hotel pan of asparagus and one of string beans. He placed the veggies on the line, garnished a dinner, and then whipped up a creamy hollandaise sauce in a stainless-steel bowl.

Mr. Difda scurried into the kitchen, splaying his thick black mustache, and plucking a bit of white lint off his satin vest. "You can fire that four-top, chef," he announced.

The French chef clapped his hands twice to wake up his expediter.

"I don't pay you to sleep!" he yelled. "Let's go with that baked sea bass, prime rib, rack of lamb and steamed lobster *s'il vous plaît*."

Pierre's nose-less sous chef removed a sizzling rack of lamb from the oven; he placed it on a cutting board, reached for his French knife and handily carved the rack into mouthwatering portions. The meat's savory juices flowed like rivulets along the board while the sous chef decoratively arranged the chops onto a large round platter. Meanwhile, a line cook added roasted red potatoes, and asparagus streaked with hollandaise. The chef garnished the plate with fresh parsley sprigs and a lemon crown.

Mr. Difda picked up his serving tray with the four entrees and carried it out to the dining room, setting the tray on a stand and taking the plate-covers off the first two dinners.

"Be very careful these plates are extremely hot," the waiter cautioned while serving Rita her lobster and Rachael's fish. Next, he gave Ron his rack of lamb and Rosco's prime rib.

"Does the Escoffier Room still give tours of its wine cellar?" Rachael asked the waiter.

"We do," he replied. "I'd be happy to give you ladies a tour of it after dessert. I'm sure that wouldn't interest your husbands much."

"How do you know?" Rosco tersely spoke.

"Oh, you're certainly welcome to join us, sir," the waiter said.

"Thanks. But the husbands will be going to the casino after dinner," Rosco growled.

"Don't lose your shirt, sir. I'm just kidding," the waiter said with a brief laugh.

"I might take you up on that tour, Mr. Difda," Rita said.

"Excellent. And how are your lamb chops cooked, Mr. Levine?"

"Perfect."

"Superb. Enjoy your entrees," the waiter said. "And if you need anything else, just give me a shout."

After Rita devoured the last bite of her scrumptious lobster, she untied her bib and placed it on the plate. She wiped her chin and slowly got up.

"Excuse me, I need to use the little girl's room."

Rachael said as she pushed out her chair, "Wait a sec, Rita—I'll come with you."

Rosco swallowed a bite of prime rib and poured himself a little red wine.

"She's acting kind of strange."

"Who?" Ron asked.

"My wife."

"What makes you say that?"

"I thought she and the waiter were getting a bit too chummy before," Rosco replied.

"Really?"

"Didn't you see how he put that lobster bib around her?"

"I wasn't paying that much attention," Ron replied as he appeared to be more interested in his final lamb chop.

"Yeah. And I didn't particularly care for the way he was looking at her either. Undressing her with his eyes," Rosco irascibly spoke.

"These lamb chops are out of this world," Ron stated. "You wanna a taste?"

"No, I hate lamb. You think I'm joking?"

"What about?" Ron asked.

"The waiter!"

"Calm down, Rosco. I doubt you're joking—but you want my opinion?"

"Shoot—"

"Your wife looks quite seductive in that dress."

"You think I don't know that? I told her not to wear it tonight. It's so damn revealing the bartender couldn't take his eyes off her."

Ron crossed his knife and fork on the plate and looked up at his friend.

"A little jealous, are we? —Is she wearing a bra?"

"Quiet. Here comes the waiter," Rosco warned.

Mr. Difda loomed large beside the table. He stood cocksure, his blue eyes luminous, shiny blue-black mustache splendid and thick. He questioned in a tongue-in-cheek manner, "What's the matter gentlemen? Your wives leave you?"

Rosco crossly looked up at the waiter with a stone-crab stare.

"They've gone to the wine cellar without you," Rosco replied.

"*Touché*, Mr. Applebaum," the waiter said. "I'll be coming around with the dessert cart shortly. We have a great selection of cheesecakes, tortes and pumpkin pie tonight. Are we ready for coffee or tea? Perhaps an after-dinner liqueur?"

"I'll take a double espresso, please," Ron replied.

"Just a regular black coffee for me. And a pumpkin pie. With whipped cream, please."

"Certainly."

In the restroom Rachael applied some more flesh-tone makeup to her cheeks while Rita lightly penciled a rubicund shade of lip gloss.

"Got a pen, Rachael?"

"I'll check my purse."

She foraged through her Gucci bag while Rita smiled at her image in the mirror and adjusted her slinky fitting dress.

"Is lobster an aphrodisiac, Rachael?"

"Raw oysters are supposed to be. Why?"

"My nipples are a little hard right now."

"Really. Here's a pen. You ready, Rita?"

"Soon as I powder my face. I'll meet you back at the table. Order me a cappuccino."

"See you later, alligator."

27

While Rita hung out in her suite and digested her dinner, she turned on the TV and watched the last ten minutes of Jeopardy. With his perfect head of full green hair, eyebrows, and a matching necktie: a garrulous, brick-faced, and ageless Alex Trebeck look-alike hosted the popular game show that aired on NBC TV.

"Presidents, for $200, please, Alex," a contestant wagered.

"The daily double!" a voice announced.

The show's theme music played.

Downstairs in the Escoffier's dining room, Mr. Difda helped a busboy do the set-up for lunch the next day, he loosened his bowtie, punched out, and then wandered over to the bar for a cold one.

"How's it going, Rupert?" the waiter greeted the squat Italian bartender.

"The usual, Dif?"

"Please."

"Wanna glass?"

"Don't bother."

While the bartender placed a napkin and a chilled bottle of Guinness on the bar, the waiter thought about something that occurred earlier that evening. A driblet of condensation ran down the dark brown bottle; Mr. Difda picked it up and took a swig, letting the cold stout swirl around his small throat sack awhile before swallowing.

"Busy tonight?" the bartender asked the mustached waiter.

"Slow compared to last night. Tips were okay, though. How bout you?"

Rupert blew his nose and tossed the snot rag in the trash. "Eh, nothing to write home about. Are you working the banquet tomorrow night?"

"Yeah, then I got a few days off, thank God," the waiter replied.

"Doing anything special?" the bartender asked while polishing a wine glass and placing it on the top shelf behind the bar.

"Not really. I'm going out for a cigarette. You wanna join me?"

Rupert shook his head no. "I quit a couple days ago."

The waiter grabbed his bottle off the bar and said goodnight. He went through the kitchen and poked his head inside an office.

"Evening, Chef."

"*Monsieur*, Difda. What's shaking?"

"Same old shit. You're working late."

"I have to finish up an order for a wedding next week," the chef replied while filling a shot glass with Tequila. "Want one?"

"No, thanks."

"C'mon! It's Friday night, live a little."

"No way. The last time we drank Tequila, you had me running around Saratoga like a madman. In a blinding snowstorm no less."

Pierre laughed and sucked on a lemon wedge.

"Didn't we drive to Lake George that night?" the chef asked.

"We did. You insisted on going swimming, but the lake was frozen solid. I can still see us slipping and sliding on that black ice like a couple of drunken penguins."

The chef laughed and filled his shot glass once more.

"You put out some amazing dinners tonight."

"Thanks. You did an awesome job yourself, Dif. Sure you don't wanna shot?"

"Positive. Have a good night."

"You too, Dif."

Mr. Difda zipped-up a winter coat, put on his blue ski cap, and then went outside to the loading dock, where he drank the last of the Irish stout. He lit a fag and watched the smoke drift in the air like a pearly white ghost. The waiter reached into his pants pocket and took out some folded cash. While counting the tips, he discovered a cocktail napkin someone had slipped him earlier in the evening. He unfolded the napkin and held it up to the light.

Come up to my room later. We could have a drink and chat. My husband will be at the casino for a few hours. 9:15 is good. Room 31. Knock three times and wait.

Rita

Mr. Difda smelled the fragrant lipstick-smudged napkin; he thought before crumpling it up and making a foul shot into the dumpster. A silvery moon crept above the tree line as the waiter finished counting his tips. He placed the empty Guinness bottle in a crate before opening the back door to the warm kitchen.

28

In his room at the Clinton, Mr. Difda sat on the bed and donned a pair of blue socks with white polka-dots. He stepped into his favorite boxer shorts decorated with red chili peppers, then posed in front of a full-length mirror. He did a couple of push-ups, a deep knee-bend, and exercised his elastic biceps with a pair of three-pound hand-weights. After the brief work-out, the waiter slapped on a musk cologne, put on corduroy pants, a cowboy belt, a turtleneck shirt, a fake Rolex, and a snazzy blue smoking jacket with black velvet lapels and shiny copper-colored buttons. The waiter pulled two red roses out of a vase and grabbed an unopened. bottle of cognac he was saving for a special occasion. He turned off the light in the room and left.

"Getting laid tonight, Mr. Difda?" asked a Guatemalan dishwasher who was plodding down the stairs to his minimally furnished room.

"I can only wish, Jose."

The waiter locked his door and placed the key into the pocket of his smoking jacket.

"This is true, *señor*," the dishwasher said. "You look handsome all-the-same. Good luck and *buenas noches.*"

"*Gracias*, Jose. And *buenas noches* to you."

Mr. Difda swiftly climbed the back stairwell to the third floor and slunk through the hallway. Before arriving at room 31, he saw a light above the elevator, signaling it'd arrived at the floor. The waiter's jaw locked when he heard the ding. He froze. (If Ms. Cooper or another employee caught him visiting guests in the hotel, he'd be fired for sure.) The elevator door rolled open. And outwalked a woman breathing from an oxygen tank and wearing an Anti-Virus Protection suit. She wheeled a plastic covered suitcase and held a short leash with a small white dog on the end of it. A Pomeranian, or a Shih tzu perhaps. The little canine was also dressed in a protection suit, and an infant size gas mask muzzled its snout. Startled, Mr. Difda, the woman and her dog crossed paths and walked to opposite ends of the hallway.

The waiter's heart beat fast as he stood in front of room 31. He knocked three times and waited, suddenly remembering that famous hit single, Tony Orlando and Dawn had recorded, *"Knock Three Times"*. He quietly hummed a verse and knocked once more. Like Bedouin nomads riding camels in a windswept desert at night, a perplexity of thoughts came into the waiter's mind: Perhaps she's taking off that sexy dress of hers and slipping into something more comfortable. She might've fallen asleep. Or stood me up and went to the casino with her husband. They could be in the room screwing their brains out. Mr. Difda placed his ear canal against the door, but he couldn't hear a peep. What'll I say if her husband opens the door? I'll look like a big shmuck standing here all spruced up holding flowers and an expensive bottle of booze. I could always say it's from room service then tell him I had the wrong room number. Maybe this wasn't such a good idea after all. I'll give it one more shot. If she doesn't answer this time, I'm leaving. The waiter quietly sang another verse and knocked three times.

Rita heard the knocking while she sat on the toilet and finished rolling a joint. She hopped off the seat, pulled-up her black satin undies, rearranged her naughty silk dinner dress, and washed and dried her hands. Before walking to the door, she hid the stash in the medicine cabinet and spritzed on a little patchouli scented perfume. She went to the door and observed the waiter through the peep hole. He was about to walk away when she opened the door.

"Mr. Difda. I'm so thrilled you could make it," Rita's voice rang through the corridor.

"Please, Mrs. Applebaum not so loud. I probably shouldn't even—"

Before completing his sentence, she seized his lapel, pulled him close, and then kissed him lightly on the cheek. She took him inside the room and immediately closed and locked the door.

"You look handsome."

"Thank you. Is your husband still at the casino?"

"No, silly, he's hiding in the closet with a loaded 45 magnum. Of course, he's at the casino."

"I brought us something to drink. Didn't know if you liked cognac—or not."

He handed her the glass bottle and the two red roses. Their hands touched briefly, and a charge of electricity passed between them. Perhaps this hadn't been a mistake after all, he thought, and felt more of an attraction.

"That was sweet of you," Rita said. "I happen to love cognac. Thanks. And flowers? How romantic."

Rita expressed with a blush.

"You're welcome."

After her cheeks faded a pinkish green again, Rita put the bottle on a coffee table, then placed the roses in an empty vase. She filled it with water from the bathroom sink and set it on a nightstand by the bed.

"Do me a big favor and take off your shoes and leave them in the foyer," Rita said.

The waiter did as he was told and stood awkwardly between the hall and the main part of the suite.

"Enjoy your dinner tonight?"

"I loved it. Especially that scrumptious chocolate mousse. It was almost better than an orgasm. Have a seat and make yourself comfortable."

When Mr. Difda sat on the love seat, his pants elevated four inches, revealing the blue socks with white polka dots. They terribly mismatched his outfit, causing him to feel a tad self-conscious. Rita sat beside him and wrapped one of her rubbery legs around his.

"What's your first name by the way?"

"Aristotle."

"Are you Greek?"

"Yes, I was born in Athens. My full name is Aristotle Demetrius Difda. But I've been called Dif ever since I was eleven years old."

"I think Aristotle is too formal. I like Dif better. It's much easier to say. Dif. Dif Difda, Dif Difda. I just love the way that rolls off my tongue. Dif Difda. Woops, I'm sorry."

Rita slurred her words and her long tongue accidentally slipped out of her mouth.

"What are you sorry about?" he asked, lengthening his trouser legs to hide his nerdy socks.

"My tongue. See—"

He straightened himself and looked at Rita.

"From the virus, huh?"

"Yeah, the long tongue syndrome," she replied.

"Was it hard to get used to?"

"At first. Comes in handy sometimes, "she answered with a gleam in her eye. "Except for your throat sack your face doesn't look bad at all. That's why I was attracted to you. And it's good your ears and nose didn't shrink much either."

"I was luckier than most people. My feet are webbed though. And I have other problem areas," he stated.

216

"Oh?"

Rita got up and noticed Dif's funny looking socks.

"Why don't we open that cognac?" she suggested. "Unless you prefer something from the mini bar. There's beer, wine and whiskey."

"I'll have a cognac."

"What's wrong, Dif? —you look a little nervous."

"I do?"

Rita grabbed two glasses on a shelf above the small fridge.

"My husband wouldn't care if we had an innocent drink together. I told him we might."

"You did?"

Rita laughed and put the glasses on the coffee table.

"I'm only kidding. Rosco has no clue we're doing this. Besides, he's way too busy playing the slot machines right now."

Rita lowered her eyes and noticed Dif's tented pants.

"Does that excite you? We've got plenty of time you know."

"To tell you the truth it does a little," he replied.

"A little?" She giggled. "Do you have any condoms with you? Rosco and I never use them. We

217

could do it on the love seat. Or in the shower maybe. Do you have a favorite position, Dif? My husband just likes it missionary style. I get so bored with that sometimes, I could scream. Now you probably think I'm a sex maniac or something. I'll share a little secret with you. My husband gets erectile dysfunction sometimes. We think it's from the virus. You don't have that do you?" she whispered into his ear.

"Huh?"

Dif's jaw dropped, and his bright blue eyes expanded. Rita's topic of conversation totally caught him off-guard. And he did have condoms. Just forgot to bring them.

"Shouldn't we have a drink first?" he quickly suggested.

"That's a wonderful idea."

Rita twisted off the cap on the Hennessey bottle and poured the liquor.

"It feels kind of cheap drinking fine cognac out of these," she said.

Rita picked up her water glass and toasted:

"Here's mud in your eye, Dif."

"Cheers."

The waiter almost felt like he was off the hook. They clanked their glasses and drank.

"It's delicious cognac," she said.

"I was saving it for a special occasion."

"Well, I think you've found it."

Rita put down her glass and scooched closer to the waiter. She placed her hand on his knee and playfully walked her fingers up his leg, fondling the soft corduroy material on Dif's pants. He felt his spine tingle and a noticeable twitch in something else. He swirled the amber liquid around his shallow throat sack while Rita's restless pheromones lingered in the air like a thick London fog.

"How long have you lived in Saratoga Springs?" she asked, gently pulling on his belt buckle.

He swallowed nervously.

"Ten years. I lived in Portland, Oregon before."

"Rains a ton there doesn't it," she said.

"Ever been?"

"Only in the airport. Rosco and I were on our way to a cruise in Alaska a couple years ago."

"Does your husband like to gamble? I heard him mention at dinner he lost a fairly large sum of money on a college football game recently."

"Unfortunately, he loves to gamble. How 'bout you, Dif?"

"I go to the track and play the horses in the summertime. Don't get the opportunity much."

"Why not?"

"The hotel is swamped during horse racing season," he replied. "Once a month, I play poker with the chef, Ms. Cooper, and a couple of other waiters who work at the hotel."

"Play for big money?"

"Not really."

Rita stroked the waiter's velvet lapel. He could smell her scent now.

"I bet you're a damn good poker player," she stated.

"I'm not too bad. I once won first place at a tournament in Atlantic City. I beat Tom Jones with a royal flush."

"That's impressive. I play on occasion. Pour me another drink sweetheart?"

"Sure."

He reached for the bottle and replenished her glass.

"Wanna have a smoke with me?" she asked.

"Why not."

He took out a lighter and a pack of cigarettes.

"I meant a joint."

"Oh?"

"Do you get stoned?"

"Not that often," he replied.

Rita held up a long joint and Dif's eyes brightened.

"It might help you relax."

"What the heck. You only live once, right?"

"So, they say. I'll grab my coat. We can smoke it on the balcony."

Dif slipped into his double-wide loafers while Rita put on her down jacket, a ski cap, and a pair of bedroom slippers.

He opened the sliding glass door for her. "After you, *madam.*"

"Merci beaucoup monsieur."

Dif followed her out onto the balcony.

"Parlez-vous Francais, Rita?"

"I know a few words. What about you?"

"I can hold a simple conversation. The chef speaks to me in French sometimes. Mostly when he's drunk or angry."

Rita took the lighter from Dif and fired up the joint. She blew a purple sinsemilla cloud off the balcony. After another hit, she exhaled the smoke into Dif's face and handed him the joint. He just stood there and admired it.

"You gonna smoke it, or look at it all night?"

"You do such a nice job rolling. He puffed on the joint and started a violent hacking.

"Careful, it's pretty potent stuff," Rita said while rubbing her hands together and sticking them inside her jacket pockets.

Dif took a long manly drag and held it in for a few moments. Again, he coughed severely while exhaling the smoke.

"Okay?"

"Yeah."

"It's medical marijuana. I need it for the pain in my hip. I had it replaced two years ago," she said.

He looked at Rita bug-eyed. "Does it relieve the pain?"

"Most of the time."

Rita took another hit and asked if Dif wanted anymore. He didn't, so she put out the joint and moved closer to him.

"You wanna know something really strange, Dif?"

"What's that?"

"I've never kissed a man with a mustache. On the lips that is."

She put an arm around his waist and lightly pressed her thigh against his groin. His body warmed her's.

"Your husband never grew a mustache?"

"Not since I've known him. Mind if I kissed you?"

"What would your husband think?"

"Don't worry about him. It's just an innocent little kiss."

"Okay, then."

When Rita pressed her body against Dif's, she felt his unmistakable manliness through her soft chiffon dress. She wrapped both arms around his waist, closed her eyes, and then planted her lips on his for a moment or two. She opened her eyes and watched their white breaths mingle in the frozen night air.

"How was that?" he asked.

"It tickles. Could we try it again?"

"If you want."

While they made out, a screaming police siren wailed and faded in the distance. A whorl of freezing air scattered a sheet of wispy snow off the gabled roof of the hotel. The sudden squall lifted Dif's toupee slightly. He secured it with his hand. A cat screeched and darted across the road. A traffic light turned yellow then red. A checkered cab cruised to a stop at the intersection of Broadway and Congress. The clandestine couple came up for air. The traffic light turned green.

"That was delightful," Rita said.

Dif looked into her eyes, almost feeling guilty they had kissed.

"Now you can say you kissed a man with a mustache," he said. "But please . . . don't ever tell your husband that."

"Don't worry, I won't. Shit—it's freezing out here. Let's go back inside."

He opened the sliding glass door again. They heard someone knock on the door. Dif looked at Rita, turned around, and was about to hide under the bed.

"Don't panic, Dif. I'm sure that's not my husband. He won't be back for a couple hours at least."

She went to the door and peered through the scope. Rachael was making funny faces out in the hallway.

"The coast is clear, Dif. It's not my husband."

"Who is it?"

"My girlfriend."

He took off his shoes again and sat on the love seat. His pant legs rose once more, revealing the circus style socks. Rita opened the door for her friend.

"What are you doing here stranger? I thought you went to the casino."

"I changed my mind," Rachael said showing her friend the cover of her paperback novel.

"*A Murder in Boca Raton.* Any good?"

"It's not your typical murder mystery. Sort of intriguing."

"Coming in for a drink?" Rita asked.

"Only if you twist my arm. What's-a-matter you cold?"

"Why do you ask?" Rita said while closing the door.

"You're wearing your hat and coat."

Rachael removed her triple-wide heels and placed them beside Dif's orthopedic penny loafers.

"I didn't know Rosco wore those kinds of shoes," Rachael said.

"He doesn't. They're Aristotle's."

"Who?"

"Our waiter," Rita said. "We were just out on the balcony getting stoned. That's why I have my coat and hat on."

"You should've told me you had company, Rita."

Dif waved from his seat; one hand still trying to conceal a polka-dotted sock.

"Oh, hi, Mr. Difda," Rachael greeted. "It's so nice to see you again."

"Good evening, Mrs. Levine," he said with a funny expression on his face. He was obviously baked from the cannabis sativa.

"What are you drinking, Rachael?"

She noticed the bottle of Hennessy.

"I'll have a little cognac."

Being a gentleman, Dif got up, found a glass and then poured her a drink.

"Here you go, Mrs. Levine."

"Cheers. So, what do you do for fun around here?" Rachael asked Dif.

"I mostly work."

"I'm sure you don't work all the time. Are you married? Have any kids? Hobbies?"

"Stop being so nosy, Rachael," her friend said.

"I was just trying to be sociable."

"I'm divorced. I have a grown son who lives in Portland."

"Maine?"

"Oregon."

"I'm bored to death," Rachael announced. "It's too bad we don't have a Monopoly game."

"Dif said he plays poker. He's a card shark," Rita mentioned.

"Really?"

"She's exaggerating of course," he said.

"Why don't we play a game? I have an unopened deck in the room. I'll go get it," Rachael said. She grabbed her book and ran across the hall in her stocking feet.

"Don't know about you, Dif, but I'm beginning to get the munchies. We could order something from room service. How's the pizza 'round here?"

"Pretty good."

"I'll call up for one, then. A large should be enough for the three of us, right?"

"They're big pies."

Rita picked up the room phone and dialed the number for room service.

Meanwhile, back in her suite, Rachael found the brand-new playing cards while rummaging through her suitcase. She used the bathroom before going across the hall. She returned and sat next to Dif, noticing his socks while tearing the plastic off the deck of cards.

"Those are cute."

"Thanks—."

"I just realized something," Rachael said.

"What's that?" Rita asked.

"We don't have any poker chips. Do you, Dif?"

"I lent mine to the chef."

"Darn—"

"We could play strip-poker," Rita suggested. "Don't need any chips for that."

"Are you serious?" Rachael asked.

"Why not? Dif wants to play, right?"

"I really should be going soon. Have to work breakfast in the morning."

"Oh, come on! The night is young," Rachael said while shuffling the stiff cards.

"You in, Dif?" Rita harped.

He hesitated a moment. How could he say no? This might be his chance to see two naked women. *I'll easily beat them.*

"Eh, what the heck…"

"That's the spirit," Rita said. "I'll throw on some other clothes."

Rite5 grabbed a pair of white socks, sweatpants and a navy-blue sweater and ran into the bathroom to change.

"Hey Rachael, I ordered a pizza from room service. If it comes, put it on the room and sign for it please. I left a tip on the table."

29

Aristotle Demetrius Difda licked his thumb pad and shrewdly fingered his five cards: An ace of diamonds, king of diamonds, queen of diamonds, jack of diamonds and ten of diamonds. Otherwise known in poker as a royal flush. Dif wasn't quite sure of what he was getting himself into when he agreed to a game of strip poker with two married women, but at least he had more clothes on than they did. He lost the first four rounds but was now on a winning streak. Unbeknownst to him, Rachael once worked as a professional poker player at the casinos in Biloxi, Mississippi. She won so many tournaments there, her competition had nicknamed her 'Lucky L'. To make matters worse, over the years, Rita learned some of her friend's favorite poker moves. And she was a decent card player herself.

Rachael started the next round in her white blouse, purple silk panties, and sheer nylons. Rita sported a scarlet red bra, sweatpants, and a pink wool cap with a fuzzy white ball on the top.

Rachael nonchalantly inquired before starting a new round: "Where'd we leave off?"

"Dif smugly replied, "I believe it's your turn to deal, Mrs. Levine. You lost the previous round. And aren't you forgetting something?"

A snarky grin curled from the corner of Dif's upper lip.

"Guess I have to remove an article of clothing," Rachael said without being overly concerned.

The man watched her seductively undo five mother of pearl buttons; she removed her slender arms from the blouse and draped it over the love seat.

"My girls are going to be chilly now," Rachael stated.

"Girls?" Dif questioned.

Rachael pushed up her B-cup bra and winked at the man.

"These."

Dif inspected the shirtless women's mediocre size chest, and laughed in a contemptuous manner.

"Don't worry, Mrs. Levine. You'll be taking your bra off soon, too," he pompously boasted before swigging more cognac.

Rachael shrugged off Dif's insulting demeanor while she shuffled and dealt the cards.

"Thanks for ordering the pizza, Rita. I loved it."

"You're welcome, Rachael. Anyone want another slice?" Rita offered while lifting the top on the pizza box. "They're still warm."

"No, thanks," Rachael replied.

"How 'bout you, Dif?"

Did just smirked and defiantly inflated his little blue throat sack.

"Not right now," he said. "I seldom eat when I'm on a winning streak."

The women looked at each other and puffed out air.

He slouched on the love seat and felt a cool breeze tickle his bare feet and ankles.

Dif had a look of disbelief when he examined the new hand Rachael had dealt him. It was one of the crappiest he'd seen since the poker game started. A two pair: A ten of diamonds, a ten of clubs, a six of hearts, a six of spades, and a three of clubs. *Where'd that come from?* Dif wondered. He lost that round to Rachael's straight flush and Rita's full house.

A bead of sweat glistened on his brow. From that moment on the poker game got progressively worse for him. Dif stood, unzipped his pants, and then peeled them off, exposing his tawny-brown legs which were hairless and sinewy. He neatly hung the trousers over the love seat and sat again.

"Can I freshen your glass girlfriend?" Rita asked while lifting the bottle of cognac.

"Yes, please. It's your turn to deal, Dif," Rachael said.

"Yeah, don't rush me," he snapped.

"What's the matter, Dif? Losing your touch?" Rita questioned.

The two women laughed and tapped their glasses together.

"Here's mud in your eye, Rachael."

"Cheers."

Dif couldn't understand why his luck had turned sour all of a sudden. He felt like a putz sitting there in his boxer shorts. In the company of two married women no less. After rushing a couple bites of lukewarm pizza, he anxiously shuffled, cut, and dealt the cards. Everyone organized their hands and the poker game quickly got underway.

After five minutes Rita broke the silence: "The guys must be winning, or they'd be back by now."

Without looking up from her cards, Rachael agreed. She scratched her wrist and slyly glanced at the waiter from the corner of one eye.

It was quiet again in the room for a few moments; then a whistling wind stirred from the balcony. An excited couple started practicing the Kama Sutra in the room next door. Their bed springs bounced repeatedly to the couple's screams, moans, and erotic conversation.

Dif checked the time on his watch, and despondently glanced at his cards again.

Rita heard the couple laughing in the room next door.

"They must be newlyweds," she mentioned, and casually placed her cards on the table. "I'm out."

"A straight of spades. Good show. Me too," Rachael said as she slapped down a royal flush. "What do you have Dif?"

He sighed while making a futile attempt at wiping the rubbery green skin off his forehead. Without speaking, he slowly raised his bloodshot eyes and sheepishly displayed a three of a kind.

"Guess I'm shit out of luck."

"I'm afraid so, Monsieur Difda," Rita said.

"We could turn off the lights if that would make it any easier for you," Rachael suggested.

Dif conceded by nodding his head and glancing at the yellow moonbeams that came through the curtain. Rachael stood in her dressy undergarments; she darkened the lights in the room then quickly returned to her seat. A gust of wind rattled the glass door to the balcony. Dif wanted to grab his clothes and run out of the room in his boxer shorts, but he scrapped the idea when he distinctly heard Ms. Cooper and Chef Crepaud laughing and carousing in a drunken stupor outside in the hallway. Instead, he swallowed a shot of cognac and reluctantly came to a standing position. He glanced at the time, cursing himself for making the rule of excluding watches, rings, and all other jewelry from the game.

The moon seemed brighter now as it boldly shined through a blue curtain on the sliding glass door. Its inquisitive sallow rays mingled with the LCD on a clock radio, Dif's illuminated fake Rolex, and the hall light that slipped underneath the door.

Rachael habitually thumbed through the deck of cards. Rita bit her fingernails. And they anxiously watched and waited, as a corona of greenish yellow light encircled Dif's dark hair. He placed his hands on the waistband of his boxer shorts and slowly pulled them down. Now, the lunar glow mixed with a mysterious luminosity in the room.

Rachael gasped while Rita nearly fell off her chair when they gazed upon Dif's belittled, glow-in-the-dark penis. His balls were as white as the snow outside. The women briefly shivered after noticing them.

Rachael whispered into her girlfriend's ear, "Oh, my, God! I've never seen one like that before."

"And quite a beautiful color if I may add," Rita said.

At that precise moment, the door flung open. And closed.

"Honey, I'm back," Rosco announced in a cheery sounding voice.

When Dif heard, his heart skipped a beat, and he immediately went into a kind of shock. His naked body became as still as a bronze statue in the New York Metropolitan Museum of Art.

"Hi, Rita," Rosco called from the vestibule.

"Hi, sweetie. You're back early."

Her husband flicked on a light switch by the door, and he hung his down jacket in the closet. He unlaced his boots and removed them.

"What are all these shoes doing here, Rita?"

There was a momentary silence while Rosco used the bathroom.

Wishing they were somewhere else, the two women looked at each other with their eyes raised.

"We're fucked now," Rachael said.

"Watching TV, Rita?" her husband called from the bathroom.

Rita cleared a significantly large frog from her throat.

"Ah, not exactly, dear."

Rosco did a double take when he saw the naked man.

"Who's that, Rita?"

"Our waiter."

"Why in God's creation is he here? —and how come he ain't wearing any clothes?"

"Because he lost."

"Lost what?"

"The poker game we just got through playing. Hi, Rosco," Rachael said.

"Oh, hi Rachael. Didn't see ya there, it's so dark in here. You were playing strip poker?"

"Yes," Rachael answered and quickly put on her blouse and buttoned it part-way. "You guys have fun at the casino?" she asked while stepping into her skirt and pulling up the zipper on the side.

"Not as much fun as you girls appear to be having. What's wrong with him?" Rosco inquired.

"He's been like that since you came in. G'night all," Rachael said.

"Good night."

Rachael walked past the petrified waiter. She quickly grabbed her heels, opened the door and left.

Rosco clapped his hands twice, and Dif suddenly snapped out of the trance he was in. His eyes appeared like two red marbles with a thin streak of white.

"Maybe you should put on some clothes before you catch a cold," Rosco suggested.

With a confused look on his face, the waiter inquired: "Where am I?"

"You're not in Kansas anymore, I can tell you that much," Rosco replied.

Dif hastily dressed, picked up his shoes, and then ran out the door barefoot.

30

Rita unhooked her red bra, playfully tossed it across the room, and she slipped into a velour negligee. Her husband poured himself a drink and suspiciously asked while noticing the two red roses on the nightstand.

"Where'd you get the cognac from, Rita?"

"Mr. Difda brought it."

"That was nice of him. He give you the roses too?"

"Yes."

Rita sat on the bed and applied some collagen-based beauty cream to her face.

"I see you got pretty friendly with the man, having a big party and all."

Rosco opened the pizza box and fingered a cold slice.

"It wasn't that big."

"Oh, no?"

"You win or lose?" Rita asked.

"I won for a change."

Rosco got undressed and put on his flannel Fred Flintstone pajamas.

"How much?"

"Close to $600, minus the tax."

"That's great!"

"At least I got the money back, I lost on the football game. Now we can paint the bedrooms. What do you think of teal?"

"We should probably stick to antique white," his wife replied.

"Yeah, maybe."

Rita got under the covers and opened a National Geographic. She turned to the article Ron had written.

"Are you mad at me, Rosco?"

"Should I be?" he asked while adjusting the thermostat to make the room warmer.

"I just thought—"

"What did you think?"

"Never mind."

"You think I'm mad because you had a little party, played an innocent game of strip poker, and got to see our waiter's big fluorescent ding-dong? That's no reason to be mad. Is it?"

Rita flipped the magazine page. She laughed when she saw the old Jewish man in the velvet loincloth.

"You're being sarcastic, Rosco. It wasn't so big."

"Love the taste of this cognac. I'll have to get a bottle when we get back to Florida. Wonder how much it costs? Maybe your boyfriend, Mr. Diffy can find us one in the wine cellar at a discounted price."

"His name is pronounced Difda," she said without looking up from the magazine.

"Yeah, whatever."

After Rosco brushed his teeth and washed up, he climbed into bed and frigidly laid next to his wife.

"I suppose Rachael talked you into playing strip poker."

"No, she didn't. Why don't you see what's on the television, Rosco? Maybe there's a late movie on."

"Don't try to change the subject, Rita."

She dropped the magazine to the floor and darkened the lamp by her side of the bed.

"I bet it was the waiter's idea. That fucking jerk."

"Actually, it was all my doing. I'm exhausted. And I'd prefer not to discuss it right now. If that's okay with you."

"I don't give a crap. Just hope I never see the guy again. At least not without his clothes on."

"I'm going to sleep. Good night, Rosco."

"Yeah, sweet dreams. And try not to snore so loud."

Rosco surfed the channels on the TV while brooding over the bizarre episode he witnessed earlier. He really wanted to give the waiter a good swift-kick in the ass before he left the room. The guy sure had some big balls playing strip poker with two married women. I wonder what else he was up to. Rosco drank the last ounce of cognac, lowered the volume on the TV, and then tried to relax by focusing his attention on a late-night movie: Casablanca, featuring Humphrey Bogart and Ingrid Bergman. He figured he wouldn't have to think about the creep, if he occupied his mind on something else.

31

Under an obsidian sky shinning like a sparkling dome, Rosco dreamed he was at the wheel of the rented honker, speeding along the New York State Thruway. He stopped for a hitchhiker; a man wearing dress shoes (ultra-wide), black pants, a white shirt, and a loosened bowtie. Rosco rolled down the window.

"Where ya headed pal?"

"Miami Beach," the hitchhiker replied. "Collins Avenue to be exact."

"It's your lucky night. That's where I'm going. Hop in the front—my wife's sleeping in the back."

(Mrs. Applebaum was reclining there, but only in the form of a surreal naked blow-up doll.)

The hitchhiker opened the car door and climbed in. From the overhead light, Rosco got a better look at the man's face.

"Hey, aren't you the waiter that works at the hotel I'm staying at? What's your name again?"

"Aristotle Demetrius Difda, but I've been called Dif, ever since I was eleven."

"It's funny meeting you here. Put your seat belt on. You just getting off work?" Rosco asked.

"Yeah."

Rosco shifted into drive and headed south down the interstate. He traveled a few miles until he got off at the exit for New Paltz. A hip little college town snuggled in the foothills of the Shawangunks, a steep and rocky mountain range in Upstate New York. At a toll booth Rosco handed a man a hundred-dollar bill. The toll-collector checked to see if it was counterfeit or not.

"Here's your change meester," the man said while dropping ninety dollars in quarters into Rosco's hands. Most of the coins spilled onto the pavement and rolled away.

"Are there any gas stations open around here?" Rosco asked the toll collector. "One of my tires is low on air."

"It's two-thirty in the morning, man. Ain't a damn thing open 'round here, 'cept for Joe's 24-hour diner and maybe one of those sleazy looking oriental massage parlors."

The man spit a glob of chewing tobacco and suspiciously glanced at the apparition sitting in the front seat. The curious toll-collector pointed to the naked blow-up doll sprawled in the back seat.

"Who you got back there?"

"My wife. Why?" Rosco asked.

"Excuse the pun, mister, but she looks kind of winded. Maybe she ought a put on some clothes — you could get arrested for that sort of thing around here."

"So, is the food any good at the diner?" Rosco inquired.

"It's okay if you like roadkill."

Once more, the toll collector laughed in a cynical manner.

Rosco rolled up the window and drove onto Route 299, entering the sleepy little village of New Paltz. No other vehicles traveled the wistful gray road except for the honker and a solitary Hell's Angel riding an extremely noisy chopper with his bitching naked girlfriend on the back. They passed Joe's Diner, shuttered shops, restaurants, taverns, red brick houses, Dutch stone architecture, an oriental massage parlor with a blinking open sign, and several clapboard shacks thrown together in the wee daylight hours. The honker coasted down a hilly Main Street.

New Paltz hadn't changed much since Rosco and his wife had attended her class reunion a few years before. The small college town still resembled the bohemian, laid-back, hippie hangout it was in the psychedelic Sixties. The big difference now was how people looked. And sounded.

"New Paltz was my old stomping grounds, Dif."

"What were you doing here?"

"I taught biology in high school for 18 years."

"You cut up a lot of frogs, huh?"

"I had my share. My wife went to college here. She majored in Art and Dance but dropped out after we got married and had our first child."

"You meet her at the university?"

"No, up at Lake Minnewaska. Boy—we had some wild times up there. Life was one big party in those days."

"Where's Lake Minnewaska?"

"A few miles north of here," Rosco replied, signaling to turn right.

"How'd you meet?"

"My wife? I was fishing at the lake one sweltering summer day, when I noticed this gorgeous young woman skinny-dipping in the freezing cold water. She had the prettiest blue-green eyes I'd ever seen."

"Then what happened?"

"She swam to the shore, dried herself off, and then started laughing at me."

"How come?"

"'Because I was fishing. She said I wasn't gonna catch one fish. Not even a minnow. There were no fish in the lake. Has something to do with the acid rain, or the low temperature of the water. Who knows."

"You probably felt like a big jerk after she told you that," Dif said.

"Not at all."

"Why?"

They stopped at a red light and watched some inebriated college students hop across the street.

"Because we fell madly in love that fine summer afternoon. We started dating, got engaged, and then married a few months later."

Rosco looked over his shoulder at the blow-up doll. The traffic light turned.

"I still say Rita's eyes are the same turquoise green as the water in Lake Minnewaska. She always laughs when I tell her that. Ain't that right, honey? She must be sleeping."

Dif reached back and caressed the arm on the blow-up doll.

"Hey, your wife is really hot."

"Keep your hands off her!"

"Sorry. It must be a beautiful lake. Can we go there?" Dif asked.

"It's a little out of the way. And you won't see much. It's too dark out."

"I don't care," the waiter said. I'd really like to see it."

"Okay, but only under one condition," Rosco said, making a U-turn.

"What's that?"

"Promise me you won't play strip poker with my wife ever again."

"I promise."

"Scout's honor?"

"Yeah, sure. I'll even throw in a cross my heart and hope to die."

Since the flying gargoyles were blinded by the bright lights on top of a cell-phone tower, the grotesque creatures had lost their way and descended through a night sky and splattered onto the windshield of the honker. Rosco had to stop on the side of the road and wipe the bloody mess off the glass with a rag. Somehow, one of the winged gargoyles crawled into the back seat and snatched the blow-up doll out of the car. The ugly creature ran down the road and flew up into the air with it. Neither man noticed.

"These are disgusting!" Rosco exclaimed.

"They stink—what are they?"

"I don't know."

"Watch yourself!" Dif warned while a mangled gargoyle hung from the car hood and sunk its nasty little fangs into Rosco's hand. He bled.

"Ouch!" he exclaimed while slapping the creature off the car and kicking it away with his foot.

Rosco got behind the wheel again, put it in gear, and then sped over a bumpy metal bridge that was painted an industrial green. Because the fog was thicker than chutney, he missed the crooked sign pointing to Lake Minnewaska. Instead, he made a sharp right turn onto Springtown Road and almost flipped the car over to avoid hitting a devilish little man in a sleigh pulled by eight reindeer.

Rosco swerved around the sleigh and continued driving along the dark country thoroughfare.

Silver grain silos portentously loomed over pastoral dairy farms. The statuesque luminaries kissed the diamond night sky while golden blocks of hay sat perfectly stacked on frozen red earth. Poisoned by Monsanto, withered cornstalks leaned downcast in bleak windblown fields. Local farmers and their families, livestock, poultry, and beasts of burden all slept peacefully. Outside, reincarnated hobgoblins, renegade Indian spirits and hungry ghosts despairingly roamed the nocturnal landscape along Springtown Road.

Three turkey vultures contemptuously sang a cappella. Kssssshhh-uhhh, kssshhh-uhhh, kssshhh-uhhh. The sullen birds hovered directly above the bedraggled custodians who watched over the farmers' fields. Not a weary soul awake to light their corncob pipes, or help them labor in the fields, gardens, barns, wood-lots, or vineyards. The country bumpkin effigies wore tattered pants, dresses, and three-piece suits that were three sizes too large or too small. Their raggedy ties and scarves wrapped snuggly about their knotted necks. Solid, plaid, paisley, and striped blouses and summer dresses were stuffed with hay scraps, newspaper, and rags. Their stick-thin arms and legs all crafted from contorted wire hangers, umbrellas, tennis rackets, bent golf clubs, pool sticks, and ski poles. The pumpkin headed scarecrows danced to a ragged rhythm and blues while they madly swung around their rake, hoe, spade and broken-shovel dance partners like fools in a Harlem dance marathon. Roundabout they flew in a mud-caked jitterbug, foxtrot and bluegrass nightmare. The scarecrow revelers suddenly stopped dancing when they saw the headlights of a car coming up Springtown Road. They waved their wheat-thin arms and bird-eaten hats to the passing vehicle. Rosco beeped the horn twice as he drove by.

"There's a friendly looking bunch."

"Why are you slowing down?" Dif asked.

"I'm lost."

"I thought you knew the way."

"It's so dark here I can't recognize a damn thing," Rosco stated. "Besides, it's the first time I'm up here like this."

"What's that supposed to mean?" Dif asked.

"Beats me."

"There's an old hippy lady walking her dog up ahead. Why don't we stop and ask her for directions," Dif suggested.

"Good idea."

Rosco stopped and rolled down the window. Before he said a word, the woman's large brown dog looked up at the obsidian sky and immediately started howling at a purple moon.

"Quiet, Wildman," the hippy woman kindly told her dog while stroking his large fuzzy head.

"Sorry to bother you, ma'am, but I believe we're lost."

"Where you headed?"

"We're on our way up to Lake Minnewaska."

The dog sneezed and cocked its head sideways. He perked his folded ears and then jumped up on the car door and ecstatically started licking the skin on Rosco's hand and wrist.

"Get down from there, Wildman!" the woman ordered her German short-haired pointer. "Sorry, mister, he gets excited when he hears the name of the lake. He loves for me to bring him up there so he can run around. Whenever he hears it, he goes wild. That's why I named him Wildman."

"So, where's this Lake Minnewaska?" Dif stupidly questioned.

Once again, the dog insanely barked at the purple moon; he scrambled around to the passenger side, jumped on the car door and then immediately started licking Dif's face 'til it was covered with a layer of warm and sticky dog slobber.

"Yuck! That's disgusting," Dif declared.

"Behave yourself Wildman. You're going the wrong way," the woman said. "The lake is about ten miles in the other direction."

"What town is this?" Rosco inquired.

"Rosendale."

"Rosendale?"

"I take it you fellas aren't from this neck of the woods."

"We're not," Dif answered, still wiping off the dog saliva that dripped from his ears.

Wildman whimpered. He sat his rump down and quietly contemplated the moon. The woman noticed Rosco's injured hand.

"Looks like a gargoyle bit you. Why don't you come inside the house. I'll clean and bandage it for you. You don't want it to get infected."

"It'll be all right."

"Oh, no, I insist," the hippy woman said. "A gargoyle bite can be pretty nasty. And your friend can wash off that dog slobber. Afterwards, I'll make you boys a pot of hot herbal tea to warm your bones."

"Gee, that's awfully neighborly of you," Dif stated.

"Folks are like that in these parts. My name's Althelia, by the way. I'm the High Priestess of the Gunks."

"Gunks?" Rosco asked.

"That's what the locals call these mountains up here. It's short for the Shawangunks," Althelia replied.

"Oh. I'm Rosco. That's Dif. My wife is sleeping in the back seat. At least she was a minute ago."

"Nice meeting you, fellas."

"Likewise."

"Pull in the driveway here," the High Priestess said. "And be careful you don't run over the little toads. They like to come out and play this time of morning. I'll tie up my dog."

Rosco parked the car in the woman's driveway. From the side of Althelia's old white garage, an inquisitive possum observed the two men get out of the car and follow the woman along a flagstone walkway which led to the entrance of the house.

The men looked up at a white door that stood twelve feet high.

"This place is huge. How many rooms does it have?" Rosco asked.

"There's fifteen bedrooms, five bathrooms, a library, a living room, a lounge with a bar, and three kitchens. One for the servants. It used to be an old inn and tavern back in the 1800's," Althelia described. "Welcome to my humble abode."

She showed them inside, and they followed her through a hallway lit by kerosene lamps. The wood floor made an eerie sound as they walked upon it.

"You can use this bathroom here, Dif."

To attend to Rosco's wound, Althelia used a bathroom at the other end of the hall. She disinfected and sufficiently bandaged his thumb and forefinger.

"There. You're as good as new," she said.

Althelia ran the hot water and washed and toweled her hands.

"I appreciate your help. Thank you."

"You're quite welcome. Let's have some tea now, shall we?"

Rosco followed Althelia up a staircase, down a hall, and into the main kitchen of the house. He sat at a table while she poured steaming hot water into a teapot filled with hibiscus and morning glory flowers. She placed it on the table along with three cups, spoons, buckwheat honey and cloth napkins embroidered with tiny quill-wort blossoms. All this time, Rosco admired a large-framed poster of the Beatle's Yellow Submarine album on a wall.

"Great band," she stated.

"Certainly was. How long have you lived here?"

Althelia turned off the burner on the stove.

"Seems like forever. I purchased the property from Timothy Leary. After I came back from the Woodstock 69' music festival. Have some tea."

The hippy woman arranged some brownies and raspberry-walnut scones onto a plate, and she offered Rosco one. Dif stumbled into the kitchen.

"Thought I'd never find you — this place is so big," Dif stated. He sat in a chair opposite Rosco.

"I was wondering where you were," Althelia told him. "You're just in time for tea. Don't be shy, fellas, help yourselves to a brownie or a scone if ya want. I baked them myself."

Althelia poured some of the steaming hot tea into Dif's cup. He grasped the glowing vessel and sipped some of the hot beverage.

"What kind of tea is this your Highness?" he asked.

"Hibiscus and morning glory. I grow the flowers in my garden," Althelia said proudly.

"It's a most stimulating and deliciously uplifting tea, I must say. Pass me a brownie, please," Dif requested.

"I should warn you fellas about a couple of important things."

"What's that?" Rosco asked.

"Lately there's been some really weird things happening in the Gunks at night," she replied. "For one thing, hamadryads have been sighted in the woods around Rosendale. About a quarter mile northwest of here."

"That some kind of wild animal?" Dif inquired before he polished off another brownie.

"No. They're beautiful tree nymphs who inhabit the forest at night. They sound, look, and pretend to be women. But they're not."

"What are they then?"

"Evil spirits who wait for men to wander into the forest and get lost all night. They like to seduce men and trick them into falling in love. Their only desire is to steal a man's heart and possess his soul."

Dif laughed.

The High Priestess added a spoonful of honey to her tea. She stirred the hot liquid while biting into a scone.

Dif inquired with a captivated expression: "What are the chances we'll meet any of these ravishing young tree nymphs?"

"You probably won't," Althelia replied. "They mainly keep to the deeper parts of the forest. But just in case, I'll give each of you a bottle of this magic water. If any of the tree nymphs happen to come near you, just sprinkle some water on them, and they'll be dispelled. Understand?"

"You mean they'll disappear?" Rosco asked.

"Precisely. Did you hear what I just said, Dif?"

"Are these hamadryads as beautiful as you say they are?" Dif asked.

"Even more so, but that's only a false appearance. A mirage so to speak. They're nothing but hungry ghosts."

"If we get thirsty, can we drink the magic water?" Rosco inquired.

"By all means. The water can't harm you. It's a healing elixir for humans."

"If the tree nymphs look so much like women, then how will we know they're not?" Dif inquired.

"By their pointed green ears or big woolen feet. It's difficult to see their ears, though."

"Why?" Dif asked as he greedily eyed the last brownie.

"Cause their thick locks of hair usually conceal their ears. It's better to tell by their feet, because hamadryads never wear socks or shoes," Althelia explained.

Rosco reached for the last brownie, but Dif selfishly snagged the sweet cake before he could.

"Hey! —I was going to eat that," Rosco declared.

"I saw it first."

And Dif gobbled it down in a couple of bites.

"Widow Jane's place is the other thing I wanted to warn you fellas about."

"What's that?" Rosco asked while pouring himself a half cup of tea.

"It used to be an old, abandoned cement mine in Rosendale. A horrid old witch by the name of Widow Jane owns the property now. She converted the mine into a restaurant and bar with live music and topless dancers. Some extremely bad characters frequent the place, and I'd definitely stay away from there. At all costs."

"You said they have topless dancers at this Widow Jane's?" Dif asked with a sparkling glint in his eye.

"Yes, they do. Here, take these roses. One's for you, and one's for Rosco." She handed each man a glowing red rose, alive with a powerful scent. "Don't lose them. They'll protect you from the evil spirits out there. And you'll need these flashlights. It's awfully dark at the lake this hour."

"Wow! Those brownies were delicious, Matilda," Dif exclaimed. "And thanks for your kind hospitality."

"My name is Althelia. And you're quite welcome. I believe it's time for you fellas to be on your way. It looks like your friend has fallen asleep."

Dif shook Rosco's shoulder.

"Wake-up, we have to go."

Althelia showed her guests to the door, and she went outside for some fresh air.

"Good luck finding the lake, fellas. And remember what I told you."

The high priestess waved good-by to the men, brought her dog inside, closed and locked the twelve-foot door, and then she got herself ready for bed.

32

Rosco was still asleep when he drove along Route 213, through Rosendale, NY. He suddenly heard a loud noise come from the car. Pop! thud, thump, thump, thump, flump, flump, flump-flub, flump-flub, flump-flub, wobble, wobble, wobble, wobble-flump.

"What was that?" Dif asked.

"Sounded like I blew a tire."

They pulled off the road. The two men got out and inspected the damage on the front right wheel.

"Looks like a simple fix to me," Rosco stated.

Rosco opened the trunk for a spare tire and a jack, but all he found were empty bottles of cheap Russian vodka and a thread-bare leisure suit.

"Shit!"

"What's the matter?"

"There's no spare tire or jack."

"How we gonna get to the lake now?" Dif grumbled. "There won't be any gas stations open this time of morning."

"You're probably right."

Dif walked to the edge of the forest and leaned against a white birch tree. He lit himself a cigarette while a whippoorwill sang a short distance away.

Rosco picked up a small flint rock and dejectedly tossed it into the woods. He looked above and saw a shooting star speed across the heavens. The wind picked up some.

"— hear that?" Dif asked.

"What?"

"Sounded like a flute."

"It was probably just a bird."

"You need to get your ears checked, Rosco. I distinctly heard someone playing a flute."

"My hearing is fine. Must be from all those pot brownies you ate back at Althelia's house. You're probably stoned out of your mind right now. She put about an ounce into the brownie mix."

"That's crazy. And I suppose the tea was spiked with something too," Dif said.

"— was."

Just then a twig snapped in a nearby briar patch. The men saw a small red fox run past while a pleasantly perfumed breeze disrupted a bed of birch leaves at the foot of the tree they stood under. Dif felt a warm breath softly caress the waxy blue skin on his neck. A feminine, yet husky sounding voice whispered into his ear:

"Well, hello, handsome. I've been waiting for you all night."

Dif turned to Rosco: "What did you say?"

"I didn't say anything."

"You just whispered into my ear."

"I'm telling you, it was only the wind."

Again, a deep womanly voice quietly spoke to Dif:

"I think you're adorable. And that mustache really turns me on."

"Would you please stop whispering those sweet nothings into my ear," Dif said. "I'm gonna look for a gas station past these woods. There's gotta be something open somewhere. You look tired, Rosco. Maybe you should take a nap in the car."

"I think I will, handsome."

Ida, Lola and Pingala were three sisters who regularly frequented the Shawangunks late at night. They would hang in New Paltz or Rosendale, hoping to meet a man. The sisters weren't women, but the nocturnal hamadryads, or tree nymphs, the High Priestess had warned Dif and Rosco about. The three temptresses slept, only after the morning sun rose above the Hudson River.

Ida was the oldest sister, and by far, the tallest at six foot eight inches. She claimed to be the prettiest and the most educated as well, with a bachelor's in forestry and a master's in herbal folklore. Her fair skinned, slender, big-boned Amazonian physique was a stunning sight to behold. She had long voluptuous legs, loving arms and broad feet that were covered by a soft brown fur. Ida's deep blue eyes, Marilyn Monroe smile, and wavy blonde locks could easily spark a man's romantic desires. When she wasn't gallivanting barefoot and semi-naked around the Gunks, Ida played soothing music on her Celtic harp and fantasized about falling in love some lonesome night.

Pingala was the middle sister, and easily the shortest at four-seven. A shrewd, brown-eyed angelic looking hamadryad; she was buxom yet rounded. Ringlets of auburn hair hung to the cleft of her lower back. She possessed an unusually happy disposition, although a mischievous tree-nymph at times, she was blessed with effervescent hips and syrupy-sweet-lips. On wet spring evenings, especially during a lunar eclipse, Pingala would sneak onto the local dairy farms and suck goat's milk straight from the animals' udders, without the farmers or hired help ever knowing. That's probably why she had such a portly figure. In the early days of summer—right before the crickets sang and the flowers closed at night—Pingala savored the wild-flower nectar that bees, butterflies and hummingbirds love. When bored with those activities, the little tree nymph would wait in the darkling chestnut oak forest and play melodies on her pan flute, eager to entice a man some moonstruck evening.

Lola was the youngest sister. She couldn't play a musical instrument but loved to dance, sing and drink Champagne all night. Her short, cropped hair was tinted a platinum blonde, a silk scarf always concealed her pointed green ears. Despite the youngest sister's pretty face and hour-glass figure, her arms, hands, legs and feet were built quite masculine. Lola had the stormiest personality and would frequently throw temper tantrums that disturbed the neighbors on Springtown Road. She also dreamed of catching a fine-looking bachelor to fall in love with. And adamantly believed she was the most attractive sister, often teasing Ida and Pingala about it. Lola sure had them fooled all right; because she — was a he.

33

In the pitch-black chestnut oak forest, Dif pointed his flashlight and saw a woman who appeared to be floating two feet off the ground. She was wearing a-blue sarong which covered her hairy feet and a head scarf that covered her moss green ears. She approached him.

"Well, hello sweetheart," she spoke in a baritone. "I've been waiting for you all night."

"And who might you be?"

"My name is Lola. I spoke to you earlier, but you were too busy talking to your friend."

"He's not my friend. He's just some loser, I picked up hitchhiking. Hi, my name is Dif. It's a pleasure to make your acquaintance, Lola."

"The pleasure is all mine, darling. What are you doing out so late sugarplum?"

"My car had a flat tire, and I was looking for a gas station to get it fixed. Do you know if one might be open this late hour? I was on my way up to Lake Minnewaska."

"Oh, I love it up there! The nature is so breathtaking," Lola stated.

"Is it?"

"Yes."

Lola gave Dif a flirtatious smile while readjusting her headscarf to make sure her earlobes weren't showing.

"There's a 24-hour gas station open at the bar and grill," she stated. "After you get your tire fixed, we could elope at the lake."

"How far is that from here?"

"It's just past the sugar maples," Lola replied. "Smack in the middle of the chestnut oak forest. It's a short walk from here."

"Could you take me there?"

"I'd be delighted to. That's a sweet-smelling rose. Is it for me?"

"You can have it," Dif unthinkingly replied.

Lola quickly snatched the flower from Dif, and she placed it in her sarong. She pressed her body against his and passionately kissed him on the lips.

"Wow! —you sure don't waste any time—do you?" he asked.

"I noticed you were admiring my figure before. Do you think I have a sexy body?"

"Without a doubt. What's that in your hand?" he asked.

She held up a bottle and grinned. "Champagne. Care for a glass?"

"I'd love one."

"C'mon, let's have a drink and get to know each other better," Lola said while she grabbed Dif's hand and hurriedly led him over to a picnic table under a dark pine grove. She popped the cork on the bottle and poured the cool sparkling liquid into two glasses.

"To our everlasting love," she toasted.

"Cheers."

Lola and Dif chit-chatted while they quickly drained the bottle of its contents. The tree nymph snuggled up to Dif and ran her manly fingers through his straight black hair.

"I bet you're a great lover," she said.

"Boy, that went fast," Dif said, eyeing the empty bottle.

"I have more Champagne at my house." Lola held out her strong hands. "May I have this dance?"

"There's no music playing."

Dif smiled. Still transfixed by Lola's mysterious beauty.

"I'll arrange the music."

She clapped her hands twice and two semi-clad women instantly appeared underneath a willow tree close by. They started playing an enchanting melody on the pan flute and Celtic harp. Lola grabbed Dif's hand, and they got up to slow dance. He looked over his shoulder and observed the two women, immediately taking a keen interest in them.

"Is the music romantic enough for you?"

"Yes, but who are they?" he asked while stretching his neck.

"They're my sisters. Ida and Pingala. Pay no attention to them. I'm all yours now."

"They're gorgeous," Dif stated as he looked back again.

"True. But I'm much prettier than they are. Don't you agree?"

Dif thought a few moments, and then Lola stomped on his toes with her big snarly foot.

"Ouch! That hurt. Yes—you're definitely the prettiest sister."

"Now that's what I like to hear," Lola said.

While they continued dancing, the ornery tree nymph grew sexually aroused, and she fondled one of Dif's buttocks. Lola's envious sisters kept serenading them, until Dif became exhausted and thirsty.

"What do you say we go to my house now and consummate our love?" Lola asked.

"I'd like that, but first I need to drink some water."

"Wait here. I'll get your bottle."

Lola walked to the picnic table and unscrewed the cap on Dif's bottle of magic water. She turned it upside down and poured most of the water out, leaving only a few drops. The cunning tree nymph returned with the glass bottle and handed it to Dif. He raised it to his parched lips, yet there was barely enough liquid for a sparrow to drink.

"Did that quench your thirst, my love?"

"Most certainly not." Dif held up the empty bottle and gave it a shake. "I thought there was more in it than that."

"Don't worry, sugarplum. There's a clear stream that runs by my house. The water is pure and refreshing. And it tastes just like wine."

Lola rubbed her body against Dif's, gently stroking his hairy chest. She latched onto his balls with her man hands and squeezed so hard it almost made him cry.

"Hey. That's a little too rough!" he declared. "I was really thirsty. And I don't particularly like the taste of wine. I'm more a beer drinker myself."

"Oh, shut up! —and give me that fucking bottle!" Lola yelled. She snatched the empty glass container and smashed it against some rocks.

Dif was horrified.

"Why'd you do that?"

"Because I felt like it. Now, let's go!"

Rosco awoke from the loud noise. He climbed out of the car and walked into the woods with his flashlight. He heard Dif and the three tree nymphs laughing. Lola pulled on Dif's arm, escorting him deeper and deeper into the dark chestnut oak forest; her two sisters followed close behind, still playing their musical instruments. Soon the man would be gone, and his soul forever lost beyond the nether world.

Rosco shined the flashlight, and he caught a glimpse of Dif and the three tree nymphs wandering off into the bleak woods.

He screamed: "Dif, come back! Come back!"

Dif paid no attention to the desperate calls. Rosco ran until he caught up with them. He doused the three tree nymphs with his magic water; they instantaneously vanished. And the glowing red rose that Lola had worn fell to the earth.

"Hey. Where'd those beautiful women go?" Dif inquired.

"Are you insane? Those weren't women. They were the hamadryads the High Priestess warned us about."

"They were?"

"Come on. Pick up your rose and let's get the hell outa here."

34

Several candles shed light upon three dog skulls atop a stone monument. The bright illumination cast spectral shadows of mythical beasts in the forest. An epitaph engraved on the stone wall read:

Here rests the bones of Cerberus

Faithful guard dog of Hades

"It appears to be some sort of ancient tomb," Rosco stated. "You're Greek, Dif. Do you know anything about this?"

"According to the Greek mythology I've read, Cerberus was a vicious dog-like monster that had three heads, a serpent's tail, a mane of living snakes, and the claws of a lion. The monster supposedly guarded the entrance to the underworld, preventing ghosts of the dead from leaving. In his twelfth labor, Hercules traveled down to Hell and fought the mythical beast. He overpowered the three-headed dog and brought it up to Earth, but somehow it managed to escape down to Hell again. That's all I know."

"That's a very interesting story but we should get going already," Rosco said.

"I see a light up ahead. Maybe it's a gas station," Dif announced.

Only a short distance from the tomb site: the two men came across a wooden post with several directional arrows on it. A light shone down from the post. One arrow pointed 5 miles to New Paltz, 8 miles to Lake Minnewaska, 27 miles to Woodstock, 86 miles to Manhattan, 1,366 miles to Miami Beach and 5,400 miles to the North Pole. A bottom arrow pointed east, 150 feet to Widow Jane's Bar and Grill. The sign next to it advertised a 24-hour service station, gourmet food, live music, and topless dancers.

The two men stared at the signs. And wondered what to do next.

"It's an awfully long way to the lake from here," Rosco said.

"That Widow Jane's place is close by," Dif stated. "They have a gas station. Maybe we could get someone to fix the flat tire."

"The High Priestess warned us about going there, Dif."

"Oh, come on. Are you gonna believe some crazy old lady who says she's the High Priestess of the Gunks? Besides, the place can't be all bad. And I'm hungry and dying of thirst."

Dif was already walking in that direction.

"All right. But only long enough for us to grab a quick bite and get the tire fixed."

At that very moment the two men saw something short, black, and white dart through the trees and disappear.

"What was that?" Dif asked.

"It looked like a black bear cub."

"Bear?"

"Yeah, we're in the forest. There're probably all sorts of wild animals running around here at night."

The two men approached a poorly lit billboard. A horrid odor filled the air. Rosco pointed his flashlight and read:

Property of Widow Jane's

Ghouls, Ghosts, Werewolves & Bogymen Welcome

All others keep out!

They disregarded the lower part of the sign and walked up a dirt road and approached a cave-like entrance to the bar and grill.

"This must be the place," Rosco said.

"Doesn't look that bad to me."

Rosco raised his nose and shivered.

"Something smells foul. There must be a landfill nearby."

Rosco clamped the ends of his nasal cavity with his thumb and forefinger.

"That's probably your upper lip you're smelling."

"Wise guy."

Dif chuckled as they walked toward a line of people outside the entrance to Widow Jane's. Dressed in a clown suit, a man stopped them at the door.

"Hey knuckleheads! The back-a-the-line is that-a-way. Whatsamatta? You guys from the sticks or somethin'?" he asked in a distinctive New Jersey accent. A red rubber ball was attached to the end of his nose. He was juggling three buzzing chainsaws.

"Sorry it's our first time down here," Dif told the clown.

"Fuget about it. Welcome to hell, fellas. Hey . . . are you guys from Jersey? I'm from Jersey. Are you from Jersey?" the jester asked without breaking his concentration on the revolving chain saws.

"No, I'm from Florida," Rosco replied. "You're not Joe Piscopo by any chance?"

"Why? You from Jersey? I'm from Jersey. You gotta problem with that?" the clown asked.

"No, Mr. Piscopo. I've seen all your shows on Saturday Night Live."

"Good. I'm from Jersey…"

Rosco stepped past the psycho clown.

"Let's get on the line, Dif. We don't wanna piss anyone else off here. Besides, I don't like the looks of that guy holding the Samurai sword."

The line was long, and everybody in it wore the most bizarre clothing and masks. Many of the party goers gave Dif and Rosco unfriendly stares.

"Everyone has a costume on here," Dif said. "There must be..." he started to say while a shrill train whistle drowned the last words of his sentence.

"What did you say?"

"Looks like they're having a masquerade party here."

"Apparently."

A blaring train horn startled the two men. A locomotive screeched to a halt behind them. Rosco heard shrieks and banging come from inside the boxcars. The metal doors were opened, and the screaming mixed with barking dogs, gunfire, bullwhips cracking and soldiers shouting orders in an unfamiliar dialect.

"You hear that?" Rosco asked.

"It's just the local train letting off some passengers," said a woman casually standing in front of the two men. She wore a cloud of perfume, a black Victorian gown with dark red ruffles, a tightly laced corset, and a pair of nine-inch heels with rhinestone studded straps. Her knobby fingers, scraggly wrists, neck and earlobes were festooned with diamond earrings, pearl necklace, gold bracelets and rings. A long black veil covered her face. She held a sculptured wooden cane and a glittery silver handbag. When the greatly pretentious woman looked down and saw the costumes Dif and Rosco were wearing, she burst out laughing.

"What are you fellas supposed to be dressed as, Frogs?"

"Yes, ma'am," Dif meekly replied.

"Well, those are pretty original costumes I must say," she said.

"Thanks, yours is too," Dif mentioned.

"Eh, it's only some old rags I got from my dead daughter-in-law's closet. That good for nothing bitch," the over bloated woman flagrantly spat her words into Dif's face.

"I'm sorry to hear that, ma'am," he said while wiping the spittle off with his coat sleeve.

"Well, don't be!" she shouted.

"If you don't mind me asking. What actually happened to your daughter-in-law?" Dif asked.

"I smashed her pretty little head in with an iron skillet. Then I ran her skinny little ass over with my pickup truck."

"Why would you do such a horrible thing?" Rosco asked.

"She made me scrambled eggs for breakfast one morning, and I had explicitly ordered over-easy. Anymore stupid questions scrotum-face?" the cavernous-eyed lady asked while jabbing the fleshy part of Rosco's arm with the end of her cane.

"No, ma'am."

"Good!" the ostentatious woman said while she turned her back on the men and expunged a horribly smelling flatulence.

"I just caught another whiff of that stinking landfill."

When Rosco and Dif reached the front of the line, a woman in a Bugs Bunny outfit greeted them. A long carrot dangled from her mouth. A fat smelly cigar burned in her hand. The door woman said: "Badeh, badeh, badeh, badeh. Welcome to Widow Jane's annual Fall Equinox masquerade party. You guys have tickets?"

"No."

"It's $20 bucks to get in."

"Is there a live band?" Dif inquired.

The woman looked the two men up and down and

sneered. "No, they're dead."

Dif reached into his pants pocket and pulled out a wad of cash.

"It's my treat, Rosco, since you're giving me a ride all the way to Miami Beach."

Dif waved the money in the air, then peeled off a crisp hundred-dollar bill and gave it to the woman at the door.

"Keep the change honey-bunny."

"I wouldn't do that if I were you," Rosco warned.

"What?"

"Flaunt your cash around like that. People might get the wrong impression."

"Why? Everyone around here seems decent and trustworthy," Dif said as they were about to walk away.

"Wait a minute fellas, I need to stamp you," said the rabbit at the door. And with her cadaverous hands, she clenched the two men's wrists and stamped a blue serial number on the inside of their forearms. "Don't forget to take off your shoes before you go inside. Widow Jane hates anyone tracking in dirt. Badeh, badeh, badeh, badeh. That's all folks."

"Silly wabbit," said the guy dressed in the clown suit. "Are you guys from Jersey? I'm from Jersey. Did someone fart?"

In the foyer of the restaurant, Rosco noticed a tall pile heaped with boots, sneakers and shoes.

"Look at all those shoes!" he exclaimed. "Must be a couple thousand at least."

"Yeah, you wouldn't think the place held that many people," Dif said while they unlaced their shoes and placed them on the mountain of leather. They went inside the dark gray cave-like restaurant, and the hostess who greeted them looked as if she stepped right out of the *Night of the Living Dead*.

"You guys want a table or a booth?"

"A table is fine," Rosco replied. "What's that disgusting odor I keep smelling?" he asked the zombie-like hostess.

"They're barbecuing out back. Don't you just love the smell of burning flesh? Your server will be along shortly."

The hostess smiled and some of her teeth fell out.

"I wish we hadn't come here."

"Oh, stop your whining already, Rosco."

Skimming through rays of violet and wading on a drop of dew, a soupçon of wisteria in her bleached-blonde hair, and a regal crown of barb-wired roses fitted 'round her skull: a skin and bone waitress approached Rosco and Dif's table.

"Hi, my name is Sugar. Sugar Magnolia. I'll be your server tonight. Our soups are a lovely cream of caterpillar and a tomato-based goat's head chowder. Both are very delicious. And gluten-free, if I may add. Are you frogs ready to order?" the skeletal-framed waitress inquired in a pleasant-sounding voice.

"I'll have a Guinness, four shots of Tequila, a very rare non-gluten-free cheeseburger, and an order of extra greasy and extra salty French-fries please," Dif said.

"For you sir."

"Black coffee and a bowl of that goat's head chowder," Rosco replied.

"I'll put your order in and get your drinks," Sugar said.

Dif got up from the table, "I'll be back in a few."

"Where ya going?"

"Check out those dancing girls. Hot cha, cha, cha, cha!"

"Don't be long. Our food should be ready soon," Rosco stated.

35

At a table inside Widow Jane's, Rosco felt a pull on the cuff of his pajama bottom.

"Psst," someone loudly whispered.

At first, he thought someone was playing a joke on him. Then it happened again.

"Psst, Rosco!"

Under the table, stood a dark-skinned dwarf dressed like a Catholic priest. He held a small bible in one hand and a scepter in the other.

"You and your friend, Dif are in grave danger here, Mr. Applebaum," the tiny man said.

"Who are you? And how'd you know my name?"

"I'm Father Jay. The High Priestess told me you might come here."

Rosco laughed.

"What's so funny?" the little man asked.

"Are you supposed to be a man of the cloth?" Rosco inquired.

"I am. It's not a costume. I'm the High Priest of the Gunks."

Rosco raised his eyebrows.

"You're the High Priest of the Gunks?"

"That's what I said."

"Oh, my sincerest apologies, Father Jay. Was it you I saw running in the forest earlier?"

"Yes, it was. Althelia warned you about this place. Why didn't you heed her advice?"

"I figured since there's a gas station here I could get my flat-tire repaired. And Dif was hungry and thirsty."

"You're only dreaming this, Rosco. That gas station hasn't been in operation for a hundred years or more," Father Jay stated. "Both of you must leave right away, or you'll suffer grave consequences."

"Yes, of course, Father."

The High Priest vanished into thin air, but he left his miniature bible. Dif caught part of Rosco's conversation as he returned to the table. He sat down and had himself a shot of tequila.

"Delicious! Who were you just talking to?"

"Father Jay."

"Who?"

"The High Priest of the Gunks. He forgot his bible."

"Are you hallucinating again? That's a box of matches."

Dif laughed while he prepared to do another shot of tequila.

"I swear. He was under the table a minute ago."

"Yeah, sure. Keep dreaming, Rosco. Here's our food."

"Careful, fellas. These plates are hot as hell," the waitress warned.

"When you get the chance, sweety, I'll take four more beers and six shots of Tequila," Dif told the waitress.

"Refill your coffee, sir?"

"Yes, please. Maybe you should ease up on the sauce," Rosco lectured Dif.

"Maybe you should mind your own damn business. I can handle my alcohol just fine," Dif haughtily stated.

"It's your liver."

"I was talking to a truck driver up at the bar," Dif said.

"What about?"

"The man said we could catch a ride with him to the lake. He's heading that way after he eats."

"That's great."

"Yeah."

"So how were the topless dancers?" Rosco asked.

"They put on a good show—but you're never gonna believe this."

"What?"

Dif sprinkled salt on his hand and prepared to do another shot. "Your wife works here."

"You're pulling my leg."

Dif drank the liquor and slammed the shot glass on the table. He bit into a lemon wedge.

"I saw her at the bar a few minutes ago."

"She's a bartender?"

"No, a topless dancer."

"What?!"

"Go see for yourself," Dif said.

"I'll be right back."

"Hey, don't forget your stupid rose," Dif said, handing it to Rosco.

36

Dressed in madcap costumes, a rock and roll band increased the volume on their amps and tuned their electric guitars, piano, sax and bass. A drummer tested his snare drum, tom-tom and high-hat cymbal while the ghosts of Widow Jane's left their comfortable tombs and gathered above the stage the live band was about to perform on.

At the smokey bar, four imposing characters drank Jack Daniels and watched two topless dancers shake their stuff. The four men wore identical black robes; matching hoods covered their hairless skulls; their vacant eyes and high prominent foreheads were barely visible. Each man possessed a lethal weapon: one, a gleaming steel broadsword, another, a decoratively carved crossbow, the third, a razor-sharp scythe; and the fourth man held a barbaric weapon consisting of an iron chain and spiked metal balls on the ends of the chain. The foursome exuded an extremely sour body odor while their massive white hands had sharp and blackened fingernails. The man with the crossbow mumbled something and pointed his ugly finger at Rosco; he was busy drinking expensive cognac at the far end of the bar, unaware of the men watching him.

Dressed in a gorilla suit, a bartender casually licked a chocolate, strawberry and vanilla ice-cream cone. Rosco waved him over.

"Yeah, what can I do for you, pal?" the ape-like barman asked.

"I was told that my wife dances here. Have you seen her by any chance?"

The bartender gave Rosco a dirty look and smashed the ice cream cone onto his forehead. He laughed as some of the melted ice cream dripped along Rosco's face.

"This place is open 24-seven, pal. Plenty of women dance here. What's your old lady look like?" he asked while peeling a banana.

"She's got blue-green eyes, a pretty face, long brown hair, medium height, and a real nice figure."

"She have a big green wart on her left butt cheek?" the bartender asked.

"Yeah, that's her."

"I saw her dancing earlier. She left with some truck driver about five minutes ago."

"Serious?" Rosco asked.

"Serious as a heart attack. I should know, I had three. The third one killed me. You want another cognac, toady boy? You can't sit here and watch the titty show unless ya drink."

"Yeah, sure. Put it on my tab."

Rosco then noticed the four mean looking men at the opposite end of the bar. They glared at him.

"Better make it a double this time."

On top of the bar a sprightly blonde wench danced directly in front of Rosco. The scantily dressed dancer smiled and eyed his magic rose. She squatted and wiggled her fleshy behind inches from his flat-nosed face. Rosco downed a cognac and stuck a couple of dollars into her skimpy G-string. The dancer flirted with him, stole his rose, and then blew him a kiss before she departed.

Meanwhile, back at the table, Dif finished his food and washed it down with another beer and tequila. Tremendously bored, he picked up his rose and recited that old rhyme, "She loves me, she loves me not. She loves me, she loves me not." He tore off another rose petal and repeated the verse until there were no petals left on the stem. "She loves me not." He pushed the rose petals and the stem to the floor, and in a glowing crimson pile, the red petals turned black then shriveled.

Suddenly, Dif felt a sharp pain in the top part of his foot.

"Ouch!" he loudly yelled.

Dif looked under the table and saw a gremlin-like fellow dressed in a Santa Claus outfit, holding a miniature staff in one hand and a white pillowcase slung over his shoulder. It was filled with colorfully wrapped gifts tied with ribbons and bows.

"Did you just poke me with that thing?" Dif asked the white bearded gremlin.

"Yes. I've been trying to get your attention for the last ten minutes," the gremlin said. "Hello Aristotle Demetrius Difda. Are you enjoying the party?"

"I am. And who are you supposed to be?"

"I'm a friend of the devil but tonight I'm Santa Claus."

Dif chuckled a moment.

"What are you getting me for Christmas, Santa?"

"That all depends."

"On what?"

"Whether you're naughty or nice."

"Ho, ho, ho," Dif sang off key.

The gremlin scowled.

"Don't say I didn't warn you," the devious little Santa said before he disappeared.

While Dif had been distracted by the mean little hobgoblin, somebody had cleverly lifted the thick roll of cash from his pants pocket. He went back to drinking his beer and shots.

The waitress came to the table. "Can I get you fellas any dessert? Perhaps some nice chocolate covered tarantulas? I highly recommend the banana maggot pie, but the red-velvet swamp cake is to die for," said the skeletal waitress with the roses 'round her skull.

"We'll just take the check, Honey," Dif replied.

"My name is Sugar."

"Yeah, whatever," he rudely spoke.

Dif reached into his pockets but found no dough aside for what was in his wallet: a ten-dollar bill, some quarters and a credit card. He searched the cold stone floor under the table, only seeing the charred rose petals, and an empty white pillowcase. Sugar returned and slapped the check down.

"My shift is over soon, and I gotta cash out. I'd appreciate it if we could settle-up now," she said.

Dif looked over the bill and noticed the exorbitant total: "$598. 99!"

"What's the matter, sir?" Sugar asked.

"I think I've been robbed. And it looks like you've made a mistake on the bill. What's this 'all you can eat' buffet charge? We didn't eat off the buffet," Dif argued.

"Your friend did," she said. "And he ran a tab at the bar and finished three bottles of expensive cognac. You drank twenty-six shots of Tequila, twelve beers, and your food."

"And you include a 66 percent gratuity?"

"That's right. Plus, the State, Federal, and Ulster County culinary tax."

"Culinary tax? This place is just a lousy greasy spoon!" Dif shouted.

Sugar leaned over and stared Dif in the face. Her eye sockets were sullen and empty looking.

"Sorry you feel that way, sir, but please . . . keep your voice down. Other people are still dining."

Dif gave the waitress his credit card.

"I'll go run your card and be right back."

He twiddled his thumbs in the meantime. And guzzled more beer.

When the waitress returned this time, she stuck a steak knife in the table and almost stabbed Dif's hand in the process.

"Are you some kind of fucking wise guy, frogman?" Sugar asked.

"What's the matter?" he asked.

The waitress held up Dif's credit card and stuck it in his face.

"Your shitty card expired two years ago," Sugar angrily replied. "And the name on it says Santa Claus."

"Don't worry, my friend will pay the bill. He has plenty of cash on him."

"Where is he?" the waitress inquired.

"Up at the bar, watching the dancers."

Sugar crossed her arm bones.

"Well get his dumpy ass over here. And make it quick," she said, tapping her skeletal foot.

Dif searched the whole joint, including outside, but he couldn't find Rosco anywhere. He went back to the table, lit a cigarette and started blowing pink smoke rings in the air. Sugar Magnolia returned with Widow Jane this time. A tall, mean, fat-boned woman with a scarred face and dressed in a nun's habit.

"Is he the guy who called my place a greasy spoon?" Widow Jane asked the waitress.

"Yes, boss. That's him. I don't know where his friend ran off to."

The restaurant owner smacked the side of Dif's head so hard it knocked the cigarette out of his mouth and the toupee off his head and onto the floor.

"What was that for?" Dif exclaimed, holding his swollen face with one hand.

"There's no smoking in the dining room, sir. And I don't appreciate your offensive remarks about my business either," Widow Jane replied.

"Yeah, well," he said, looking away from her.

"Well, what?"

Widow Jane noticed the spent pile of cigarette butts, an empty pillowcase, and the black rose petals on the floor.

"Did you make this mess, sir?" she asked.

"No, ma'am."

"Well, somebody must have."

Widow Jane bent down and picked up Dif's toupee, and she slapped it onto his head backwards. She and the waitress looked at Dif, and they both had a good belly laugh.

Sugar asked in a sinister tone, "Did you find your buddy? The guy with all the money."

"No, I didn't."

"So, how are ya gonna pay the bill?"

"I have absolutely no idea."

"Well, I do," Widow Jane broke in. "Since that slimy friend of yours has dined 'n' dashed. You are going to scrub some pots and pans, wash a few dishes, mop the floors, and clean the toilets 'til they shine. How does that grab you smart ass?"

"Oh, I can't wash any dishes, or go near any harsh cleaning detergents like bleach or ammonia," Dif replied.

"And why not?" Widow Jane asked, crossing her bulky white arms against her nun's habit. She sulked.

"Allergies," Dif answered. "My skin breaks out. Even if I wear gloves."

"I'm terribly sorry to hear that, sir. You'll just have to pay some other way," the restaurant owner casually stated.

"And what's that supposed to mean?" Dif inquired.

"Give me a minute. I'll show you. Sugar, would you go tell Bruno, I would like to see him please."

37

On his way back to the table Rosco stopped dead
in his tracks. The rockabilly band had taken a break
while the bar and dining room grew utterly silent. The
light man aimed a spotlight onto Dif; he put down his
beer and shielded his eyes from the glaring round
light. A hooded security guard approached him and
put a boney white hand on his shoulder. He
whispered something.

"Dig the Gothic costume, man," Dif told the
hooded man.

The man in the black costume moved a couple
feet away from the table and removed his hood,
revealing a hairless skull and skin-less face,
uninhabited eye sockets, no nose, ears, or lips. A
listless void.

With the spotlight still shining on Dif, a drumroll
sounded while Bruno, the security guard, gripped the
handle on his tempered-steel broadsword. He raised
the sharp blade and rapidly spun around a half-circle,
severing Dif's head clean-off, right above his Adam's
apple. His headless body slumped in the chair and
blood splattered everywhere while patrons kept on

eating at the surrounding tables. The light-man darkened the spotlight and shined one on the stage. The rock and roll band belted out a tune as Dif's head dropped to the floor, rolled through the dining room, past the smokey bar, and then onto the dance floor.

A couple stopped dancing, and they glanced down at the severed skull.

"Look dear, someone is playing a practical joke," the dancer stated.

The other dance partner observed the head with its eyeballs turned up at him.

"It's probably just one of those crazy Deadheads again," he said.

Widow Jane swiped her hands together and walked up to the security guard and patted him on the shoulder.

"Job well done, Bruno."

He mumbled a thank you while he wiped the blood off his sword. He asked her if she needed him for anything else.

"Yes, Bruno, I do. Now, you and the rest of your gang can go find that other toad-faced scumbag. And bring him back alive if you can. And Sugar?"

"Yes, boss."

"Have the dishwasher clean this mess. I have to seat a party of eight."

38

Rosco bolted from Widow Jane's dining room and pushed open a swinging door to hell's kitchen. He opened a walk-in freezer stocked with a plentiful supply of chocolate ice cream on one half. Body parts on the other. He quickly left and escaped through a back door. Outside, he hid himself behind a dumpster crawling with all sorts of undesirable things. Two brick smokestacks nearby billowed a methylene gas that strangled the air of oxygen, leaving a horrendous smell of death in his nose. Rosco retched from it. Once again, he heard the shrill whistle and a blaring horn of a locomotive. A train pulled up with a long string of boxcars in tow. Uniformed ghouls ripped open the doors, and the sardine-packed occupants were unloaded.

The frightened mortals on the train platform formed two lines and were ordered to start moving. Rosco spied the haggard parade of young and old men, all ages of women, adolescent boys and girls, small children, and pregnant mothers holding crying toddlers wrapped in soiled blankets. The wayfarers looked like they'd come from different countries; many foreign languages were spoken. They marched to the woods where they were forced to undress before entering a cold cement building.

Still hidden behind the dumpster, Rosco warily watched two spiritless men dressed in ragtag clothes. They donned filthy work gloves and opened an iron door to a sizzling hot oven. The hatchet-faced men lifted the corpse of a naked girl off the back of a wagon; they shoved her inside and slammed the oven door shut. The scrawny men removed their caps and gloves and then wiped the black filth and sweat from their brows with grungy rags. A horridly stinking odor permeated the air.

"I'm starving," one of hatchet-faced men said.

His companion announced: "I vill get us some food now."

"Potato skins and roadkill?"

"Vhat else is there to eat, comrade?"

"If you can get me an extra piece of meat, I would appreciate it."

"I vill try comrade."

"Good. After we eat, we can finish burning the bodies."

"Da."

While the spiritless man went inside the kitchen, his helper plopped onto a dilapidated couch alongside a wagonload of fresh corpses. He drank a tepid liquid purported to be coffee, and he bent his lice-infested body between his knees and sobbed. Rosco listened to the man's shameful crying, as a silky blue smoke poured from the chimneys and drifted far above his head, up into the diamond night sky.

...

From the edge of the chestnut-oak forest, Father Jay picked up a pebble and threw it at the dumpster. It caught Rosco's attention, and he saw the High Priest jumping up and down and waving his stubby arms in the air.

"Father Jay?"

The dwarfed man whispered as loud as he could.

"Yes, come quickly."

Rosco snuck past the man who was sleeping on the couch and safely reached the woods just when a black robed man walked outside to smoke a cigarette. A twig abruptly snapped under the high priest's shoe, and the robed man suspiciously looked in the direction of the woods. Rosco and Father Jay held their breaths and stood motionless.

The other spiritless man kicked open the back door of the kitchen, and he carried out two plates heaped with hot grub. The robed man stuck out his high boot and tripped him as he passed. He fell onto his face and the plates of food went flying. The robed goon laughed and tossed his burning cigarette in the air. He returned to the kitchen, while the hatchetfaced man got on his hands and knees and salvaged as much food off the ground as he could. His helper remained asleep on the filthy couch.

Rosco and Father Jay breathed again.

"Father, I saw Dif get his head cut off in the dining room. It was horrible."

The man who was collecting food off the ground picked up his ears and looked suspiciously toward the woods.

"Speak softly, my son," the high priest said. "I saw it too. If you had stayed much longer, your head would be rolling on the dance floor also. We must leave this place now."

Rosco looked down at his feet. "My shoes are back there."

"Too dangerous. I brought you a pair of running shoes. Quick—put them on."

After Rosco tied the laces, he and Father Jay sped along a trail that led through the woods, not stopping until they reached the crypt of Cerberus. Only a few burning candles remained. Father Jay unfolded a map and marked out a route with a red pencil. He traced it with his tiny index finger.

"Look, Rosco. This is where we are right now. Rosendale. New Paltz is over here. This is the apple orchard. Lake Minnewaska. And Gertrude's Nose is about ten miles east of the lake. I'll circle the landmarks for you. You don't have much time. Dawn will be arriving soon, and you'll have to get to the lake as fast as you can. If Widow Jane's men catch up to you they'll kill you for sure."

"What's Gertrude's Nose, Father?"

"It's a rocky precipice on top of the Gunks."

"Why do I need to go there?" Rosco asked.

"I don't have time to explain."

"But the car has a flat tire."

"You won't be driving a car. You'll travel overland on horseback."

"A horse?"

"Of course."

"But I've never ridden a horse in my life."

Father Jay shrugged his small shoulders and folded the map. He put his hands together and prayed.

"It's a piece of cake. First you must get to the apple orchard. That's where I keep the horse."

"You're not coming with me, Father Jay?"

"No. You'll meet me in the orchard by the tree with the golden apples. You can't miss it. It's the largest and most magnificent tree in the orchard. And the only one with golden apples on it. Take the map. Hurry. And may God be with you always."

39

A large colony of bats congregated over a church steeple in Rosendale before fluttering above Widow Jane's property. The multitude of black winged creatures entered a barn through a broken side window, flew up to the rafters, and then hung themselves upside down. The horses in the back stable nervously scuffled their hooves while a dozen foul-mouthed, unwashed, and exceedingly bad-tempered souls fed and groomed the animals.

A one-legged spineless man on crutches hobbled toward the musty barn. He opened a rickety door, and the family of bats watched him enter. He reluctantly approached the stables where the horses were boarded.

"That Widow Jane bitch said to tell you guys to shake a leg," the skinny messenger announced to the twelve vermin who called themselves men.

One of them threw a horseshoe at him and narrowly missed his head. Another ghoul flung his hunting knife which shaved the skin off the messenger's exposed earlobe. The blade twanged as it stuck into a wooden post behind him.

"Listen, you little half-ass prick. Go tell that Widow Jane she can shake this leg," one of the ghoulish horsemen said while urinating onto a pile of hay before placing his crinkly yellow penis back inside his manure-stained pants.

Another demon slid the edge of his scythe against a sharpening stone. He looked up and said to the messenger: "Yeah, go tell that ugly witch we'll be on our way when we're good and ready."

The others laughed.

"I'm just following orders," the one-legged messenger stuttered while holding a hand over his bleeding ear lobe.

A scowling equestrian raised his sharpened sword.

"Get lost you dirt-bag, 'fore I amputate that other stump you call a leg."

At exactly five hours after midnight: Widow Jane's phantom horsemen mounted their powerful steeds and departed the ramshackle barn in Rosendale. Blanketed by a thick dewy air, six equestrians held burning torches and led the way along a trail through the densely wooded Shawangunks. The other six followed, armed with swords, ball and chain, crossbow, and scythe.

Deep within the forest, Rosco stopped running to remove the prickly burrs that had stuck to the bottom of his night clothes. While plodding through the brush, he tripped over a blue-stone slab and stumbled upon an old Jewish cemetery. The grave sites were sadly overgrown with weeds, nightshade, monkshood and lobelia. The names and dates of the deceased were barely recognizable, except for one monument with the moniker 'Rosco Applebaum' clearly engraved on a black marble stone. *Why is my name on a gravestone?* he asked himself. Fresh brown dirt had been piled to one side of the crypt. Rosco teetered along the edge of the open grave and almost fell in. When he reached the cemetery limits, a ten-foot chain-link fence prevented him from leaving the graveyard. He put his flashlight on a gravestone and started climbing the fence. At the top, he felt someone's large hand clamp around his ankle and try to pull him down. Sharp nails dug into his calf muscle; he screamed as he felt his skin tear open. He freed himself and climbed over the fence. On the ground, Rosco rolled up a pant-leg and examined the lacerated muscle. He poured some magic water onto it, and the open wound instantly healed. The ghoul picked up the flashlight and angrily shook the fence, while Rosco got up off the ground and left.

Planets Mercury, Venus, Saturn, and Mars, along with some early morning stars barely illuminated the cobblestone road Rosco tread upon. He stopped under a streetlight to look at the map. Not far from there, a bright orange trail marker indicated the direction to Old Orchard Trail. Rosco followed it and hiked up a steep and rocky incline. At the top he heard banshee screams and horse hooves pounding in the distance.

The twelve phantom horsemen rode fast out of the chestnut oak forest. They charged through the catacombs and cleared the ten-foot fence with one powerful leap. The horses' hard shoes clattered upon the cobblestone road; they madly galloped for Old Orchard Trail.

A gaseous shard of sunlight burned through the dense haze while Rosco observed a sprawling apple orchard from a summit. None of the trees he saw had golden apples on them, only some frost-covered Cortland, water-logged McIntosh, or worm-eaten Granny Smith. It was late fall, and most of the trees stood barren with heaps of fermented fruit on the ground. When the morning light grew brighter, Rosco noticed the unmistakable brilliance of one thick-trunk tall-branched tree. A mere bushel of apples hung on the very top branches. The sun's rays alighted upon the golden fruit.

In his black and white priest's garb, Father Jay stood beside the tree of golden apples. Big as day, and taller than the high priest, two large greenback turtles: brothers, William and Jerry Blumenthal, stood upright on their hind legs next to the short priest. Older brother Jerry sang and finger-picked a banjo while Billy danced and shook a tambourine.

"Rosco! Rosco!" Father Jay shouted while jumping up and down and waving his stubby arms in the air.

Rosco heard the melodic song, and he wiped the grit from his eyes. He slowly descended the hill into the orchard.

Father Jay looked at his crossword puzzle and labored over an eleven-letter-word.

"Will you please stop dancing, Billy. I need to concentrate on my puzzle," the priest reprimanded the turtle.

"I would, Father but Jerry won't stop playing his banjo."

"Jerry?"

"Yes, Father?"

"Why don't you take a break," he said to the musically inclined turtle.

"Sorry, Father. We'll practice our routine when we get to Terrapin Station."

"That's the word. Inspiration!" the little man declared as he took out his red pencil and wrote the eleven-letter word into his crossword puzzle.

The turtles leaned their instruments against the apple tree, and they retreated to their shells.

Rosco ran toward the tree of golden apples. He was breathing hard and soaked with perspiration.

"Morning Rosco, I was just thinking about you."

"Good morning, Father. I hope I'm not too late," he emphatically said.

"Not at all. But forgive me for the pun. You're not out of the woods yet."

Rosco wiped the sweat from his forehead while glancing at one of the turtles who was laughing inside its shell.

"I thought you said I was riding a horse to the lake."

"You are, Rosco. Don't worry. Those are my friends, Bill and Jerry Blumenthal. Bill happens to be an excellent dancer. And Jerry picks the meanest banjo this side of the Mississippi, but they would take forever to get where you're going. You'll be riding Peggy 'O.'"

"Is she the horse?"

"Of course."

Behind the tree of golden apples, a praying mantis kneeled, put its tiny green hands together, and then faced a saffron yellow sunrise. Nearby, a persistent group of horse flies and midges hovered about a large white mare who was lazily eating her breakfast of oats, hay, and red clover. Except for its orange tail and mane, the horse displayed a lustrous white coat. She was larger and stronger than a Clydesdale. Much quicker than any Thoroughbred, Appaloosa, Arabian, or Quarter Horse on earth.

"She's a tad shy in front of strangers. Come ere, Peg, I want you to meet someone," Father Jay said.

The large mare bashfully poked her head around the tree. She snorted and lazily clomped over.

"This is Peggy O,' Rosco. You'll be riding her to the lake."

"Holy Mackerel!" Rosco declared. She's huge."

"She's a beauty all right. And faster than the four winds."

"Hello Peggy O'," Rosco greeted.

As if she wanted to tell Rosco something, the horse neighed and scraped her left front hoof along the frozen ground.

"That means she wants you to feed her an apple."

Rosco picked up a large McIntosh off the ground. It was soft and noticeably bruised on one side.

"Not one of those," Father Jay said. "She only likes the golden apples." He pointed up at the tree.

"I won't be able to reach them."

"With a ladder you could," the high priest said. "There's one on the other side of the tree."

Rosco climbed the long ladder to the top, stretched his arm out, and picked one of the golden apples. He slowly descended the ladder, polished the glittering fruit in his nightshirt and fed it to the horse. She sniffed and rubbed her nose against Rosco's shoulder. He stroked her smooth white coat.

"See, she's friends with you already," Father Jay said. He knelt and placed his ear against the frozen earth for a few moments. "I can hear them coming. They'll be here soon. C'mon, I'll help you into the saddle. Step onto the turtle's back and I'll give you a boost up."

With an earnest effort, Rosco straddled the tall horse.

"Gosh! She's even bigger up here," he said with some trepidation in his voice.

"Don't be afraid. She's actually quite gentle."

"How do I do this?" Rosco asked while looking down at the priest.

"Place your feet in the stirrups and hold onto the reins. Pull on them when you want her to slow down. Pull on them twice and say whoa to make her stop. Say faster girl or giddy-up when you want her to gallop. And if you really want her to fly, crack the whip on her flank, but not too hard."

"How do I make her turn?"

"Just pull the reins to the left or right. Got it?"

"That sounds pretty straightforward to me."

"Good."

Father Jay nervously pointed his finger towards the crest of Old Orchard Trail.

"Look! —they're here," Father Jay announced.

"Holy Moses —go horse," Rosco ordered.

"Giddy-up, Peggy O," the high priest shouted.

She didn't budge an inch, only interested in a bothersome apple seed which had lodged between her teeth. Father Jay jumped in the air and struck the horse's hindquarter with a skinny apple branch. Peggy 'O suddenly rose up on her hind legs and almost threw Rosco out of the saddle. She came down and took off like a bat-out-a-hell.

"Hold on tight," Father Jay yelled, as he and the musical terrapins quickly evaporated into the sprawling apple orchard.

40

On a cold mountaintop above the Gunks, a ghostly wind cried Mary while a rising black sun pierced the hollow skull of a phantom horseman. His disgruntled bones prattled beneath his moth-eaten trench coat while he aimed his crossbow and shot a burning arrow that struck the tree of golden apples and exploded into a radiant orange fireball. The macabre archer laughed as he slowly guided his mount down the rock-strewn hillside.

A second ghost-rider reached the summit, and he gleefully watched the apple tree burn. The demon-possessed man defiantly raised his sword to the sky as he descended the slope, and one by one, the other ten horsemen scaled Old Orchard Trail, carefully guiding their mounts down the steep embankment. The twelve black war horses trampled fruit and scattered clumps of frozen earth in the air. The horsemen thundered past the tree that burned yet wasn't consumed.

Rosco and Peggy O' had blown out of the apple orchard and sped up Clove Road; the slate-rock plummeting around them. The horse slowly cantered about a twisting S-curve then regained momentum. They flew by Split Rock and swiftly climbed the mountain toward their destination.

Lethal projectiles spun past the horse and rider while burning arrows singed the mare's coat and Rosco's hair and nightclothes. The inflamed arrows ricochet off boulders and set the Shawangunks ablaze. They reached the top of the mountain, and the surreal blue waters of Lake Minnewaska appeared.

With the phantom horsemen only a few lengths behind, Peggy O' quickly circled the shimmering lake and swiftly approached the trail head for Gertrude's Nose. Rosco saw the posted sign for the trail, but the horse kept straight. He pulled on the reins to go left, and she abruptly swung around to correct her mistake. When that happened, a horseman lashed out with his curved-bladed scythe. Rosco ducked in time, and the sharp blade got stuck in the bark of a maple tree. The mad horseman fell off his mount, into some hedges with razor sharp thorns.

Another phantom horseman furiously pursued Rosco. The rider sliced the air with his sword, just missing Peggy's broad hindquarter. The phantom horseman lost control of his horse, and both tumbled off the slate cliffs and plummeted 1,800 feet to the ground below.

Peggy O' galloped full-speed for Gertrude's Nose; the sheer drop only two lengths ahead of them.

A phantom horseman let go of a spiked iron ball and chain, whirling it straight for the back of Rosco's neck. Before the deadly projectile could reach its target, Rosco slapped the whip on Peggy O's flank, and she jumped off the rocky palisade. The great white mare ascended into the purple haze.

Rosco woke-up.

41

At half-past six in the morning Ron put winter clothes over his thermal underwear and tucked his snowshoes under an arm. Rachael slept soundly, while her husband quietly left the room. Ron caught sight of a blue sock with white polka-dots on the floor by the elevator door. Ron pressed the call button and the door slid open; Mr. Fowler, the bellhop, unexpectedly appeared. He was examining his clean-shaven face from the mirror inside the elevator. Both men awkwardly smiled while Ron stepped inside. The bellhop panicked after he realized his face was exposed to the guest. He quickly put on his ten-gallon cowboy hat to hide his warty countenance, shriveled blue ears, and weepy green nose. His bloated throat sack was hidden behind a high, turtleneck collar.

"Good morning, Mr. Fowler. There's really no need to hide. We all seem to have our unique imperfections."

"Morning, Mr. Levine," the man croaked from underneath the cowboy hat. "See you're going for a walk in the snow."

"I need a little exercise. Eating all that rich food in the Escoffier Room. I must've gained a few pounds.

"You're dressed appropriately for it, it's twenty degrees out," the bellhop said.

"I got my thermal underwear on. Listen, Mr. Fowler, I know it's none of my business, but I don't think your face looks that bad. At least not in my opinion. What I mean is, it's not much worse than anyone else's face I've seen lately. In fact, I think I look uglier than you do."

"No!" The bellhop lifted his head. "Honest?"

"Yeah—"

"Your face doesn't look too bad either, Mr. Levine."

"Thanks. I thought about getting me one of those cowboy hats. They're rather stylish. They come in white?"

"I believe so," the bell hop replied while touching the wide felt brim on his hat. "L.L. Bean sells 'em for sixty dollars. Plus, tax and shipping."

"That's where I got my snowshoes from. I'd have to get me a horse and a pair of pistols if I wore a hat like that. *Who was that masked man?* Remember him? The Lone Ranger?"

Mr. Fowler removed his hat and laughed. Something he hadn't done for quite some time.

"I do, indeed remember. Loved the show. My favorite was his side-kick, Tonto, the Indian."

"Yeah. That was a trip."

The elevator reached the lobby and the door rolled open. Ron lingered a few moments inside, looking at himself in the mirror.

"I could use a shave myself. You have a wonderful day, Mr. Fowler. And don't ever be ashamed of what you look like."

"Thanks, Mr. Levine. I appreciate that. Enjoy your walk."

Ron got himself a coffee from the lobby and went outside; he immediately felt the frosty air against his face. He zipped his down jacket, pulled a hat over his ears, and walked around to the back of the hotel, where he attached the snowshoes. Ron scissor-legged it across a quiet field. The stars still twinkled while he ventured toward a broken wooden fence; a fringe of tall spruce grew nearby; a fresh snowfall had weighed-down its branches. He smelled the evergreen scent while meditating on the early morning solitude.

Ron waffled out into the clearing again. The snow was five feet deep where he stood. The sky had lightened to a dark blue while most of the stars had faded into yesterday. Two of the luminaries shone in the east; one a big bright star, the other, a planet maybe. He approached the brick hotel again while a nebulous sun unfurled its cool orange light above the frozen Hudson River. He removed and cleaned the snow shoes, then stowed them in the truck of the rental car.

Inside the hotel's warm dining room, Ron greeted the Applebaums at a table.

"Morning."

"Well, if it isn't Nanook of the North. Good morning, Ron," Rita said. "Take off your coat and stay awhile."

Ron smiled and hung his down jacket over the back of a chair. He sat next to his friends and reached for a container of coffee.

"You out snowshoeing?" Rosco asked.

"Yeah. Walked in a big field in the back of the hotel. Snow is pretty deep out there."

"Sounds like fun," Rosco said.

"— was. Anyone see Rachael?"

"She's up at the buffet table," Rosco replied.

"I heard you girls had a pretty wild night," Ron mentioned.

"I'm paying for it this morning," Rita said while rubbing her temples. "I have a hangover the size of Texas. What time do you think the drugstores open around here?"

"Alice should know. Here she comes now," Ron replied.

"Good morning, everyone," Ms. Cooper greeted.

"Morning."

"Hope you were all warm enough last night."

"We were. Morning, Ms. Cooper," Rachael greeted as she put down her plate and sat beside her husband.

"Hi, sweetheart. Why don't you grab yourself some breakfast?"

"Soon as I have a coffee."

"How was your walk?"

"Fun. It's nippy out, though."

"I bet."

"Does your gift shop sell aspirin, Ms. Cooper? I have a terrible migraine," Rita stated.

"It doesn't open till 9:30. I should have a bottle at the front desk if you need some right away."

"That'd be great. Where's Mr. Difda this morning?" Rita asked from the side of her mouth.

"He called in sick. Mentioned something about a bad sore throat," the hotel manager replied.

"Oh, that's a shame," Rita said, biting into her buttered English muffin.

"Are you checking out today, Mr. Levine?" Ms. Cooper asked.

"Unfortunately, we are, Alice."

"What strange and wonderful adventures are you off to next?" she asked.

"After breakfast, the girls wanna do some shopping in town. We'll spend a couple days in Woodstock before flying home."

"You be sure to stay with us the next time you're in Saratoga, Mr. Levine."

"Will do, Alice."

42

While Ron drove the Delta 88 honker along the Adirondack Northway, he noticed a carbon black smoke above the horizon. Farther down, an old red Buick had been parked on the side of the road. Its engine overcooked and steamed like a pressure cooker ready to blow its lid. The Buick looked like one of those old gangster cars driven in a James Cagney, or Edward G. Robinson movie. Its whitewall tires and wide chrome grill and bumpers, a stark contrast to the more modern vehicles on the interstate. The debilitated vehicle clicked, clacked, and sputtered while a wiry man stood next to it. He was dressed in patched jeans, cowboy boots, a brown wool poncho and a multi-colored skullcap. He flung his arms up in the air and cursed something in Spanish. Ron slowed down and put on his hazard lights, approaching the old Buick.

"Why don't you pull over and see if he needs any help," Rachael said. "He looks awfully familiar to me."

"— know."

Ron drove up behind the car and stopped. He zipped up his jacket, grabbed his cell phone, and then went over to greet the man.

"How's it going?" Ron asked.

"I've had better days. Appreciate you stopping though."

"What's wrong with your car?" Ron asked while he pondered the man's face for a moment or two.

"I'm not exactly sure, but I might need a fire extinguisher soon."

"Why don't you call 911?" Ron suggested. And suddenly, the man's colorful cap jogged his memory.

"I think it'll be all right. You know much about fixing antique car engines amigo?"

"No, but I believe we've met before," Ron replied. "Are you Carlos Calaveras? The shaman from Peru."

"I am. How do you know me?"

"Does Iquitos ring a bell? I'm Ron Levine."

The stranger stepped back in surprise.

"The writer from Florida?"

"That's me. What are you doing here, Carlos?"

"My car broke down."

"I see."

"I can't believe it's you." Carlos grinned. "How'd you recognize me?"

"By your colorful skull-cap. I remember you always wore it when we were in Iquitos."

"That's right," Carlos said, placing a hand on the top of his head.

"You still live in Peru?"

"We left about a year ago," Carlos replied. "Right after the pandemic got too crazy in Iquitos. My wife and I live in New York now."

"Where?"

"Woodstock."

"That's a coincidence. We're just on our way down there," Ron stated.

"No kidding. I need to call a tow truck. Can I borrow your phone a minute? My battery died."

"Here."

Ron stared at Carlos's disfigured face while the Peruvian man took a business card out of his wallet and made a call.

"Triple Z Towing. Can I help you?"

"My car broke down on the Northway. About a mile south of the Saratoga exit," Carlos replied.

"Are you, or anyone else injured? Are you in a safe place?"

"There's nobody injured. I just need a tow truck."

"What's the make and model of the vehicle?" the dispatcher inquired.

"It's a 1951 Buick Special-Deluxe."

"What color is it?"

"A faded red. It's got white wall tires and a chrome grill and bumpers. I'm a couple of miles south of Saratoga."

"We'll have a truck out there in thirty-five minutes. In the meantime, wait somewhere warm and safe," the dispatcher advised.

Carlos handed the phone back to Ron.

"Thank you. A tow truck will be here in a half-an hour," Carlos said.

"You're welcome to wait in our car 'til it comes— there's plenty room."

"That's okay, Mr. Levine. I don't wanna hold up your vacation."

"No, I insist. It's freezing out. And you can't wait in that smokey vehicle."

"All right," Carlos said as he reached into the Buick and shut-off the ignition. He grabbed a bouquet of flowers from the front seat, and the two men walked over to the rented honker.

Ron opened the door and leaned inside the car.

"This is Mr. Calaveras everyone. You remember Carlos, right, Rachael?" he asked.

"Of course, I do. You're the shaman from Peru. What a surprise seeing you here."

Carlos asked while he briefly glanced at the other two faces staring at him, "How are you, Mrs. Levine?"

"Great. How's Ranita doing?"

"She's fine, thank you."

"Carlos has to wait for a tow truck, so I figured he could sit in the car 'til then," Ron said.

"Oh, absolutely," Rachael said.

"Here—why don't you sit up front," Rosco said while he got out and offered Carlos his seat.

"*Muchos gracias.*"

"*De nada.*"

After Rosco squeezed in the back, Ron introduced Carlos to the Applebaums.

"They live near Woodstock now, Rachael."

"What a coincidence. That's where we're going."

"I told him already," Ron said. "Are you still doing the Ayahuasca ceremonies, Carlos?"

"I have them at my retreat center in Bearsville."

"If you're unable to drive your car we'd be happy to give you a ride down," Rachael said.

"Terrific."

Rachael admired the red long-stemmed roses on Carlos' lap.

"Those are pretty."

"It's our 30th wedding anniversary today," he proudly announced.

"How nice. Congratulations, Carlos," Rachael said.

"Ours too," Rita added.

"Muchos gracias."

Forty minutes had passed when a black and yellow wrecker drove up and stopped in front of the old red Buick. Carlos got out and met the driver by his car.

"What happened?" the tow truck driver asked.

"Don't know for sure. I was going about 60, when I heard this loud clanking noise. Think I blew a gasket, or a piston."

"Crank it up."

He got in, turned the key and then gave it some gas. The engine coughed out smoke; it backfired three times while Carlos shook his head in frustration.

"You can kill it," the man said.

"What do you think it is?"

"I'm not a mechanic but I'd say your car is shot."

"The camshaft?"

"No. The whole freakin' ingune."

"Really?"

"I've heard these old injunes make that sort of noise before," the tower said. "Want me to take it to a garage?"

"You think they could get it running again?" Carlos inquired.

"All depends."

"On what?"

"If you replace the whole darn injune."

"Just take it to the junk yard," Carlos said.

"Cost ya fifty bucks, pal."

Carlos handed him a fifty-dollar bill.

"Write me out a receipt please."

"Sure. Get everything you want from the car," the tow truck driver said. "Remove the license plates too. Got a screwdriver handy?"

"Yeah."

Carlos grabbed a small brown box from the front seat, the registration, and a screwdriver from the glove compartment. After removing the plates, he took the car key off his key chain and placed it back in the ignition. The tow truck driver connected the chains and hooked the winch. He pulled the lever to tighten the slack and the mechanism locked into place. After the man scribbled Carlos a receipt, he hopped in his truck, closed the door, and then released the emergency brake. He stuck his hand out the window and waved goodbye.

Carlos sadly viewed his antique Buick for the last time. He sat in the honker, and Ron headed south.

After they traveled well past Albany, Carlos broke the silence, "I really appreciate your help, Mr. Levine."

"Don't mention it."

He took a ten-dollar bill out of his wallet. "Here, let me give you some gas money before I forget."

"Don't be ridiculous. Put it away. Is that a gift for your wife?" Ron asked about the small brown box in Carlos' hand.

"What this? No—it's a part I ordered for my gonkulator."

"What's a gonkulator, Carlos?" Rita asked as she rested her arm on the back of the front seat.

"It's a digital device I developed to measure a person's brainwaves while they're hallucinating. I use it in my work sometimes."

"You hallucinate at work?" Rita asked.

Ron laughed. "Carlos doesn't have what you'd call your typical nine-to-five job, Rita. He's a shaman."

"You mean like a witch doctor?" she asked.

"A healer or medicine man is a more appropriate term," Carlos stated.

Rosco woke up from a nap, stretching his arms overhead, he yawned and inquired, "How'd you get into that line of work, Carlos?"

"My father and grandfather were shamans. They taught me the ropes."

"That's so cool," Rita said.

"You should visit my retreat center in Bearsville," the shaman said. "I have many wonderful classes and workshops there. Tomorrow afternoon I'm having a traditional American Indian sweat lodge. You're all invited as my guests."

"That would be fun," Rachael said. "We should go, Ron. Maybe take lunch at the Bear Cafe."

"That could be a plan," Ron stated.

"Where are you staying in Woodstock, Mr. Levine?" Carlos asked.

"At the Old Bones Hotel. Up on Meads Mountain Road. It's one of the last hotels in the Catskills that still serves authentic kosher food."

"I know," Carlos said. "My wife is the head chef there."

Rachael beamed a smile. "That's wonderful."

Several miles down the interstate, Carlos pointed to a green sign on the New York State Thruway.

"The exit for Woodstock is coming up," he mentioned.

"I usually get off at the Kingston exit," Ron stated. "I find that route a little more scenic."

"That's true," Carlos said.

Ron gave the Delta 88 some gas, and he scaled the steep hills of Route 28. The sky became a tapestry of colors as the late afternoon sun descended into the Catskill Mountains. He made a righthand turn onto the Levon Helm Memorial Highway, drove through West Hurley, past the Maverick, and then onto Mill Hill Road. They passed a boarded up and defunct Joyous Lake, once a popular venue for live music in Woodstock. Ron slowly cruised up Tinker Street, the main drag in town. Local families, tourists, philosophers, and hippy throwbacks bravely gathered for a drum circle on the snowy village green. Off the Millstream, Ron pointed to an upstairs dwelling above an artsy-fartsy boutique.

"Dylan used to live in the apartment up there. Once upon a time," Ron stated.

"As in Bob Dylan?" Rosco asked.

"Yeah," Ron replied while making a U-turn by the Twin Gables Bed and Breakfast. He drove past the Millstream and circled the village green again. "Where do you live in Bearsville, Carlos?"

"On Wittenberg Road. You can drop me off at the 'Old Bones. I'll catch a ride home with my wife after she finishes work."

"Are you sure?" Rachael asked.

"Positive," Carlos replied.

"I just love this place," Rita said. "We should buy a summer home up here. Huh, Rosco?"

"Wish we could afford it," he dreamily replied as the car passed a small building which housed a visitor center and the Woodstock Chamber of Commerce.

Grandfather Woodstock, (an ancient hippy the locals claimed was over 100 years old) balanced his bicycle heaped with every kitschy looking thing known to man. His tall peace flags proudly waved, as he walked his bike around a corner and disappeared.

Ron drove onto Rock City Road and rambled past a familiar white landmark, the Colony Cafe. After several sharp turns up a precipitous Meads Mountain Road, he pulled into a gravel driveway that led to the Old Bones Hotel. He parked the honker beside a white van placard with purple peace signs and 'Imagine' bumper stickers. It was dark now, and a magical vibe pervaded the enchanted Catskill surroundings. Everyone lazily got out and stretched their arms and legs for a minute. The temperature had dropped. They listened to the gurgling Esopus Creek while the smell of home-cooked food filled the air. The two women hurried into the rustic looking lodge, and the three men followed with the luggage.

43

In the Old Bones kitchen Carlos went behind the line and greeted his wife with a kiss, the bouquet of red roses, and a small blue gift box.

"Happy anniversary *mi amor*," he announced while the kitchen and dining staff clapped and cheered.

"What a surprise!" his wife exclaimed. "*Muchos gracias* my love. And same to you."

"*Gracias.*"

Ranita clapped her hands and told everyone to go back to work. "And what's this?" she inquired about the gift wrapped in spangled blue paper.

"Open it," her husband said with a wide grin.

She gave her husband the flowers, and opened the present. Inside the box, on a cushion of black-velvet sat a sparkling diamond necklace.

"Oh, Carlos! You shouldn't have."

She hugged and kissed him.

"They're real diamonds," he said.

"Better be."

"You like it?"

"It's amazing, I love it," his wife replied.

She held the glimmering necklace up to her chest a few moments, then placed it back in the small box and slipped it into a pocket of her white chef uniform.

"Did you get the part for your gonkulator, Carlos?"

"*Sí*, but the car had some mechanical difficulties right outside of Saratoga," he reluctantly told his wife.

Ranita's mouth contorted into an upside-down smile.

"What happened this time?"

"The engine died on me. I had it towed to the junkyard."

"Again?"

Something smells delicious," Carlos said.

His wife picked up her French knife and put an edge on it with the knife steel.

"That's the second car in six months you've had towed to the junkyard. I don't know why you keep buying those beat-up old jalopies, Carlos."

"It wasn't a jalopy. It happened to be an antique."

"Antique shmantique," Ranita said.

"What's for dinner, sweetheart?"

"Guinea pig. I need three ceviches, *pronto, por favor!*" the chef yelled over to the cold station.

"Guinea pig? Are you serious?" her husband asked.

"Maybe. How'd you get back here anyway?"

"I caught a ride with the Levines."

"Who?"

"That sweet American couple we met when we lived in Iquitos. The journalist from Miami Beach."

"Oh, really?"

"They're in the dining room having dinner with two of their friends," Carlos said. "The four of them checked into the hotel a little while ago."

"I hope you gave them some gas money, Carlos."

"I offered but they refused. I'll treat them to a nice bottle of wine."

"I should go say hello, and see how they like their food," Ranita said.

"I'm sure they would appreciate it."

"*Bueno.* I have a lot of work to do," Ranita said. "I made your favorite adobe chicken and rice. It's in the back oven. Go fix yourself a plate and eat some hot soup."

"I will. I love you sweetheart."

"I love you too, Carlos. Now put the roses in water for me, *por favor.* There's a vase in my office."

"*Sí.*"

In the unpretentious yet elegantly furnished dining room at the Old Bones Hotel, Rachael reached into a bread basket and nimbly handled a freshly baked jalapeño biscuit. She cut the roll in-half, watched the steam come out, and inhaled the spicy aroma. She spread some soy butter onto it. Rachael looked up and asked with a straight face: "You wanna know something, Rita?"

"What's that?"

"Miami Beach was so hot one day last summer, I looked out my kitchen window and saw a bird using a potholder to pull a worm out of the ground. Can you believe that?"

Rita laughed as she cut into her jalapeño biscuit.

A waiter came over and stood next to Ron. It was Jorge Kohani, from Iquitos. He placed a bottle of Chateau Baret 2010 on the Floridians' table.

"*Señor* Levine, this is compliments of the gentleman who is eating at the bar," Jorge said while taking out his corkscrew. Carlos looked over at Ron's table and waved. Ron saw him and waved back.

"That was sweet of him," Rachael said. "Please tell Carlos we said thank you, Jorge."

"I will, Señora Levine."

After dinner the Applebaums and Levines donned their coats and hats and strolled over to the Old Bones nightclub located across the street from the main lodge of the hotel. A few guests socialized inside. The two couples ordered drinks at the bar before meandering over to a comfortable leather couch near the fireplace. Forty-five minutes later, a man with an acoustic guitar stepped onto a small wooden stage. He plugged-in, tuned, played a couple of chords, and then blew a few riffs on his rusty harmonica.

"Good evening. See we got a good size crowd tonight. My name is Bob Wilbury. It's always a great pleasure to perform at the 'Old Bones stage. Feels like home. I'm gonna do some original folk tunes for you. I wrote this song a few years back," the musician told the small audience. He strummed his Gibson guitar and warbled into the mike:

"Well, I was comin down the mountain one day, and a dog bit my left foot . . ."

"Want another Molson, Ron?" Rosco asked before he went up to the bar.

"I don't think so. Rachael wants to leave soon. You and Rita coming with us to the Tibetan-Buddhist monastery in the morning?"

"What time are you going?"

"Right after breakfast," Ron replied.

"I suppose a little meditation couldn't hurt. I'll be right back," Rosco said.

The young folk singer ended his ballad on a twangy minor chord. He played three more songs, finished the set, and then acknowledged the audience's applause with a bow, a throaty "thanks", and an "I'll be right back after a short break". In his bare webbed feet, Mr. Wilbury squish-squashed off the Old Bone's stage and procured himself a drink.

Up at the bar, Rosco accidentally bumped Mr. Wilbury's arm. "Sorry about that," he said, while the folk musician turned to face him.

". . . it's all right," Mr. Wilbury sang, smiled, and then tasted his whiskey.

Rosco returned to the couch and placed a bottle of beer and a hot cider onto the table.

"Hey, this guy ain't a bad musician," Rosco said. "His voice is a little strange though."

"You ready, Rachael?" Ron asked while he put on his coat.

"Yeah, let's go."

"We'll see you guys bright 'n' early," Rita and Rosco said.

"G'night."

Outside the 'Old Bones nightclub Ron and Rachael listened to the Esopus Creek slosh over some moss-covered rocks. In the distant hills the haunting cries of a coyote gave them shivers up and down their spines. Rachael exhaled and watched her breath sculpt a ghostly silhouette upon the frozen mountain air. An otherworldly silence enveloped them while a starburst gathered in the lucent Catskill sky. Rachael put her arm around her husband and kissed him on the cheek.

"It's a beautiful night," she mentioned after gazing at the stars.

Ron didn't speak.

"What's wrong, sweetie?"

"Nothing," Ron replied. "I'm just exhausted. It's been a long day."

"We'll be in bed soon."

The couple walked across Big Indian Road, and they followed the twinkling constellations back to the main lodge of the hotel. A plump white moon appeared above the roof; they stopped to admire it for a spell. In the rustic lobby a large grandfather clock tick-tocked in a corner. It chimed midnight as the night manager added a couple logs to the fire before sitting down again. Ron and Rachael walked up to the front desk, as the night manager raised an eye from his game of solitaire.

"Hi," the couple greeted him.

"Supposed to get down to the teens this morning," the night manager mentioned. "If you need, there's extra blankets in your closet. Wanna wake-up call?"

"No, thanks," Ron answered as the man handed him the room key.

The Levines climbed a creaking wooden staircase to the second floor. They walked down the hall and unlocked their guest room door.

"Chilly in here," Rachael said.

"I'll crank up the heat."

Ron went over to a clunky iron radiator and turned a stubborn metal knob. The dinosauric heater hissed, knocked and banged out a cantankerous rhythm for a couple of minutes. The radiator gradually put forth heat.

44

"Where am I?" Ron asked.

"You're on what I call the ethereal plane, Mr. Levine," the shaman replied. "It's a much different reality than usual."

"Why am I here?"

"You're going on an astral projection. You said that you wanted to see what it was like."

"The out-of-body experience we discussed in the sweat lodge?" Ron asked.

"That's right. I'll be guiding your departure and return," the shaman explained.

"Exciting."

The two men floated in their astral bodies until they started drifting farther and farther apart.

Ron panicked. "Wait! How am I supposed to find my way out of here?"

"The blue light will guide you, will guide you, will guide you, will guide you," the shaman's voice echoed. "I'll help you when you're near the end of your journey, end of your journey, end of your journey, end of your journey."

The shaman's voice resonated far inside a tunnel while his astral body gradually faded from Ron's visual perception. When Ron asked, his voice also echoed through the long conical passageway.

"End of my journey? End of my journey? End of my journey? End of my journey? And where will that be? And where will that be? And where will that be? And where will that be?"

"Follow the blue light, follow the blue light, follow the blue light, follow the blue light . . ."

Ron looked back but no longer heard the shaman's reverberating voice. Both men shrunk smaller and smaller 'til they were only blue dots floating in a cosmic sea. Ron found himself alone, in a conical tunnel, surrounded by a vaporous blue light. A supernatural realm where nothing appeared familiar. He stretched his arms out and touched the gaseous walls of the passageway, feeling a powerful, yet gentle force push him out and up into a vast open sky. Ron was flying.

Everything around him was colored an aery blue like the tunnel. It wasn't the light of day there, or the darkness of night, more like at dusk or dawn. His ears popped when he softly gravitated downward, landing onto a parking lot of the Blue-Mart shopping center in Plattsburg, New York, not far from the Canadian border. Ron noticed that all the vehicles in the lot were painted a silvery blue. He entered the store and browsed the aisles. Because of Ron's black-green complexion, the employees and customers rubbernecked him. Except for Ron, everyone in the store had a blue barcode tattooed on their wrist. Their hair, skin color and clothing were that strange aery shade of blue. Same for every piece of merchandise, meat, fish and grocery in the store. Large signs advertised a big sale. Today only. Ron inspected a bunch of blue-skinned bananas, wondering if the fruit was real or not. A blue-green grocer cheerfully approached Mr. Levine.

"It's absolutely astounding, isn't it? They're ripe by the way," he said and smiled, revealing a set of blue front teeth.

"Huh?" Ron inquired.

"The bananas, man! It's amazing what science can do today."

"What are you talking about?" Ron asked.

"Haven't you heard?" the grocer asked. "It's all-over social media. How's your day going, sir?"

"Fine, thanks," Ron replied. "Although, I'm not sure if I catch your drift."

"You talk like you're from the Sixties," the grocer said. "The fruits and vegetables man. They've all been hybridized, genetically modified, organically certified and engineered according to strict government standards, regulations, and specifications. Plus all the produce has been taste-tested to consistently have the same damn taste 365 days a year. How do you like them apples?" the grocer said while he picked up four shiny blue apples and started juggling them.

"You're pretty good at that, but what you're saying is rather alarming," Ron stated.

"Better get used to it. All the supermarkets and malls are gonna be that way soon."

The grocer kept his eyes on the fruit he was juggling.

"It's our government's new monopolization and ultra-gentrification programs. Before you know it, those bastards will control everything. Even our thoughts."

"You can't be serious?" Ron said.

"Oh, I definitely am. And by the way, everything in the store is half-off the regular price today."

"Why is that?" Ron asked.

The grocer let the apples he was juggling fall, and he rearranged them on the display.

"It's Blue Friday. Haven't you heard?"

"No, but where can I find a birthday cake?"

"In the bakery section, of course. It's right over there," the grocer said pointing.

"Thanks."

Ron went over to the bakery and picked out a chocolate layer cake from a glass showcase. He had the clerk write 'Happy Birthday Earl' on the blue buttercream frosting, and the cake was gently placed inside a box and tied with a string. Ron balanced the box on top of his head, and he glided over to the sporting goods department. He grabbed a fishing rod with an easy-action reel and a smooth cork handle. *This'll be perfect.* He thought.

Dressed in a spanking blue uniform, a charming saleswoman approached Mr. Levine.

"Need some help, sir?"

Ron showed her the fishing rod.

"Are these on sale too?"

She wiped the perspiration from her forehead and unbuttoned her blue, eye-popping blouse.

"Everything in the store is half-off today, sir."

"Great."

"Will you be you purchasing it with your blue mart prime card?" she asked while walking to the register.

"I don't have one," Ron said.

"It's unbearably hot in here today. Excuse me, sir," the charming saleswomen said while she removed her blouse, unhooked her bra and exposed a delightful set of indigo breasts which were pierced with silver-blue nipple rings. "Would you like to apply for a blue card today? You'll save fifteen percent on all your purchases."

"No, thanks. Can I pay for the cake here, too?" Ron asked.

"Sure. Just leave it on your head. I can scan it from there," the saleswoman said while one of her icy blue nipple rings brushed against Ron's arm. He shivered.

After she scanned the cake and the fishing pole, the woman noticed that Ron was checking her out.

"Is there something wrong, sir?"

"Why do you ask?"

"You're staring at me," the shirtless saleswoman replied.

"Sorry. I was just admiring your pretty blue eyes."

"Thank you, sir. With the discount your total comes to $85.69."

Ron squinted, massaged his chin for a moment, and then gave the clerk a hundred-dollar bill."

"I feel like I know you from somewhere," he said.

"Having a déjà vu moment—are you?"

"I guess," Ron replied while she handed him his change.

"Happy fishing, sir."

"Thanks. I don't need the receipt."

With the fishing rod in his hand, cake box on his head, Ron left the store and flew out into the wild blue yonder again.

45

Passing a shop that sold custom-made doors, Ron soared over Steam Mill Road and gradually touched down by a four cornered junction, where he patiently waited for a tight-lipped flock of wild turkeys to scuttle across the road and vanish into the woods. He was lost, so he decided to ask for directions at a gas and convenience store on one of the corners. The fuel pumps appeared to be from the early 1950's. On the store front hung an advertisement of a spirited young woman drinking an ice-cold Coke from a thick glass bottle tinted green. A blue neon sign indicated that Gleek's Gas and Grocery was open for business.

Bells jingled and jangled when Ron pulled the door handle. A dog snarled in a corner behind the front counter.

"Hello? Does anyone work here?" Ron called from the open doorway.

Nobody answered except for an impetuous gust of wind that whistled through the entrance. The air clenched Ron's shoulder and scattered dust from shelves stocked with cheap red wine, canned goods, bell-jars, Crackerjacks and brown bottles of home-brew. After the dust cloud settled, Ron entered the store. The door slammed shut behind him, vibrating a row of glass bottles on a shelf. One bottle teetered and took a nosedive, exploding on the floor and making a foamy mess in front of him. The dog barked again.

"Hello?" Ron announced a second time, as he carefully stepped over the broken glass and spilled beer.

Entangled by a cluster of spider webs, Ron pushed them out of his way and noticed an old pinball machine light up and make all sorts of weird noises. He pulled the lever for the ball release and watched the colored lights blink on and off. Suddenly, a door opened and closed from the back end of the store.

"Howdy—," an old geezer announced. The dog barked. "Quiet, Buddy!" he commanded while leaning his shotgun against a wall; it accidentally discharged and tore a gaping hole in the ceiling. The dog whimpered while Ron was about to shit his pants.

The old geezer hung his plaid hunting jacket on a meat hook and shook the snow from a colorful winter cap. He cleaned his muddy Sorel boots on a door mat while blowing the snot from his crooked blue nose.

"God damn jackals are after my chickens again!" the old geezer declared. He suspiciously viewed Ron. "They killed a couple of 'em just last week. Sorry, I was outside in the shitter. My toilet here needs a new thingamajig. Yur not a plumber by any chance?" he asked in a crustaceous sounding voice.

"No, I'm not a plumber. I just came in to ask for directions to my friend's place."

"Who are you?"

"Ron Levine."

The old man wiped his hand on his grease-stained blue jeans, and he firmly grasped Ron's webbed hand.

"Don't worry, I washed em. I'm Charlie Gleek. Welcome to Gleek's Gas and Grocery."

"How's it going?"

"That's a very unusual hat ya got there," Mr. Gleek said about the tall square box balanced on top of Ron's head.

"What hat?" Ron asked.

"The one on your freakin' head. Ya know."

"Oh, shoot! I almost forgot. That's not a hat, it's a birthday cake."

Ron lifted the cake box off his head and placed it on the front counter.

"Well, ya better be careful it don't turn into an upside-down cake. That's a fancy fishing pole ya got there. Going ice-fishing on Lake Champlain are ya?"

"No, it's a birthday present for a friend of mine."

"Well, that should make a fine gift. Ya know."

"I thought so myself. Hey, I'm really sorry about the mess on the floor."

"Eh, no worries. That home brew recipe is so darn volatile. Sometimes I'll be sitting here, and a bottle will explode for no reason whatsoever. It's because of the barometric pressure in the Adirondacks. It's got an excellent taste, though. Wanna try one?"

"Is it beer?"

"North Country's finest. And it tastes much better than the pig-swill they sell at the Shop and Drop in P'burg. I brew it myself."

"Sure, why not."

The old geezer opened a cooler and took out two bottles of home-brew. He handed one to Ron.

"Don't shake it or you'll blow the roof off this place," Mr. Gleek warned. "Here, let me open it for ya."

"Thanks."

"To your health," Mr. Gleek toasted.

"Yours too."

Ron swallowed a taste of the yeasty liquid and licked his lips.

"What do ya think?"

"It's not bad."

"I told ya."

Mr. Gleek reached into a glass bowl and grabbed a handful of chocolate covered confections. He popped a couple in his mouth and chewed.

"Want one?" Mr. Gleek asked.

"What are they?"

"Chocolate-covered truffles. My old lady makes em from the wild mushrooms that grow out in the cow pasture. She uses real Belgian chocolate."

"No thanks, I'm allergic to chocolate."

Napping in a corner, on a small Persian rug, Mr. Gleek's musty old hound dog lethargically raised his head. It yawned, licked its testicles, barked twice, got up, and then lumbered over to Ron to sniff his crotch.

"Good boy," Ron said as he stroked the canine's head.

"That's Buddy Washburn. Don't mind him. He wouldn't hurt a fly. Go lie down, B.W. By the way if yur tanks empty, I don't have any gasoline. My pumps are bone-dry 'til next April."

"I didn't come by car."

"How'd ya get here then? Passenger train?"

"No."

"Jet plane?"

"No."

"Betcha took a boat up the Saranac, right? I thought the river was frozen this time a year," Mr. Gleek said. He scratched his head and indulged in another chocolate truffle.

"I didn't come here by boat either."

"Well, fuck me running! How on God's good earth did ya get here? —the Goodyear blimp."

The store owner shrugged while his dog quietly whimpered and scratched his ear.

"To be honest with you, I flew here," Ron stated.

"So ya did take an airplane."

"No, I flew by myself," Ron explained.

"Well, that's the most peculiar thing I ever heard. But ya know what they say?" the old geezer asked.

"What's that?"

"Don't stuff the small sweat."

"I think you mean don't sweat the small stuff," Ron said.

"That's right. My long-term memory ain't what it used to be. The main thing is yur here right now. Ya know. Be Here Now. Ram Dass wrote the book. I've read it close to a hundred times. You get into all that new-age esoteric crap, La-vine?"

"Occasionally."

"My wife takes yoga classes," Mr. Gleek stated. "I would but my knees don't bend like they used to. So, what are your long-term plans in the North Country?"

"I'm going to my friend's birthday party."

Mr. Gleek guzzled some more home brew.

What your friend's name?"

"Earl Tosh."

Charlie nodded. "I know Earl. Used to see him buy'n tofu down at the health food co-op on Thursdays, happy hour at the Monopole on Fridays, square-dancing on Saturday nights, church on Sundays, and the bank in P'burg on Mondays. Did you know that Plattsburg has more bars than banks?"

"No, I didn't," Ron replied. "So where does Earl live?"

"In the old stone house on Quarry Road, right off the Northway. It's just beyond Uncle John's pumpkin field. Ya can't miss it. It's the second driveway on the left. Not the third driveway on the right, or the first one past it. That'll take ya to an old, abandoned bunkhouse in the woods. The locals reckon it's spooked."

Ron shivered. "You mean ghosts inhabit the place?"

"That's right. A friendly bunch of long-haired hippies had a commune down there once upon a time. Good neighbors though. Never bothered me any. Mostly self-sustaining carpenters, artists, philosophers, musicians and college students. They grew their own food, raised their own grass-fed livestock and helped the community. Lived what I'd call the good life. They were nature lovers. And really serious about preserving the environment. Ya know?"

"Sounds pretty sensible to me," Ron said.

"I remember when they used to have these wild gatherings from time to time. Called em poobahs."

"What's a poobah?"

"A big celebration that went on for days. Lots of folks came up and camped in the woods and meadows. They put up tents and teepees, or just slept out under the moon and stars. They played live music all night, danced naked, smoked a little weed, drank some wine, ate lots of great tasting food, and had themselves a good 'ole time. I showed up for one or two of them poobahs. I'll tell ya one thing, La-vine. Those hippies sure knew how to throw a party."

"They still come around?" Ron asked.

"Haven't seen em in years. Believe they moved to a farm in Tennessee. They sold the place to a Mr. and Mrs. Keerowax. The husband worked as a poet. And his wife handknitted colorful wool sweaters and hats."

"Well, I better get going, or I'll be late for my friend's birthday party," Ron said as he placed the cake box on top of his head again.

"By the way, the radio said there's supposed to be a real hard rain comin through Keene Valley later. Gits awfully muddy on that road to Earl Tosh's place. I'd park yur car by the main road and walk to his house. If I were you."

"I didn't come with a car—remember?"

"Hey don't forget yur fishing pole. Ya won't catch many fish without it."

"Thanks for the home brew, Mr. Gleek. And the directions." Ron opened the door to leave, and the hanging bells chimed again.

46

Ron approached a lonesome-looking cottage that looked like it hadn't been lived in, in years. The sheathing on the A-frame sadly drooped while its dilapidated roof was covered with branches, bird shit and pine needles. The front porch was strewn with a hodgepodge of leaves, acorns, empty beer cans and wine bottles and stacks of old magazines and newspapers. Gangly weeds, tall grass, and wildflowers infested the front yard, while a motley collection of junked cars, a paint-peeled tractor, and bikes with flat-tires instilled a terrible eyesore on anyone who looked upon it. Rusted tools and wrought iron sculptures, a broken drum set, piano, mike stands, string-less guitars, bass, a soprano sax, scratched and warped records and a phonograph, old telephones, bones, abandoned toys and lawn furniture had been scattered about the disheveled property.

Ron place-kicked a beer can off the porch, and rapped twice on the front door; the bell didn't work. He went around the side of the house and peeked through a white framed window. Inside, he espied a neatly made bed; a kerosene lamp burned beside an old black sewing machine. On the floor lay spools of thread, wool, yarn, swaths of colored fabrics and knitting needles. A rainbow of mittens, scarves, winter hats, wool socks and cashmere sweaters warmed a table nearby. Ron walked to the back of the cottage, where a screen door had been left ajar. Fuzzy moths and mosquitoes fluttered in and out. He stuck his head through the doorway and called, "Earl? You home? It's me, Ron." *This sure is a funny looking stone house. There's not one stone in sight.* He entered and walked through a short hallway, passing the bedroom, and into a minuscule kitchen where the bold aroma of freshly brewed coffee caught his attention. He found himself a mug and poured the hot liquid into it. When he opened the fridge for some milk, a small appliance bulb emitted an incandescent blue light. It escaped through the door and brightly illuminated the kitchen and the rest of the cottage. Next to a quart bottle of milk, sat a bowl of mixed fruit. Ron picked out a succulent strawberry and ate it. He suddenly found himself in a slightly different reality.

A trail of fragrant juniper and purple-red trillium flowers led him up to a meadow on top of a grassy knoll. Up there, Ron followed a spiraling pathway inside a stone labyrinth. He eventually came out the other side, where he viewed the high peaks of the Adirondack Mountains.

Under waning stars and moonlight, Ron observed a mirthful young woman in a raven-black dress. Along with a bevy of lighthearted spirits, she danced around an Indian tipi, before floating away upon the early morning mist.

The meadow was completely overgrown with strawberry plants that appeared to go on forever. Ron bent over and plucked a red berry. Just when he was about to bite into it, he found himself back in the kitchen of the small cottage. He stuck his head in the fridge again and smelled the milk inside the quart bottle. It'd gone terribly rancid. He closed the refrigerator door, sat at the kitchen table, and then drank his coffee black.

Before him, a stack of unopened mail, a manual typewriter, a ream of paper, scissors, pens, pencils, a stapler and a roll of Scotch-tape. A large bible had been opened to Psalm 23. He recited a verse or two out loud:

The Lord is my shepherd; I shall not want.
He makes me lie down in green pastures.
He leads me beside the still waters…

Ron picked up an envelope and read the name and address on it. "Mr. and Mrs. Jack Keerowax, 5 Old Abandoned Bunkhouse Road."

He dropped the envelope and swore under his breath.

"Wait a minute. Holy shit—this isn't the old stone house."

From the bedroom down the hall came the voice of an old woman, "Is that you, Jack? I've finished knitting your sweater, dear. Why don't you come to bed already? You've worked on your book long enough."

Terrified, Ron knocked over the coffee mug, and it shattered on the tile floor. He bolted from the kitchen, down the hall, out the back entrance, and into the woods. He descended a long granite staircase where mushrooms, puffballs, fiddle heads, and toadstools sprang up around him. He reached the last step, bounced onto a soggy trail, and stopped to catch his breath. He cupped a hand to his ear and listened to a stream gurgle through the woods. Nocturnal birds hooted, howled, screeched and whistled. Perched in a dead elm, a sharp-sighted nighthawk scowled and licked its talons. A snowy owl swooped inches above his head. A solitary nightingale sweetly serenaded him while a family of nine raccoons secretly roamed the dream-scape woods.

Ron stumbled upon a fast-moving stream running adjacent to the trail he was following. Out of the blue, his walking stick broke in two. He dropped the fishing pole and lost his equilibrium, tumbling into the icy cold water. Miraculously, the cake box stayed balanced on top of his head. Drenched to the bone, Ron climbed out of the freezing water and picked up the fishing pole and continued along the narrow path until it abruptly ended by a wobbly wooden footbridge. It led him over to an island with a small house on it. Puffs of smoke escaped from a stovepipe on the roof. It seemed awfully small to be his friend's stone house. He walked up and knocked on the wood door.

A scratchy voice called from inside, "C'mon on in."

When Ron opened the door, a blast of hot air blew into his face. He asked, "Is this the old stone house?"

"Hey! Shut the door! —You're letting out all the heat," someone gruffly demanded. "And you better leave that cake outside, or it'll melt in here."

Ron placed the box on a bench outside the entrance. He stepped inside and a dry heat enveloped him. The only light in the place came from a single candle that burned along the sill of a stained-glass window: a vibrant red rose. He heard boorish whispers through the hot steamy air. Water still dripped from his pants and shirt sleeves.

"Well, you gonna take off your clothes? Or, are you having a sauna with them on?" someone asked in a scratchy voice.

"Is that you, Earl? It's your friend, Ron."

He heard more whispering.

"Earl? Ron? What's he talking about?"

"Do you know him, dear?"

"No. And he doesn't look like the sort of man I've seen before. Look at his hands. And face."

"How 'bout you, Beaver? You know him?"

"No. Maybe he lives down by the barn, or with the folks on Murtaugh Hill. I thought people stopped using the sauna after it flooded down here."

"I wasn't sure what time your birthday party started, so I figured I'd come early," Ron announced through the steam cloud.

"I didn't hear anything about a birthday party. Did you, dad?"

"No."

There was more whispering along with a distinct sound of a creature gnawing on timber. A fire crackled inside a wood stove a few feet away. The steam dissipated. And the bloodshot eyes of four bristly-furred animals keenly watched while Ron stood there dripping wet. Two of them sat on a wooden bench; the other two crouched on a wooden platform directly above. The four animal's hands and feet had pointed claws. Their front teeth were bucked and sharp. They had small black noses and wiry brown fur. Their bodies were the size of a large muskrat with barbed paddle-like tails.

"Who are you?" one of the creatures asked.

Shocked to see and hear the animal speak: Ron's vocal cords froze. His teeth chattered, and his knees knocked together uncontrollably.

"Poor thing. He's soaking wet. And shaking like a birch leaf," the mother creature stated.

"I see. Hi there," greeted one of the animals who appeared to be the father. "We're the neighbors who live on the other side of the pond. I'm Mr. Jones."

"I think he's afraid of us, dad."

"That's probably because he's never seen a naked beaver before."

"You think?"

Mrs. Jones filed her claws along the wooden bench.

"You really should do something about the dam, dear. It's getting a bit messy."

"I know. Me and the boys will swim out tomorrow morning and clean it up."

"Good. Has everyone had enough of the sauna?"

"Yeah, Mom, I'm ready to cool off in the pond."

"What are we going to do with the man, dear?" Mr. Jones asked his wife.

"Oh, he'll be all right. I'm sure he can fend for himself."

"Should I put out the fire, dad?"

"Just leave it beaver. It'll burn out on its own."

The four wild creatures snuffled past Ron, clawed the door open, and then dove into the ice-cold stream.

47

The spectacular aurora borealis, also known as the northern lights, guided Ron over a frozen field where pumpkins shivered, and sunflowers withered. He swooped down onto a slick Quarry Road and skated on black ice, 'til he abruptly stopped by a mailbox with Earl Tosh written on the side of it. He saw the name and declared, "Finally! I've arrived."

Ron was overjoyed to see a two-story old stone house at the end of a long snow-covered driveway. Smoke from a chimney signaled someone might be home, while frost-bitten Brussels sprouts poked out of a garden beneath the snow. One of Tosh's calico cats espied the man coming up the drive; it scampered into a woodshed near the garden.

Seated on the front porch, a humongous pumpkin wondered if it would still be around next Thanksgiving, or even survive another Halloween for that matter. A candle burned inside of the pumpkin. Through its carved-out eyes it shrewdly watched as Ron climbed the porch steps and knocked the snow off his insulated boots by kicking the squash's hard orange rind.

The pumpkin groaned in a baritone voice: "Mind not doing that, please. It's rather painful."

"Excuse me? —did you just say something?" Ron asked.

"How would you like it if someone kicked you in the ribs?" the pumpkin inquired.

"I'm sure it wouldn't feel too good. My apologies."

"I accept your apology, but try to use the door mat next time. That's what they make 'em for. I'm Big, by the way," the pumpkin proudly announced its moniker through a cleverly sculptured mouth.

"You're definitely one of the largest pumpkins I've ever seen. And the only one I've met who can talk."

"Thank you. But what I meant was, Big is my name. Uncle John named me that this past Halloween."

"It suits you."

The pumpkin coughed and sneezed twice.

"God bless you."

"Thanks. I hope I'm not catching a cold again. That Canadian cold front must be down. Care to brush some of that snow off my head?"

With his gloved hand, Ron wiped the snow from the top of the pumpkin.

"Thanks, that's much better. Three times I asked Mr. Tosh for a winter hat, but still no luck. I suppose you're here for his big birthday bash."

"How did you know?"

"Earl told me you were coming. Ron Levine, is it?"

"That's right."

"Pleased to meet you, Ron."

"Likewise."

The pumpkin raised his eyes. "That's a real nice fishing pole."

"It's Earl's birthday present."

"He'll love that," Big said. "Earl ain't home right now, or his pickup truck would be in the driveway. My guess, he's knocking back a few beers at the Monopole Tavern right now. He went fishing earlier in the day. I just hope he didn't get bit by a big black snake down by Chateauguay Lake. Go on in and make yourself at home. Earl said you can stay in the Blue Room. It's upstairs. The first room on the right. There's clean sheets on the bed and fresh towels and soap on the dresser."

"Thanks, Big."

"Pardon the banality, Ron, but I need to hit the hay. Have a good night and enjoy yourself at the party."

"Will do."

Ron opened the front door, and he was greeted by a banner of Happy Birthday Earl! And a cluster of brightly colored balloons which hung from the ceiling. He leaned the fishing pole against a wall and placed the cake box on the dining room table. He stoked the wood stove, prepared himself a hot tea, and then relaxed on a couch in the living room, expecting to see his friend Earl, walk through the front door any moment.

An old black and white Magnavox television played in a shadowy corner of the room. The programs had long gone off the air, and Ron blankly stared at the snowy gray screen. He lazily got up to change the channel, but found every station had the same audio-visual distortion. While Ron hunted for an off-switch, a blurred image of an actor appeared on the glass tube; a clean-cut gentleman dressed in a suit and tie. His familiar voice came through the speakers loud and clear. Ron settled on the couch and listened to what the man had to say.

"Do not attempt to adjust the picture . . ."

Ron quickly got up and snatched the TV cord and yanked it from the outlet. The house got quiet, except for the motor idling on the ice-box, a mouse scampering across the kitchen floor, embers snapping in the wood stove, and the occasional rumbling of a sixteen-wheeler on the Adirondack Northway. The unnerving silence gave Ron the most uneasy feeling. He walked over and flipped a light switch by the front door, and a pancreatic blue light partially illuminated the living room, vestibule and front porch. Earlier, a thrashing wind had blown out the candle inside the pumpkin's belly, and poor Mr. Big was left to the clutches of the Canadian cold front. Ron came back inside and sat on the couch again.

A radio in the living room came on by itself.

"Good evening, Plattsburg. And welcome to IRKME FM. My name is Tom Epsom. Like the salt. For your listening pleasure I have a full program of songs from the 60's, 70's and 80's. So why don't you turn up the heat, kick off your boots, and relax for a while. Here's one by Bob Dylan. It's called Tangled Up in Blue."

While Ron waited for Earl and his party guests to arrive, the fire in the wood stove burned to coals. The temperature in the living room dropped ten degrees. Ron went outside to the wood pile and split a few logs. He hauled the wood inside and stoked the pot-belly stove. The living room slowly warmed up again. He carried a bundle of wood upstairs to the bedroom that was painted blue, neatly stacking the split-wood by a stone hearth, which already had a fire burning in it.

Ron stood by the fire while shadows of azure-tipped flames danced off a large red and white mural of a Sufi Heart and Wings on a wall. He picked up an old journal and sat in a rocking chair; he blew the dust off the cover and watched the tiny white specks parachute into the firelight. As the hour lengthened, he wondered why Earl's birthday party hadn't started yet. And *why was he the only guest who'd shown up for it, so far?* He slowly leafed through the journal filled with lyrics, poetry, newspaper clippings and photographs. Ron turned a dog-eared page and saw a photo of him and Rachael taken years before the human amphibian virus had changed them.

While Ron relaxed in the rocking chair, he felt a draft, and got up to see where it was coming from. He pulled a curtain and was shocked to see a life-size bust of a plastic saint. He jumped back a couple of feet. The mannequin's piercing blue eyes, thorny crown, bleeding heart, straggly brown hair and bearded face appeared all too real. "Jesus!" Ron spoke out loud. He touched the plastic skin on the savior's shoulder, and laughed at himself for being so afraid of an inanimate object. He quickly shut the window and pulled the curtain closed. Ron returned to the rocking chair and opened the old stone house journal again.

48

Earl Tosh felt compassion for a feisty night crawler while he placed it on a fishing hook and cast his line out onto a dusky Chateauguay Lake. He adjusted his six-ball-bearing reel and settled onto his portable easy chair.

"You coming, Earl?" his fishing buddy asked.

Earl opened a tobacco pouch without looking up at his friend.

"I'm gonna stay a little longer. See if I can't catch me a nice size rainbow trout," he replied while stuffing a pipe with a cherry flavored tobacco.

"Fish ain't biting so good, Earl. Ya don't wanna be late for your own birthday party ya know."

"Yeah."

With his pebbly blue eyes, the hard-headed man stared weirdly at his weather worn fishing buddy. Earl just nodded, kept puffing on his pipe, and opened a cold beer.

"We'll see ya later then."

"Sure—"

Earl's fishing buddy grabbed his gear, and he limped to an old blue Rambler parked next to his friend's white truck. He stowed his shit in the trunk, closed it, and got behind the wheel. The car stalled a couple of times before he drove away. A mile or two down the road, he passed a wagon full of rowdies who gave him the finger and smashed an empty beer bottle against the windshield. The old fisherman kept driving while the rednecks eventually turned onto Chateauguay Lake Road.

Back at the peaceful lake, Earl sat alone and patiently waited for a fish to bite. He contemplated the distant Green Mountains beyond the fog. His pole bent forward slightly, and he lackadaisically turned the reel. Earl puffed on his pipe and thought about how much fun he'd have at his party later.

Meanwhile, a red paneled station wagon drove erratically through the parking lot of the lake. The car burned oil, and its body was caked with mud and blue-green algae. The driver spun in circles before braking next to Earl's dented white pickup. The vehicle had oversized tires jacked-up redneck style. The seats of the station wagon had been slit open by some jagged object. It idled awhile before the engine was cut.

Earl had been oblivious to the boisterous display of driving. He was too busy fighting something big on the end of his line. He tugged on the pole with all his might. Any moment the line might snap.

The passengers in the station wagon kicked open the doors and three freaky-looking characters climbed out. Their physical features had the most disturbing details. One man brandished an aluminum baseball bat. He nervously walked in small circles. One of his legs had been replaced with a wooden peg-leg. Another guy held a large nylon fishing net. He wore muddy neoprene waist-high waders that appeared to be permanently grafted onto his body. His face looked as if it had been squeezed in a bench vise. His black beady eyes, sunken jowls and skinny head made him look like a barracuda. A putrid smelling cigar hung from his scabby lips. The driver of the vehicle had a curved and pointed metal hook in place of one hand and wrist. He lost the appendage in a boat propeller mishap in upper Chateauguay Lake.

These three characters could not be called men, but menfish rather. They had faces and shark-like torsos that were slathered with an odorous gray slime. Gills bubbled in air. Each of them had a razor-sharp fin that protruded from behind their neck and upper back. Their dorsal fins were what torn the leather seats of the red paneled station wagon.

While Earl struggled with his prize catch of the day, the three menfish clandestinely walked down to the shore and quietly approached him from behind. The manfish with the baseball bat belted the tall, stone-shouldered man on the back of his head, and Earl saw stars as he dropped into the lake and swallowed a generous amount of cold water. He surfaced, gasping for air and screaming and flailing his arms. The menfish threw the fish net over his bleeding head. There wasn't a soul around to save him. He was struck again with the bat, this time cracking his ribs and knocking the wind out of him. Earl was wrestled from the water while the man with the hook for a hand impaled his mouth and cheek. They pulled him to the parking lot and hauled him onto the bed of his pickup.

The menfish hooted and hollered while they left the lot with the muddy red station wagon and Earl's Toyota pickup. They crazily drove back to Plattsburg and swung onto an icy Quarry Road. The two vehicles sideswiped and knocked over mail boxes and garbage cans along the way. They turned into the driveway of the old stone house and skid to a stop. The rowdy menfish spilled out of the truck and station wagon and rolled in the deep powdery snow. They laughed hysterically, as they picked themselves up and butted one another with their squamous fish-heads.

Earl's breathing had become labored. His blood trickled off the truck bed and tainted the virgin snow. The menfish dragged him in the net to the porch.

Semiconscious now, Earl muttered, "Have mercy. Please . . . don't hurt Big. Please . . . don't hurt Big."

Earl took his last breath. And a sudden spurt of blood and purplish-blue bile erupted from his throat.

"What'd he say?" one of the menfish asked.

"I don't know. Some shit about don't hurt Big."

"Screw that!"

"Be careful, knucklehead, or you'll pull his arm out of his socket," a clammy-eyed character warned.

"Who cares? We're gonna cook him up anyway."

"That's true. Hey, can someone get the door?"

The humongous pumpkin opened his eyes and shivered. Big protested loudly while observing the menfish drag poor Mr. Tosh through the doorway of the old stone house. They pulled him along the living room floor, and into the kitchen.

One of the menfish kicked the pumpkin's side as it complained.

"Shut up, you stupid pumpkin. Why don't I get rid of this fat bastard once and for all."

And with a great effort, the manfish shoved the pumpkin off the porch, rolled him up the driveway, and onto Quarry Road. After a couple of hefty kicks and shoves, Big hurtled down the icy street. His world turned upside down, around and around and around.

"So long, sucker!" the manfish yelled from the side of the road.

The gargantuan pumpkin gained more speed while it careened down a steep hill, making a beeline for the Northway exit ramp. A fully loaded logging truck headed straight for him. The driver blasted his horn twice before smashing into the runaway pumpkin. Big's pulpy orange and yellow innards splattered across the highway while the trucker looked in his side-view mirror and just kept going.

Back at the old stone house, the menfish gathered at the dining room table and observed the box with the cake inside.

"Oh, lookee here, fellas. Someone has left us a nice birthday cake," said the manfish with the Captain Hook appendage. "Isn't that sweet. Happy Birthday Earl."

The men-fishes' mouths watered.

"Let's have a taste, shall we?" one of the menfish suggested.

They lifted the cake out of the box and smashed their ugly fish snouts into it. They licked off the blue buttercream icing, and sang a rousing version of 'Happy Birthday', before devouring the entire dessert.

Up in the blue room, Ron heard the celebration going on downstairs. The old journal fell off his lap as he got off the rocking chair and was about to join the party when he saw an intense blue light shine through the Sufi Heart and Wings on the wall. A long conical passageway appeared, and he could vaguely see someone at the far end of the tunnel. It was the shaman waving to him. His voice echoed from within:

"Mr. Levine, Mr. Levine, Mr. Levine, Mr. Levine. Step inside, step inside, step inside, step inside, step inside."

While all this was happening, an old Chinese woman, (Earl's house maid) stood in the doorway of the blue room. She was dressed in a white silk kimono, red silk slippers, and a single braid of white hair hung down to her lower back. She hugged a bundle of firewood to her bosom and poked her head inside the room.

"Good morn-ing, Mis-ter Earl. I bring you wood. See your fire getting low."

"That's very kind of you, Miss, but I'm not Mr. Earl. I'm a friend of his," Ron said.

"Oh, I'm very sally."

"That's okay. Sounds like a pretty wild party Earl is having downstairs."

"Pity party?"

"Yeah, I heard them singing happy birthday before."

"Oh, no. Par-tee finished a long time ago," the Chinese woman said.

"You're kidding me."

"No kid–ding."

The woman entered the room and carried the wood to the fireplace. When she saw Ron's face in the firelight, she screamed: "Frog! *Ching wa.*"

Before Ron could explain, the old Chinese maid dropped the firewood and bolted from the guestroom. She ran down the staircase, crossed the living room, out the front door and slammed it with a crash! The old house shook, cracked, crumbled, and then fell into one large heap of stones. Smoke still came out of the broken chimney.

Ron had safely floated back through the vaporous blue tunnel, and he entered his physical body again.

49

A man greeted guests who were eating breakfast in the Old Bones Hotel: "Good morning, everyone. All those going on the tour of Woodstock, the Tibetan Buddhist monastery, and the surrounding Catskills, please meet outside by the white van with the purple peace signs. The driver will be leaving in twenty minutes or so."

The sun's rays came over a mountain in the east and reflected off the golden ornaments on a Buddhist monastery, creating an atmosphere of nobility and splendor.

Inside the meditation hall, a man tugged on his long gray beard while he struggled to sit in Padmasana, the full lotus sitting position known in yoga. He wasn't very successful at it. The head of the monastery, Khempo Rinpoche, saw him, and quietly approached the man to give him some timely advice.

"Good morning, Rabbi Mandelson. I see that you're having some difficulty there."

"Good morning, Khempo. It's been quite a while since we've last met."

"I'm happy to see that you're keeping up your meditation practice, Rabbi."

"I'm trying my best. What else can I do?"

"And how's the Jewish community doing in Woodstock these days?" Khempo inquired.

"Very well, thank you." The gray bearded man grimaced as he finally unlocked his padmasana legs. "We have plans to remodel our synagogue and construct a new Hebrew school by the end of next year. God willing."

"That's wonderful news. I'll have to stop down for a visit when I get the chance."

"You're always welcome, Khempo."

"Before I start the morning meditation, perhaps I should give you a little insight, Rabbi?"

"Please do. I'm beginning to feel like a human pretzel."

Khempo laughed.

"When practicing meditation, you're not required to put yourself in unneeded pain or discomfort. I would suggest you sit in a less challenging position. Or, if you'd prefer to sit in a chair and meditate, that's fine also."

"Good to know."

The rabbi got up slowly and walked over to a chair and sat. Khempo sat in the chair next to him.

"That's much better," the rabbi stated.

"Good. I'm giving a talk after the morning meditation. I'd be honored if you could join us, Rabbi."

"What's the topic on, Khempo?"

"I'll be speaking about the drastic changes in our physical appearances, how the Human Amphibian Virus has influenced the manner in which we relate to the world, ourselves, and our fellow human beings. As I'm sure you must know already, one of our most important aspirations in life, is to cultivate goodness and well-being in our hearts and minds. This is how we can show true love, compassion and understanding for one another. Like everything in life, our physical bodies are only temporal. When time fades away, the body will also. And then what will be left of us?" Khempo asked.

The bearded gentleman contemplated Khenpo's wisdom for a moment.

"That sounds like it will be a very interesting lecture."

"Enjoy the meditation, Rabbi. And remember. When your mind starts to wander off, don't forget to bring your attention back to your out-breath again."

"Blessed be his name. Your instruction is much appreciated, Khempo."

"My pleasure."

Khempo got off his chair and bowed. He walked to the altar and lit some sandalwood incense. The sweet fragrance embellished the air inside the serene meditation hall while an orange-robed monk sounded a gong with a soft mallet, signaling the morning meditation would begin in five minutes.

The driver of the Old Bone's van navigated a hairpin turn, and he arrived at the top of the mountain where the Tibetan-Buddhist monastery was located.

"I'll be back to pick you up in two hours," the driver told his four passengers.

The Applebaums and Levines climbed the steps to the monastery and entered through a tall maroon door. They took off their shoes and outerwear and found seats inside the placid meditation hall.

A monk tapped a brass gong, marking the end of Khempo's morning talk. People lethargically stirred on their chairs and meditation cushions. Visiting guests, regular attendees, and a group of resident monks helped themselves to hot tea and snacks on a table. Khempo Rinpoche put away his notes and stepped off the podium to join them.

Ron had left the lecture early, and he stood outside, on the monastery grounds, savoring the harmonious surroundings while a colorful banner of Tibetan prayer flags flapped in the cool breeze. He watched the morning sky turn a dark purplish gray, then massive black rain clouds soon settled over the mountain top and completely enveloped the sun. An elderly man approached Ron from behind.

"They're cumulonimbus," the elderly man said.

Ron turned around and saw a bearded man dressed in a long black coat, a white wool scarf, and a brown fur hat.

"Sorry, I didn't mean to disturb you," the bearded man said. "I was referring to the clouds."

"You weren't disturbing me. I was just enjoying the great view of the mountains up here. At least until the weather changed a few minutes ago."

Ron tucked a magazine under his arm and further scrutinized the man's face. The older man appeared to be studying him as well. Although Ron didn't want to believe it, he recognized his old acquaintance by his pronunciation, clothing, distinctive eye-glasses, and the familiar manner in which he carried himself. There was an obvious change.

"Rabbi Mandelson?"

"Mr. Levine?"

"I can't believe it's you, Rabbi. What are you doing here?"

"I was meditating. Khempo just finished his morning talk, and I needed some fresh air. What a wonderful surprise."

The two men hugged each other, and cried for a few moments. They wiped away their tears.

"I'm sorry," Ron said.

"Don't be sorry, Mr. Levine. Crying is good sometimes. Besides, we may not look it anymore but we're still human."

"Yes, we are. My apologies for not keeping in touch after the expedition," Ron said.

The rabbi shrugged his narrow shoulders and deeply sighed.

"That's understandable my friend. Because of the virus life became a bit traumatic for everyone."

"I've changed since the last time you've seen me," Ron said.

"Mr. Levine. As you can see . . . I don't exactly look like your typical Chasidic rabbi anymore either. So vhat brings you up to the Catskills?"

"I'm on vacation with my wife and some friends of ours. What about you?"

"My wife and I live in Woodstock now. I'm the rabbi of the synagogue here."

"That's great. Hey, I have something for you," Ron said while he showed him the magazine that was tucked under his arm. "Have you read it yet?"

"National Geographic. Not that issue."

"My article about the expedition is inside. Here, let me sign it for you."

Rabbi Mandelson's eyes lit up.

"That's terrific, Ron. Congratulations."

"Thank you."

"I hope the magazine sufficiently compensated you for the article."

"I have no complaints."

"I'm happy for you. How long are you in town for, Mr. Levine? Maybe we can drink a coffee and talk in Woodstock."

Ron signed his name by the article and gave the rabbi the magazine.

"Thank you."

"I'd love to have a coffee, but we're flying back to Miami tomorrow afternoon."

"Next time then," the rabbi said, giving Ron his business card. "My new cell number is on it. Give me a buzz next week. I'll have read your article by then. And give my regards to your wife."

"Thanks, I will. Yours too."

Rachael shouted from the parking lot, "Ron! The van is leaving soon."

"Have to run. It was great seeing you again, Rabbi."

"Likewise, Mr. Levine. Have a pleasant flight.

The End

Made in the USA
Middletown, DE
25 April 2023

29182212R00209